The Countess' Lucky Charm

By

A.M. Westerling

To Dorra,

I hope you enjoy the story
of Temple & Simone!

Astrid

a.k.a. a.m. westerling ☺

2012 /07/ 17

DEDICATION

To my boys

Acknowledgements

Thank you to the helpful staff at Parks Canada - Fort St. James National Historical Site and a very big thank you to CaRWA and my fellow Carwackians - what a great, supportive, encouraging group!

The Countess' Lucky Charm

by

A.M .Westerling

ISBN: 9781927476062
Published By:

Books We Love Ltd.
(Electronic Book Publishers)
192 Lakeside Greens Drive
Chestermere, Alberta, T1X 1C2
Canada

http://bookswelove.net

Dedication

To my boys

Acknowledgements - Thank you to the helpful staff at Parks Canada - Fort St. James National Historical Site and a very big thank you to CaRWA and my fellow Carwackians - what a great, supportive, encouraging group!
.

Prologue

London – 1795

The teeming streets of the east side did not deter the shabby form of Gentry Ted in the slightest. He skirted the boisterous crowd watching the fisticuffs between two dirt-smeared boys then briefly followed a trio of gossiping young women, scullery maids by the looks of their chapped hands and grease spattered aprons.

At the next corner, he winked at the comely matron with come-hither eyes who was selling cut flowers from the basket tilted against the wall beside her. "Ha'pence," she crooned, leaning forward to display her ample cleavage.

Ted dragged away his gaze to return to the matter at hand. "Not today, luv, can't ye see I've business to attend to?"

He pointed down toward the "business": a grubby little girl of perhaps three years. He winked again and, adjusting his grimy silk cravat, strode away purposefully, toddler in tow.

"Hell's bells", he thought, thinking longingly of the woman selling flowers. "There were an opportunity missed." And he scowled down at the matted blonde curls of the girl, squeezing tighter the little hand clasped in his fist before forging on.

His pace was much too brisk for the little one. Sometimes her feet touched the ground and sometimes she dangled from his hand as her feet wind-milled through the air. Finally, he just picked her up in one arm and held her against him as he continued toward his destination. She weighed nothing at all, perhaps two stone, if that; his gait didn't slow.

A tipped potato cart blocked the road and he turned onto Newgate Street to avoid the confusion. The aroma of oranges drifted through the air and his stomach rumbled. Without skipping a beat, his hand snaked out to grab one. He rammed it into his pocket before the cart's proprietor turned his head, then ducked behind a passing coal wagon, keeping pace for several minutes until the orange cart was well behind him.

"The tib won't do." He mimicked his ringleader as he walked. "She's much too small to pickpocket. Get rid of 'er."

His protestations to the contrary had fallen on deaf ears, which was why he was now making his way to dispose of her. The easiest solution would be to toss her into the Thames with the rest of the city's refuse, but he couldn't bring himself to do it. He may have earned his living as a thief but he wasn't a killer.

Instead, he deposited the girl on the front steps of the workhouse on Bishopsgate Street and on a whim, gave her the orange. Before he could change his mind about his uncharacteristic show of generosity, he knocked on the door then hurried down the steps to disappear into the crowds.

"Ohhhh." Mrs Dougherty sighed as she opened the door to find a little girl on her step holding an orange in both hands. "They all think they can bring me the foundlings."

She grasped the little chin in callused fingers and lifted it to take a closer look. The girl had blue eyes. Piercing blue, as blue as the sunny September days of her own country childhood. She noticed a chain around the small neck. Carefully she lifted it off and slipped it into her pocket. She would look at it later.

"Quiet one, ain't ye?"

The girl said nothing. She stared at Mrs Dougherty, eyes wide with fear, bottom lip wobbling with unshed tears, both hands grasping the fruit so tightly the little knuckles were white.

"Ye got nothing to fear." She pulled the girl inside. The door slammed shut and the latch dropped with a rattle and a clank. "Mrs Dougherty will look after ye if ye do as yer told."

Chapter One

Sixteen years later

Apprehension sat heavy in Lord Temple Wellington's gut. As his hackney coach slowed to take a corner, he leaned over to risk a glance through the window. With one finger, he lifted the leather shade a fraction, just enough to see that the street behind him was blessedly empty. Good. If the disreputable lot he had naively gotten himself involved with caught him, they would kill him with nary a second thought. Feeling twice his twenty six years, he sagged back into the lumpy cushions as they bumped down the laneway that led to the river Thames.

The driver pulled up beside the lone street lamp and set the brake. "Here ye be, my lord," he grunted. "And ye just wanted a ride so I'm not helping ye with yer luggage."

"Very well, I'll just be a moment." Temple pressed several coins into the outstretched hand and jumped down to the cobblestones before pulling up his collar against the evening fog wafting from the river. It carried the faint odour of rotting fish and human waste and he shivered with distaste. During his upcoming journey he might long for a number of things about London but the smell of the Thames would not be one of them.

The muted glow of burning oil formed a golden circle on the damp, mud-rimmed stones and he looked about to get his bearings in the subdued light. He strode to the back of the coach, dragging on his gloves as he did so. He reached in to snag his carpet bag with one hand and the smaller of two matching brass bound trunks in the other. They swung easily to the ground. He grabbed the leather handle of the larger trunk and tugged. It was heavier than he remembered and, with a grunt, he tugged harder, this time with both hands. It slid, slowly at first, then gathered speed as it tipped over the edge of the coach bed and down toward the ground. He dodged it neatly before it could catch his foot.

"OOOF!"

Ooof? Temple's black eyebrows shot up to the brim of his beaver top hat. Trunks thudded, not ooofed. Was this a jest of some sort? Had the driver heard? Alas, he couldn't ask, for, the instant the second trunk had hit the ground the driver had ridden off in a clatter of hooves.

He looked around but the few stevedores were occupied with their business and paid him no attention. For all intents and purposes he was invisible amongst the barrels and crates being ferried to the ships that lay anchored mid-river.

He turned his attention back to the trunk. With some trepidation, he opened the catch and lifted the lid. Light spilled inside, feathering across its contents.

At first glance, it was a pile of rags where his carefully arranged belongings should be. To his astonishment, however, the rags moved and sat up and he was met with the bluest eyes he had ever seen. Eyes so blue, even in the weak light they glowed like sapphires trapped in a ray of sun. He caught his breath. Stunning, simply stunning.

"Oy," said the ragamuffin girl. "Be we still in London?"

"Yes," he replied without thinking, still caught in the sapphire gaze. To say he was astonished was putting it mildly. He shook his head and closed his eyes to right his tumbled thoughts. "We are at the docks near London Bridge. We set sail for New Caledonia tomorrow."

"Ye going ta report me ta the constables?" The scrawny shoulders jutted forward.

The gesture was defiant, which rather tweaked Temple's funny bone. The ragamuffin was hardly in a position to bargain although he had to admire her boldness. Of course, as a Wellington, he was much too well brought-up and polite to laugh. He kept his lips from twitching before he answered. "No, not if you tell me what happened to my things."

"Yer things or this?" A thin, bony hand held up his favourite pistol, a gift from his grandfather.

Bloody hell, how did she find that? More to the point, how was he going to retrieve it?

"What is your name?" He grabbed for the pistol but the ragamuffin pulled it back before he could snag it. He eyed it, then her, suspiciously. The urchin let it dangle far too casually from skinny fingers for his liking.

"Simone Dougherty. Only me friends thought that too 'oity-toity and call me Mona. And who are ye?"

Temple was appalled. A girl. How did a raggedy girl get into his trunk? He squinted at her—between the dim light and the grime on her face, it was difficult to determine her age. Fourteen, perhaps fifteen? A twinge of sympathy pierced him at her undernourished figure but he pushed it away. It was his own skin he sought to save at this moment.

"Temple. And you haven't answered my question," he demanded. Ordinarily he would have introduced himself by his title, Lord Temple Wellington, but he didn't want to overwhelm the girl, let alone give her any ideas about what sort of monetary compensation she might wangle from him for the return of his pistol.

"Eh? What question might that be?" The girl stood up and shoved the firearm into her waistband then climbed out of the trunk to stand before him unafraid. Her head reached his chin, no mean feat considering he was six feet plus.

She tilted her head and the lamp light glimmered on her face revealing her to be several years older than he had previously thought. A grey bonnet, its ribbons frayed and filthy from years of use, perched jauntily on dirty blonde curls that framed her heart shaped face with its full lipped mouth, pert nose and softly rounded cheeks. Those blue, blue eyes stared at him accusingly and again he was struck by their startling cerulean intensity.

"My things, what did you do with them?" Temple tried to keep the irritation out of his voice. No point in scaring her.

"Oy, I gave them ta them that really needed them." She wiped a runny nose on a grubby sleeve.

"What's this?" he asked suddenly, reaching toward the gold chain about her neck. "Something else you stole?"

The girl pushed his hand away. "None of yer damn business. It's mine, always been mine and always will be." She folded her fist around the hilt of his pistol in warning.

Temple backed away and held two hands up. "I must beg pardon, I merely wish to determine what kind of creature I'm dealing with." Relief washed over him when she pulled her hand away from the pistol.

"Cree-chur? Ye calling me an animal?"

"Well, you hardly resemble a girl. In fact," he said thoughtfully, resting his chin on one hand while propping the elbow in the other, "you remind me of nothing more than a raggedy bundle. Which brings me to another question."

"Yer awfully nosy," she interrupted.

"What are you doing in my trunk?"

"If I tell, will ye take me with ye?"

He stared at her. What a ridiculous question—he had no intention of taking her with him. However, until he retrieved his pistol, he didn't wish to antagonize her. "'Perhaps," he replied grudgingly. "But first, I should like you to return my goods."

She shook her head. "I can't do that 'cause I gave them away already. Mrs Dougherty and them, they need them."

"Now why do 'Mrs Dougherty and them'," he grimaced at the poor grammar, "need what clearly are mine?"

She began to tick off on her fingers. "The boys need new shirts, Mrs Dougherty needs a new jacket and Pamela needs a blanket because she gets cold at night." She spoke slowly, as if explaining to an idiot. "But then by the looks of ye, ye don't spend many nights in the cold."

"Why would you say that?" For some reason, her comment made him defensive and he deliberately made his voice brusque.

"Because," the girl pointed at his coat, "only them that are rich have fur collars." Then she pointed to his feet. "And boots like them." And finally, she pointed to his head. "And beaver hats. Only gentlemen wear beaver top hats. Well, Gentry Ted wears a beaver hat," she corrected, more to herself, "but only because he nicked one."

Temple made a sudden lunge toward her and grabbed for his pistol. Simone, anticipating his move, managed to get both hands on it. They wrestled for several seconds, long enough for him to realize that although thin, she was stronger than she looked.

He tightened one hand about a slender wrist, forcing her to loosen her grip on the pistol. She cursed him but he ignored it. The last thing he fancied was his gun discharging and wounding someone. Like himself.

He grappled with her several seconds more before stepping back, triumphant, pistol in hand.

"Thank you," he said smugly, although he tempered his tone. Without the pistol, she didn't pose a threat.

And then the bottom dropped from his stomach as he remembered what she had said.

The blanket. She had stolen the blanket.

Or rather, the rectangular packet hidden in its woolen folds.

The packet containing his future.

He jammed the pistol in his waistband and leaned forward to grip her shoulders with steel fingers. "Where is it?" he demanded.

"Where is what?" Her voice was innocent but the look on her face said otherwise; her gaze slithered away. She knew very well what he meant, he thought, anger churning within him at her obstinacy.

"Miss Dougherty," he warned, resisting the urge to shake her very flesh from her bones. "The packet wrapped in the blanket. What have you done with it?" He leaned his face in close to hers, so close he could feel the puffs of her breath on his cheeks.

"Mona, me name is Mona." She tried to step back but the hands clamped on her shoulders wouldn't allow it. She tugged at his wrists. "Yer hurting me, let go."

"I shan't let go until you tell me what you've done with it."

"I hid it." She tugged again at his wrists. "Now let go."

"Hid it?" Panic mingled with the anger and his voice raised an octave. "Hid it? Where, damn it, tell me where?" This time he gave her a little shake; her head bobbed, reminding him of their disparate sizes and he loosened his grip. He didn't wish to hurt the girl but he needed that packet.

"Somewhere safe. I'll show ye where but only if ye take me with ye. I—er, I'm in a spot of trouble."

He gazed at her, breathing hard, sucking air like a hungry babe sucks its mother's teat. Could he trust her? What kind of trouble was she in?

Reluctantly, he dropped his hands. "Very well." He glanced at his watch. "But we shall have to hurry, my ship sails at half past nine."

"Follow me," she said, "it's not far." She turned to go then turned back. "Yer taking me with ye, right?"

"Yes," he lied smoothly, "a deal is a deal." *Not a chance*, he thought. First he would retrieve the package he had carefully wrapped in oiled cloth only this morning. Then he would turn her in to the first constable he could find.

Chapter Two

The two of them started down the rough lane, away from the river and back toward the city proper. She led the way, walking at a fast clip, for which he was grateful. At least she understood the need for urgency. Still not trusting her, he hurried to catch up, grabbing her elbow as he did so. She gave him a surprised glance but said nothing.

"It were easy," she remarked conversationally as they maneuvered their way past a neat pile of wooden kegs.

"What was easy." He tripped on some fish net but kept his grip on her arm. He would not—could not—lose her.

"Getting in yer trunk. Ye wanted to know."

"Do tell."

"When ye were inside the boot maker's shop. The driver were napping and yer trunk weren't locked." Reproach filled her voice. "It were an open invitation, m'lord."

"I see." In future, he would have to take more care. He shook his head at his stupidity.

"I had Davy with me so I gave him the goods. I were going to take more but I…." She stopped talking and glanced up at him as if to gauge his reaction. "I were interrupted."

"Interrupted, how unfortunate for you." Sarcasm coloured his words.

She didn't seem to notice, however, for she continued on with her explanation with nary a change in intonation. "I had to hide from a constable," she confessed. "Oy, what a close call that were."

Indeed, he thought. He glanced again at his watch.

"It's just up there." She pointed, correctly interpreting his glance. "Not to worry, we won't miss the ship."

The confidence in her voice amused him and he relaxed somewhat, more certain now that she would not bolt.

They had almost reached the intersection where the lane broke off from the main road when two shadows detached themselves from the darkened silhouette of a brick warehouse. He froze in his tracks, squeezing Simone's elbow to stop her and pull her back.

Bloody hell, he recognized those two footpads—they were cohorts of his recent associate, Peter Mortimer-Rae. He had thought he had made a clean break from them, from that whole wretched group.

And he would have, if it hadn't been for the meddlesome fingers of his companion. Jaw clenched, he tightened his grip on her elbow.

He stood for an instant, torn with indecision. Nay, no indecision at all. He only had one pistol and one shot. To proceed further would certainly cost him his life. He would have to leave the packet for now and retrieve it sometime in the future.

"Is it well hidden?" He whispered to Simone.

Comprehension dawned on her face. "They're after ye, ain't they? The packet, ye nicked it from them."

He nodded, a thick scowl curling his eyebrows.

"Aye, it's well hidden," she gloated. "No one will find it. Now ye can't double cross me for if ye want it, you need me." She flashed him a triumphant look.

"Back to the quay, then," he snarled. He had reluctant admiration for her street smarts, though, for she had had him pegged right from the start.

"I can't. I were hiding from the likes of him." She pointed back toward the river and the burly constable heading their way through the evening mist.

The smile that had crept across his lips at her savvy disappeared in an instant. It would seem his ragged pickpocket was in trouble with the law and required his intervention if he hoped to keep her with him—intervention requiring time he really did not have.

She looked as if she was going to dart off and he trapped her hand in his elbow so she wouldn't. As much as he hated it, he needed her help to retrieve his stolen goods.

"That constable," he explained through gritted teeth, "is our ticket out of this mess. Just keep quiet."

He turned to face the man, neck prickling at the thought of turning his back on his stalkers. He risked a quick peek over his shoulder to see they had disappeared, scared off, no doubt, by the face of the law. Relief settled in him like a fine cognac settled in one's stomach after a rich meal and he faced the constable with renewed assurance.

"Is everything all right here, my lord?"

"Of course," he drawled.

The constable was clearly not convinced. He cast an appraising glance at Temple and then at Simone. "She doesn't seem your type," he said, pointing at her ragged black dress. "Fit more for Newgate prison."

At his words, Temple could feel the shudder coursing through Simone's slender frame. The shudder subsided into trembles.

For some odd reason, a protective urge flooded through him at her trepidation and, yes, fear. To reassure her, and to stop her from running, he placed his hand over her fingers where they peeked through the fold of his elbow.

Recognition shone in the constable's eyes. "Well, if it ain't Mona Dougherty." He turned back to Temple. "Now I know for sure she ain't your type. Hand her over. A few words from me to the magistrate and she'll be put away."

"I can assure you, she is my type. As a matter of fact," he smiled down at Simone's upturned face, "she's coming with me to New Caledonia."

Damnation, I've done it now. The only good news was the relieved expression on her face. Beneath his fingers he could feel her trembles subside.

The constable seemed unwilling to let matters be. He shook his head. "I don't know, my lord. Mona is one of the finest pickpockets on the east side. I just haven't had the pleasure to actually catch her in the act."

Temple frowned down at her. A pickpocket? Thievery for the betterment of one's peers was one thing, but a pickpocket?

She looked at him from guileless eyes. "Your package," she whispered then she looked over to the constable and gave him a saucy wink.

Temple sighed. She had him over a barrel and she knew it. "I shall relieve you of her presence, constable. As I mentioned, I am off to New Caledonia, well away from your bailiwick."

"I don't know if that's wise, my lord, I've seen her kind a hundred times before. Sweet as pudding to your face but the minute your back is turned—" The man swiped a sausage finger across his throat.

Temple looked at Simone's suddenly mutinous face, lower lip jutted out. She must have taken offence at the other man's words. He gave her a warning look then turned back to the other man.

"Truly, my good man, this woman is my travelling companion," he said in his best upper crust voice. "Your services are not needed here."

"Well, my lord, if you say so." The constable stood there a moment longer, tapping his nightstick against his leg. "If you change your mind, ask for Constable Carstairs." He tipped his hat to Temple. "It's good night to you then and if she sticks you, don't say I didn't warn you. As for you," he turned to glare at Simone, "if I see you again, it's off to Newgate with you. I know you're guilty and you won't always have his lordship here to save your skin."

"Thank you for the warning but I swear," Temple placed his hand over his heart, "I shall be fine." He was pleased to see Simone had understood the gravity of the situation and heeded his warning—she stood silent and with eyes demurely lowered.

"It's your skin." The constable shrugged then ambled off.

"Ooooh, did you hear him? I'm one of the best." Simone grinned at the recognition, rocking from foot to foot beside him. Her words were boastful, her attitude cocky. After her initial fear, she now felt quite comfortable under his protection.

Her eyes sparkled with life and much to his surprise, he realized the slender urchin intrigued him. Nonsense, he told himself. Utter nonsense. But he couldn't stop himself from looking again at her sparkling eyes. Filled with verve, they were. Verve and high spirits.

"Come on," he growled, dragging away his gaze. "The chat with the constable slowed us and we've not much time. I've arranged with the captain to pick me up." He pointed at a small row boat pulling into shore, a shadowy shape manning the ungainly oars. "Perhaps that's the fellow."

He grabbed her hand and charged back down the lane toward the steps leading down to the river.

"But he said I'm one of the best, didn't ye hear?" Simone jogged beside him to keep pace with his long stride.

"It wasn't a compliment. It's hardly an accomplishment to be proud of."

"Maybe for me it is." Her tone was rebellious. "Maybe for me it's the difference between going ta bed cold and hungry instead of just cold."

"And if you have the skills you claim, then why can't you afford decent clothing?"

"Oh these," Simone waved her hand down. "These are my working clothes. No one notices me in them."

Temple snorted. "I dare say they do. You look like a rag bundle with feet."

"Hmmph," she sniffed. "Can a rag bundle do this?" And she held up the heavy velvet sack of coins that had been in his pocket.

That stopped him in his tracks. She tossed the bag at his feet with a disdainful attitude that made him feel like a callow youth. Appalled at his carelessness, he snatched it up and stuffed it back in his pocket. She must have dipped her hand into his pockets during their brief struggle for the gun.

"And this?" She flipped him the leather folder containing his letters of introduction and passport that she had somehow rifled from his jacket. His jaw dropped.

"Agreed," he capitulated, holding his hands palms up. "You are the best."

"Aye," she said haughtily. "I am." She took a few steps away then turned to him. "Are ye coming?"

Bemused at her sudden self-assurance and consequently feeling rather gauche and useless, he followed her.

They reached his piled belongings and waited beside them while below, the row boat bumped against the landing. The sailor, dressed in a striped jersey and pants, hopped out to secure it with a heavy twisted rope.

Temple glanced back up the lane; the constable must have scared his pursuers for they were still nowhere to be seen. Just a few minutes more and he would be gone, well out of their clutches.

And hopefully, when the time came for him to return to England, they would have forgotten all about him and he could live his life in peace. Far away from the stifling niceties of London.

He turned his attention back to the approaching sailor now climbing the stairs toward them.

The sailor approached them. "Lord Temple Wellington?"

"And who wants to know?" Temple demanded. It may be a last minute trick on the part of the foot pads.

"I am Thomas Becker. Captain Featherstone of the sloop *Annabelle* sent me to fetch you." He inclined his head. "At your service."

"Very well, let's get my things, shall we?"

* * *

Simone stood back and watched Lord Temple Wellington. He was a man of power and obviously accustomed to getting his way, as evidenced by his neat handling of the constable. He relayed instructions to the sailor with self-confidence and authority, every word uttered with an underlying edge.

He was nervous, though, for as they at last sat in the boat that would carry them to the three mast sloop tethered amongst many other ships in the middle of the Thames, he continued to scan the shoreline behind them. In some way, that nervousness made him more endearing, vulnerable somehow.

She studied his face closely. He had not shaved that day, for a dusting of black hair lined his firm jaw, over the chiselled chin and down his neck. His forehead was broad and smooth, although laugh lines fanned from the corners of his eyes. Lord Wellington, apparently, enjoyed a good laugh. An unruly lock of amber-streaked mahogany hair hung over his sharp, black brows. He wore his hair long, longer than the current mode for it curled over his stand-up collar. A fine looking man, and not one to bow to the current vogue. She liked that—it made him his own person and not under the sway of others.

His eyes shifted suddenly and he caught her staring. A half smile lifted one corner of his mouth. He knew, she thought, cheeks flaming. He knew she had been studying him and it hadn't bothered him in the slightest.

She tore away her gaze, pretending great interest in the three masts of the *Annabelle* coming closer with every stroke of the oars. Her stomach fluttered as the boat smacked into the looming hull. *Oy, Mona, me girl, what have ye gotten yourself into? Whatever possessed ye to seek refuge in his trunk? Why didn't ye run when ye had the chance?*

The flutter in her stomach became an outright pounding as she recognized her unplanned adventure had not been properly thought out. Where had Temple said they were going? New Caledonia? It sounded like somewhere in Scotland but the *Annabelle* was large, built for traversing the oceans and even with Simone's limited knowledge, she knew Scotland was not that far.

"Miss, you must climb the ladder." Thomas Becker's polite voice interrupted her thoughts and she realized Temple had already disappeared from sight, up and over the side of the ship.

"What? Oh, yes. Yes." She stood and grasped the rope ladder. It twisted beneath her hands and she began the arduous climb, bumping against the planks, scraping her knuckles, banging her knees until at last, she looked up to see Temple's lean figure lean over, hand outstretched, to help her up the last few rungs.

With his aid, she clambered over the rail. Relieved, she clung to it for a few seconds to catch her breath then turned about to get her bearings.

A hatchet-faced man sporting a battered tri-corn and neatly trimmed grey beard bore down on them as fast as two bowed legs could carry him.

"Get that tart off my ship!" he shouted. "I am the captain and this, this…." He stopped, wheezing for breath a few seconds before continuing his tirade. "She's not welcome. Get that scurvy strumpet off my ship. Or else."

Simone's heart sank at the glowering face and querulous voice. Captain Featherstone was not at all pleased to see her. Her first instinct was to dart away but the railing pressed into the small of her back, reminding her she had nowhere to run. A frantic peek at the oily, black liquid swirling below confirmed that.

Apprehension welled within her for she knew very well the captain could make things unpleasant for her. She risked a glance at Temple. The question was, how badly did he need the package? He could repudiate her here and now, leading to consequences she didn't even want to think about. She sagged back against the rail. A snippet of advice from Gentry Ted swirled through her mind: *Never show your fear.*

She pulled herself upright and boldly met the captain's gaze.

Chapter Three

The captain's reaction didn't surprise Temple and he stepped forward, unperturbed.

"Captain Featherstone, Lord Temple Wellington." He bowed. "May I present my travelling companion, Miss Simone Dougherty." He pulled Simone up beside him, pleased to see her drop a curtsy, albeit a little shaky. Thankfully, she kept her mouth shut—he didn't need her interfering in his conversation with the obviously unenthusiastic captain.

"I don't have passage for her," growled the captain, eyes harsh and unyielding. "This is a cargo ship and what few cabins I have are full."

"Perhaps she could share my cabin, Captain. Name your figure." Share his cabin? What had come over him to suggest that? No, that wasn't true. He knew why. He felt a certain kinship with her for they had something in common: they were both running from a "spot of trouble".

Either that or impudent eyes paired with a scruffy cloak of defiance had addled his wits.

Whatever the reason, there was no backing down now. He dangled the money sack in front of the captain's face, giving it a little shake so the clinking of coins could be heard.

The captain shook his head. "This is a respectable ship, my lord. My wife sails with me and she's a god-fearing woman." He pointed a gnarled finger at Simone. "I don't have a cabin for her. The tart shall have to be returned to shore at once."

Temple groaned inwardly. Damnation, what was he to do now? He couldn't return to shore with Simone or his life would be forfeit. And if she didn't accompany him, he would lose any chance of retrieving his goods.

He turned around to scowl at her. She gave him a look of pure innocence and lifted her shoulders a little. Resigned, he turned back to the captain. "Surely we can come to an agreement."

"Well, now, if she were your wife…." The captain's voice trailed away.

"What? Preposterous." His wife? Pass Simone off as his wife? Not only was her clothing outrageous, but the second she opened her mouth, everyone would know her for what she was—a street urchin.

"I could look the other way and make things smooth with the mistress." The captain stared greedily at the bag of money still hanging from Temple's fist. He rubbed his chin then named an outrageous sum.

"What?" Temple was appalled.

The captain shrugged. "That's what it will cost you."

"You must be mistaken," he sputtered, scarce believing his ears. The amount named would almost deplete him of coins.

"Not mistaken at all, my lord. This is my ship. That is what it will cost if you wish the girl to accompany you."

Out and out robbery, that's what it was. Furthermore, even though it had been his idea, the prospect of sharing his cabin was not an enticing one. Not only did he like his privacy, the constable's warning about her slitting his throat still rung in his ears.

However, he had no choice. Temple turned around to glare at Simone and she smiled back at him sweetly. Rolling his eyes skyward in a plea for patience, he turned back to face the captain.

Captain Featherstone shrugged and crossed his arms. "I've given you an honest price. Take it or leave it. "

Temple scanned the shuttered face and thought longingly of the packet hidden Lord only knew where. Among other things, it contained gold guineas which would have been eminently useful at this particular moment.

"Honest price," Temple muttered, pulling open the drawstrings on his money pouch. "Highway robbery, I dare say." He counted out the coins and passed them over. Then he reached back for Simone and pulled her forward. "May I present my, er, wife. Lady Simone Wellington."

He pretended not to notice her incredulous stare. He braced himself, expecting her to protest, but surprise must have held her tongue for she said nothing, just continued to stare at him, eyes round as saucers, mouth agape.

"Your cabin is through there." The captain pointed toward a doorway before pocketing the coins. "See that she behaves," he glared at Simone, "or it's to the brig with her." He turned on his heel and stalked away, coins jingling in his pocket.

"Aye, Captain." Scowling, Temple faced Simone to crook a finger at her. "Come. We had better go below before the captain changes his mind."

"I'm not yer wife," she hissed. "Anyone with two eyes in their head can see that."

"Never mind, just follow me." He didn't wait to see if she was behind him but strode away across the deck toward the rear of the ship.

* * *

A stunned Simone had no choice but to follow. His wife? What had possessed him to put forward such an absurd notion?

She trailed behind, through the hatch and down the narrow hallway until they reached the last cabin. He pushed open the door. "Enter." He stood back so she could go in first.

Simone squeezed past, keeping her eyes on his crisp white neck cloth, sucking in her gut so that not a speck of her touched him.

She advanced several steps into the cabin because several steps were all she could take due to Temple's luggage pushed beneath the port hole on the far wall.

Golly, the cabin was tiny—two narrow beds separated from each other by the sliver of aisle where she now stood. An oil lamp hung over one of the beds, a plank shelf and several hooks over the other.

She felt him move into the room, could feel his heat and she peeped over her shoulder to gauge his mood. He ignored her to yank off his jacket, hanging it on a peg beside the door. Oy, his manner was frosty. Losing a valuable package and gaining an unwanted wife in one fell swoop had not pleased Lord Wellington at all. She didn't like it too much either. Lady Wellington? Who would possibly believe it of her?

She turned to find him leaning against the door, arms crossed. Two almost black orbs skewered her.

"Sit," he commanded, pointing to the bunk to her right. "Yours."

Simone shook her head. He sought to intimidate her and she would have none of that. Fists on her hips, she glared back.

"You cost me a pretty penny," he growled.

"Well, I am yer wife." She regretted the impish words the second they left her mouth. "I'll pay ye back," she added hastily at the thunderous expression on his face. Now was probably not the right time to remind him he had agreed when she had asked him to take her along. She straightened her shoulders and held her ground.

"Oh?" His brows lifted and scepticism blanketed his face.

"I swear."

"How? And if you are to suggest the obvious—"
He looked pointedly at the bunk. "Your favours do not
interest me. Or maybe they would, after you've had a
bath." A mocking smile curled his lips. "I shall arrange
for that. You smell and any cabin mate of mine is not
going to smell."

"Hmmph." A wave of heat suffused her cheeks.
She smelled? She tried in vain to remember the last
bath she had and gave up. He was probably right, she
did smell. Never mind that, the rogue, to even suggest
such a thing as sharing her bunk.

*But why wouldn't he? He could have me and no
one would think twice on it. He is the lord and I am
nothing to him.*

For a frantic instant, she contemplated escape
but the die had been cast—she was on her way to New
Caledonia with him. As his wife.

A deep breath steadied her nerves. "I shall pay
ye back," she declared stoutly. "Where we go—be there
cities? I can pickpocket there. No one could best a
Londoner at that. What do ye fancy—jewels, folders,
coins? I can pick just about anything."

He continued to glower at her. Her confidence
wavered. It promised to be a long and uncomfortable
voyage if she and Lord Temple Wellington could not
come to some kind of accord.

"What's a brig?" she asked brightly, hoping to
lighten his mood. "I heard the captain say that's where I
should go." She grinned at him, willing him to smile
back at her.

"Jail. Like Newgate only a lot smaller."

"Oh." She scratched her nose. "But so long as I behave, I ain't going there, right?"

"Right," he nodded.

"I can do that," she said earnestly, hands clasped in supplication. "I can behave, ye'll see."

"Aye, we'll see." He continued to lean against the door with arms crossed, looking down on her with hooded eyes.

Her stomach grew queasy. It must be the motion of the ship. It couldn't be the frank perusal of the handsome lord causing her discomfort. Could it?

Her cheeks grew hotter as the seconds ticked away.

"First things first. Tell me, why are you so desperate to come with me?"

A hundred glib answers churned through her mind. Her gaze fell to the rich fabric of his clothes. Temple looked every inch the ton that he was. She could spot them a mile away, tantalizing her with the thought of the rich purses they carried, purses that to them meant nothing, perhaps an evening's enjoyment, but to her and the others in the workhouse meant survival for another day.

"I really didn't mean to come with you. It's just that it were a chance too good to miss. An adventure." She stopped, knowing she was lying.

A black eyebrow quirked in doubt; his mouth twisted.

The reason sounded lame, even to her ears. Nay, it wasn't adventure she wanted. She could find adventure aplenty on London's streets.

How could she tell him he presented a sudden opportunity to change her life? How could she tell him of her years at the workhouse on Bishopsgate Street, with its intolerable food, its sickness and desperation, and always, always, the cold?

She shivered at the memories.

"Are you chilled?" The solicitous question startled her, as did the sudden change of subject. He seemingly had accepted her answer.

She shook her head.

"It is late," he said abruptly. "I suggest we retire for the night." He turned to grab the latch on the door. "Tomorrow we can see about getting you organized. I shall give you privacy to settle yourself."

Tar-scented air gusted into the room as he stepped through the door, slamming it behind him.

Bemused, Simone sat for a moment, fingering the medallion hanging about her neck, the one Mrs Dougherty said had been in Simone's possession when she had come to the workhouse. Touching it always gave her courage, as if it carried some great secret; it hadn't failed her yet and it worked now. She was unhurt and in one piece, wasn't she?

She straightened her shoulders before removing her tattered bonnet and shawl to place them on the shelf above her head. She kicked off her boots and grabbed the neatly folded blanket from her bunk. Curling into the fetal position on the thin feather mattress, she drew the blanket up to her chin and held it there with clenched fists. Beneath her, the motion of the ship changed, from an imperceptible bob to a gentle glide.

The *Annabelle* had set sail.

Simone's thoughts drifted much like the ship drifted with the current. She didn't want Temple to know she had hidden in his trunk to escape prison. His leaving London had been a bonus. She didn't know how long it would take to sail to New Caledonia but it would give her extra time for the constables to forget about her. And surely a few days sharing a cabin and playing the part of Lady Wellington was a small price to pay.

She couldn't turn back, even if she wanted to. Mrs Dougherty would worry about her and she felt bad about that, but there had simply not been the opportunity to bid farewell.

And what in the packet was so important to Lord Wellington that he would willingly take a stranger with him, indeed pass her off as his wife? An inquiring squeeze through the folds of oil cloth had indicated something hard, perhaps a small box. Small but heavy. How pointless to wonder about it, though—the well-hidden packet would have to wait for their return.

No, the more pressing matters were how to appease her cabin mate and how to play her part as Lady Wellington.

Temple had demanded payment from her, knowing full well she did not have it. He had been jesting about sharing her bunk. Hadn't he?

Chapter Four

Several days later, an awestruck Simone watched the *Annabelle* cut through foam-crested waves in a spray that flared out from the bow like a glittering diamond shawl. Above her head, the sails snapped and billowed and below her feet, the deck surged, rising majestically to meet each wave before dropping, down, down, only to rise again in a never-ending motion.

England lay behind her, a barely visible line on the horizon. Before her, the Atlantic Ocean rolled away so far that it didn't stop until it met the sky.

And the sky—clean, crisp, dotted with lace white clouds against a brilliant blue such as she had never seen.

It was beautiful.

It was terrifying.

It was exhilarating

It was her road to a new life.

"I ain't ever smelled air like this before." Simone gripped the ship's railing and filled her lungs, a pleasant change from London's foul air.

She glanced sideways at Temple, draped pathetically over the handrail. It was all that stopped him from tumbling into the green swells below. She supposed she should warn him to hang tight but then decided against it. The poor man suffered too much already without her nagging at him.

"Ah, Temple?"

He grunted.

"Ye know I'm not a lady of quality." This was the first opportunity she had had to broach the subject with Temple. He had avoided her blatantly, difficult to do on the confines of the *Annabelle*, but somehow he managed it.

"What did you say?" Temple barely got the question out before another bout of retching overcame him.

"I'm supposed ta be yer wife but I'm not a lady of quality. What happens when everyone on this ship figures that out?"

"Oh that." He managed to shrug even though his hands clutched the rail so tightly his shoulders could barely move. "Once the voyage is over, we'll never see any of our fellow passengers again. What they think of us is of no concern to me. Besides, I've already introduced you as my wife. Who said you needed to be a lady?"

Amazed, she looked at him. "Ye really don't care, do ye?"

He shook his head.

"But what do I have ta do? To be Lady Wellington?"

"It's simple, really. Pretend shyness. Keep your eyes lowered. If you must converse, smile and nod."

It seemed straightforward. "Very well." She nodded. "Yer the lord. If ye don't care, I suppose I don't care."

But she did care, in fact, cared very much. It was so very, very improper of her to share a cabin with a man. Even the man who had saved her neck.

"Ohhhh," Temple moaned, interrupting her thoughts.

She looked at him, the very picture of misery, and sympathy swelled within her. "Oh my, yer face is green. Maybe ye need something ta drink? I'll get it for ye." She wanted to help him but the ship's surgeon had said the only thing that would help him was time to get his sea legs. Perhaps she could get his mind off his suffering.

"Why did ye leave London? Ye were being chased but yer a lord. No one would listen to the likes of them, ye didn't have to run."

He turned her way, his face twisted in agony. "It's not a topic I care to discuss at this particular moment."

"As ye wish." Simone looked out over the vast Atlantic for several moments before curiosity nudged her again. "Where is New Caledonia?"

He groaned and pushed himself to standing, hands gripping the rail. "In the new world. Canada to be precise."

"Couldn't ye find a closer place to hide?" She wrinkled her nose. The ton—who could make sense of them?

"I am not hiding," he retorted. "I thought to make my own way and find my fortune. To that end, I have become a partner in the North West Company."

"But ye already have money."

"Nay." He shook his head. "My family may have means but I do not."

"Yer a younger son, then," she said shrewdly. "Ye got yerself in a spot of trouble and now yer shipping off for a bit to let things mend."

"It's no concern of yours." His voice was testy and he took several deep breaths in an obvious attempt to hide his annoyance. A muscle twitched in his cheek.

She had hit a nerve. His comment on finding his fortune was not so far from the truth. Remorse surged through her at the realization her passage had cost him dearly and his demand for repayment had, in fact, had some basis to it. Her promise to repay him, an idle boast at the time, took on new meaning.

"Keep your eyes on the horizon, young man." The solicitous voice gave Simone a start and she turned to see Mrs Featherstone, the captain's wife standing behind them.

"The seasickness is nothing to scoff at," the other woman continued. "Are you drinking your ginger tea?"

"I am." He nodded.

"Good." She tapped Temple on the shoulder with her fan. "You've kept Lady Wellington to yourself much too long. I came to claim her. May I?"

"Of course." Temple's lukewarm voice clearly indicated he had reservations over the invitation.

Simone glanced at him, half expecting him to blurt out the truth about her but he stood, eyes closed, clenching the railing as if his very life depended on it.

Poor man, the voyage promised to be long and uncomfortable for him.

"Oh, don't fuss, I shall look after her." Mrs Featherstone smiled, mistaking Temple's trepidation for a young husband's reluctance to lose his wife's company. "I thought to fill our days with mending and such," Mrs Featherstone remarked as she moved off, Simone in tow.

"Mending?" She cast a frantic glance to Temple, who had now opened his eyes and looked their way. She didn't know how to mend. Or sew. Or do anything a lady of quality would know how to do.

Horror filled her. It wouldn't take very long in the other woman's company for Mrs Featherstone to realize Simone was not Lord Wellington's wife.

* * *

Temple turned to give Simone an encouraging wink. She couldn't avoid Mrs Featherstone's company forever and as long as Simone followed his instructions, all would be fine.

He watched until she disappeared around the main mast. It had been quite a battle to get her to bathe but it had been well worth the effort.

Clean, Simone was pretty. There was no denying the allure of the rose pink lips, the creamy skin and pale blonde, curly hair. A bit too skinny for his liking, perhaps, but nothing a few weeks of decent food wouldn't fix.

She wore a dress borrowed from Mrs Featherstone. It hung like a sack from her skinny shoulders and exposed her tatty boots, but its lavender colour enhanced the blue of her eyes.

An idle thought crossed his mind—what would the London seamstress so favoured by his mother do for his companion? A decent outfit would improve her already appealing looks that much more. He shook his head over the absurd thought. It would never happen so why waste time thinking on it.

He took another breath in an effort to settle his stomach. Ginger tea, ugh. It reminded him of being spoon-fed the nasty stuff by an unsympathetic nanny, of which there had been a parade throughout his early childhood.

Simone's questions, however, had set his mind to churning. Why, in fact, had he decided on a sojourn in the new world? A myriad of reasons, really, starting with his boredom with the superficiality of London society and culminating in a partnership gone awry.

The partnership with the unsavoury Peter Mortimer-Rae, a well-known fixture in London's east side, had provided him with a tidy, albeit illegal, source of income.

However, Mortimer-Rae had not taken kindly to Temple's sudden decision to leave London; words had been exchanged and an angry Temple had stormed off but not before grabbing the carved teak box inlaid with semi-precious stones sitting on Mortimer-Rae's desk. The box held gold coins and the deed to a sizeable property in North Yorkshire – in short, Temple's future as a country squire once things settled down.

Temple had won it fair and square in a game of cards with Mortimer-Rae but the man had refused to hand it over. It was that, wrapped in oiled cloth, which Simone had stolen.

Finding her in his trunk had been an unfortunate stroke of luck and, as much as he admired her bravado, he did not relish the idea of her tagging along.

He gritted his teeth. Of necessity, he would accept her company. To put it plainly, he needed the packet she had stolen from him.

* * *

"I really like the dress," Simone said shyly once she and Mrs Featherstone were seated at one corner of the ship's dining table. She knew Temple had told her not to speak but she really wanted to thank the woman for her kindness. She looked down and smoothed her hands over the soft pale lavender wool, trimmed with lace about the collar and cuffs. So finely spun, it felt like silk beneath her calloused fingers. "I ain't never had one so fine. Thank ye."

"You are welcome," Mrs Featherstone replied absently, her mind on the task before them and not on Simone. As she placed items on the table, she listed them off. "A needle, a thimble, some thread." She paused. "Now, where did I leave the scissors, they must still be in our cabin. I trimmed the captain's beard this morning." She stood up. "I shan't be a moment." Without waiting for a reply, she darted out of the room.

Simone watched her leave. The captain's wife looked like someone's granny, plump and grey-haired, her affable face unlined save for a few wrinkles about the eyes and mouth. Hopefully, her temperament matched the pleasant exterior. Simone did not relish informing the woman she did not know how to mend.

Footsteps pounded down the passage way; someone shouted. Apprehensive, Simone looked to the door. It wouldn't do for the captain to find her here unaccompanied. It grew silent; she looked out the small row of windows to her left.

There was not much to see, water then sky, water then sky as the ship challenged the waves. The shifting horizon seemed to taunt her—up, how could she repay Temple, down, she must think of something, up, how to repay Temple, down, she would think of something.

"Who gave you permission to be in here?" A gravelly voice cut the air. Simone jerked her head around.

Captain Featherstone stood in the doorway, barring her exit, fists clenching and unclenching. His eyes were narrowed, his brow creased with displeasure. He took a menacing step toward her.

Words left her; she stared at him. He was not much taller than her but stocky and well-muscled. If he wanted, he could drag her from her seat and toss her in the brig. Overboard even.

"Me passage has been paid." She pushed back her chair and stood to face him. She refused to be cowed by his bullying manner.

"That doesn't give you the right to wander about."

"I'm not wandering. Yer wife and I are sewing."

"That is so, captain." Mrs Featherstone pushed her way past her husband. "Leave us be, you have more serious matters to deal with than worry about this young woman."

"I don't trust her," he growled.

"She's under my care," she soothed. "I enjoy the female companionship."

After a few more glowering seconds, the captain turned on his heel and, without saying a word, stalked off.

Shaking her head, the captain's wife turned to Simone. "He's a good man, really he is. A bit hard-headed from time to time is all." She laid a bolt of periwinkle blue seersucker on the table along with a pile of garments. The very ones, Simone supposed with a sinking heart, needing mending.

"This is a lovely colour for you. Look what else I have." She held up a pair of tooled kid slippers. "The captain bought these for me. But they simply don't fit."

"Oh," Simone sighed, reaching for the slippers. She held them up to her face to inhale the rich leather scent, unable to picture the brusque captain buying a gift for his wife. Laying the slippers to one side, she fingered the lightweight fabric. It had an interesting texture beneath her fingers. "It's pretty."

"Go ahead and start on the new dress. I'll address the mending and then help you." The captain's wife picked up a needle and threaded it deftly. She plucked a linen shift from the pile and began to sew, head down, humming, needle fair flying through the fabric.

Feeling useless, Simone sat and fingered the seersucker. The seconds ticked by until she could no longer delay.

"Mrs Featherstone?" She hated how her voice squeaked.

"Yes?" The other woman didn't lift her head.

"I, ah, I don't know how ta sew."

"What did you say?" The needle stopped mid-air; the captain's wife did not lift her head.

"I don't know how."

Mrs Featherstone raised her gaze, her face a picture of disbelief.

Simone smiled weakly. Oy, she hated to disappoint the captain's wife, she were a nice lady.

"You're not long married to Lord Wellington, are you," she said icily. Her mouth compressed and she tilted her head to look Simone full in the eyes.

Simone bit her lip and shook her head.

"And you did not borrow my dress because you lost your luggage, did you?"

Again, Simone shook her head.

Mrs Featherstone pursed her lips; her eyes narrowed. Disbelief was giving way to anger, for her cheeks had gone apple red. "I find you a rather unorthodox choice for Lord Wellington as you're clearly not of his station. However, it is none of my concern. You are both paying passengers and it's not my place to question the captain. Or, for that matter, to question your lord about you. He has presented you as his wife and therefore I must assume you are."

"I, ah, could learn ta sew," Simone stammered, trying to steer the conversation away from her supposed marriage in a futile attempt to quiet her own discomfort. "Really, I could. I want to. I really want to."

She didn't wish to provoke the woman. As the captain's wife, perhaps she had the power to throw Simone in the brig. Which was the last place Simone wanted to be. She shivered.

"But." Mrs Featherstone held up a finger. "I don't like being lied to." Her voice was reproving; her face stern.

"I am sorry. Really, I am...." Simone's voice trailed away. Miserable, she lowered her gaze. It caught on the lovely slippers. She reached over and pushed them across the table.

The other woman pushed them back. "Keep them. They're of no use to me."

Startled, Simone looked up.

The red on the woman's cheeks began to fade; her expression settled back in its customary pleasant lines. "You must promise me that you shall not lie to me any further."

Chastened, Simone bowed her head. "I promise," she mumbled. Oy, how long had they been at sea? Three days? Within a matter of minutes in Mrs Featherstone's company, Simone had been found out. She had met none of the others on board yet and already her position as Lady Wellington was suspect.

"Our passengers are usually men." Mrs Featherstone's voice was brisk. "I'm thankful for your company. So yes, I shall teach you."

Simone jerked her head up. The woman, despite her doubts over Simone's background, had made a charitable offer. Gratitude flowed through her at the woman's kindliness and she resolved not to disappoint her. "Ye think I can learn?" She looked down at her hands, the knuckles scraped and nails broken. They looked like workman's hands, not meant at all for womanly arts.

"Without a doubt." Mrs Featherstone's voice was firm. "Idle hands beget the devil's work. Depending on the winds, we have another five or six weeks at sea. I warn you, I am going to be a stern taskmaster." She waggled a finger at Simone. "I expect nothing less than your full attention."

"Yes, ma'am," Simone mumbled, still doubtful over the whole idea. However, she didn't want to fail the kindly woman sitting across from her.

With a sigh, she picked up a needle.

Oy, she wanted to please Mrs Featherstone but sewing didn't seem nearly as important as figuring out how to portray a convincing Lady Wellington or how to repay Temple.

* * *

Lesson finished, Simone made her way above deck and spied Temple near the bow. With his dark hair blowing in the wind, he looked like a pirate, or at least what she imagined a pirate would look like. Even his expression was pirate-like, dark and brooding, and his fists still clenched the rail. She wondered about his thoughts. They must be troubling to him, for his fingers were taut, whitened against the wood.

Matching her gait to the movement of the ship, she started toward him. He glanced over and his face cleared at seeing her.

She tucked her new slippers under one arm and leaned on the railing beside him. "Ain't ye sick anymore?"

"A little." His mouth made a rueful moue. "But I had a nap and the ship's surgeon has assured me I shall live. His recommendation is for fresh air of which," he swept his arm about, "there is plenty."

"I been thinking," she began, hesitant to broach the subject. She was grateful to him for bringing her along and didn't know how to say it, or show it. "About how I could repay ye."

He cocked his head. "Yes?"

"I could teach ye a thing or two."

"Now what, precisely, do you think you can teach me," he teased. "How to sew?"

"Oh no." She shook her head. "I don't like sewing. It's tedious and makes me eyes ache." It seemed pointless to tell him this morning had been her first attempt at it. "No. A few tricks favoured by pickpockets. So ye know what to look for."

"I think not." Patently disinterested, he looked away, out over the water.

"I see." She rubbed her chin. Oy, what else could she offer, she had nothing of value. Nay, that wasn't quite true—she knew the location of his mysterious package. Which didn't do her any good at this precise moment. "I know." She brightened.

"Perhaps I could entertain ye. We could play cards. Or dice."

"Cards or dice?" Astonishment coloured his voice.

"Aye. Or don't women play that in your world?" It was the first reference she had made to the social chasm between them. He appeared not to notice and for that she was grateful. She felt awkward enough as is so close to him, sharing his cabin.

"I shall think on it. In the meantime," he slanted a glance at her, "why don't you tell me where you came from? What of your parents?"

"Mrs Dougherty is the only parent I ever knew."

"Who is Mrs Dougherty?"

"Someone who took me in." She pointed her finger then changed the subject. "Look, there's a sail on the horizon." Temple didn't need to know about the workhouse on Bishopsgate Street. She shivered as a sudden cloud veiled the sun.

"You've a chill, get your shawl."

There he went again, being all solicitous with her. It made her feel special. She straightened her shoulders and pushed back from the rail.

"Before you go, why don't you put those on?" He pointed to the kid leather slippers tucked beneath her arm.

Her head jerked around. Was he teasing her again? But no, his face was solemn. "Is it proper?"

"Is what proper?"

"To take me boots off in front of ye."

"It's not really, but...." He leaned toward her. Her heart lurched and began to beat a wild cadence; her breath froze in her throat. So close she could see the golden flecks in his eyes. So close she could smell the man scent of him—spicy and smoky and something else. With an effort, she forced herself to pay attention to his next words. He wasn't for the likes of her and she would do well to remember that.

"I shan't tell," he whispered.

She shrank back. Seemingly unaware of his effect on her, he grabbed the slippers, brushing his elbow against her breast as he did so. Lightning heat burned her skin beneath the fabric of her dress; her face heated.

Mercifully, he stepped back but not before placing the slippers at her feet. Her heart resumed its normal rhythm and she drew in a large, shaky breath. She pulled off first one boot, then the other before glancing at him. He watched her, intent, predator-like.

In an instant, Temple grabbed the boots and pitched them overboard.

"Oy," she squealed. "Them were my only pair." She dashed to the railing in time to catch the sad sight of her boots disappearing into the green murk. She rounded on him, arms akimbo and forehead wrinkled. "Why did ye do that?"

"They're disgusting and they stink." He nudged the slippers with his toe. "Now put these on. Don't worry, I shan't say a word about the hole in your stocking."

A crimson-faced Simone followed his orders.

"Much better," he remarked casually.

Yes, thought Temple, the sight of two trim ankles below the too short dress was infinitely more pleasing. He let his gaze linger on them before raising it to look her square in the face.

"Have ye looked yer fill?" Her icy voice matched her cool manner and she glared at him.

He couldn't help it—his laughter burst forth.

"Forgive me," he managed to choke out, tears streaming down his cheeks. He whipped the handkerchief from his pocket and mopped his face before bursting forth again in gales of laughter.

"It ain't funny," she sputtered. "Stop it."

"Aye, you're right, it isn't funny. They were your boots and I had no right to give them the heave ho. Once we arrive in Montreal, I'll replace them. But the look on your face as I tossed them was priceless."

"I'm tired," she said suddenly, obviously stung by his laughter. "I'm going to the cabin."

"Very well. I've a mind to stay on deck." He could tell by her relieved expression she had been worried he would accompany her.

She turned to go then turned back. "Mrs Featherstone invited us to join the captain's table for supper."

Her face still bore traces of red. She looked vibrant and alive and it gave him the strangest sensation of wanting to cosset her. How ironic, for he knew she didn't see herself as needing cosseting.

She waited for his answer so he quelled his unruly thoughts. "Then we shall have to go."

"Really? I were hoping ye'd say no. What with the captain being angry with me and all."

"You cannot evade him altogether. Besides, it wouldn't do to turn down his wife's invitation," he said, ignoring the clanging cacophony of warning bells in his mind.

Chapter Five

Three hours later, before the first course even appeared, Temple regretted accepting the invitation.

The evening had started innocuously enough.

He and Simone entered the empty dining room to find the table set with a white damask tablecloth, gold rimmed porcelain, fine glassware, heavy silver and even place cards. Several heavy silver dishes, a cut crystal decanter of red wine and a woven basket of oranges graced the sideboard.

"You sit here. I'm across from you." He pointed to her chair.

He strolled around the table to read the rest of the place cards while she sidled past the side board to her chair. From the corner of his eye, he noticed she snatched an orange and stuffed it into her pocket, looking at him all the while with a wary expression. He pretended not to notice; she was, after all, a paying passenger and perfectly entitled to an orange if she so wished.

They sat down and Simone immediately picked up her card. "This says my name?" At his nod, she tucked the card into her sleeve.

Not surprising, she didn't know how to read. How, then, would she comport herself at dinner if a simple place card held fascination for her?

Foreboding tickled Temple's spine.

However, she sat with hands demurely folded in her lap, a hesitant smile on her lips. It was a promising sign and he turned his attention to the other passengers as they trickled in.

As a cargo ship, not a passenger ship, their dinner companions were small in number and consisted of the first mate, Allan McCabe, the ship's surgeon, Dr Nicholas Taylor, and Gordon Dixon, a clerk bound for Montreal. Last to arrive were Mrs Featherstone, who smiled at Simone, and the captain. He gave Simone a fierce look then made a point of ignoring her, stomping to his seat at the head of the table.

No sooner had the introductions been completed than Simone proceeded to inspect the cutlery before declaring "This be fine silver."

She picked up the dinner plate and turned it over, running her finger along the gold trimmed edge before replacing it. The crystal glasses were inspected with the same thoroughness. These she flicked with her finger until they produced a fine ring. "Nice," she declared.

Foreboding again tickled Temple's spine. He wanted to enjoy his first real meal at sea in peace but this could be an awkward situation if he didn't handle it properly. He would have to count on her quick wits.

He made an extravagant show of unfolding his napkin and placing it on his lap; she followed suit. At least she had noticed.

"Are we having them?" Simone pointed toward the basket of oranges.

Bloody hell, what was her fascination with the fruit? He opened his mouth to answer but the captain's wife forestalled him.

"No." Mrs Featherstone shook her head. "Perhaps later. Why do you ask?"

"They're me favourite," she replied enthusiastically. "I don't know why, I've just always liked them." Her voice trailed away when she noticed Dr Taylor looking at her.

"Good choice," Dr Taylor said. "We have a barrel of oranges on board. They're good for the scurvy."

"Scurvy?" Simone's brow wrinkled.

"Aye, scurvy. It's caused by a deficiency of ascorbic acid. Its symptoms are bleeding gums, loose teeth, aching joints and red spots." Dr Taylor stopped. "Oh, dear, I must sound like a medical encyclopaedia. I just finished my studies last week," he explained apologetically.

"That sounds like spring sickness." Her brow smoothed in understanding.

"Spring sickness, scorbutus, scurvy, it's one and the same."

"And oranges fixes that?"

"Well, fresh food of any kind is good," interjected Allan McCabe, the first mate. "It's just that citrus fruits keep well."

"I see." Simone was silent for an instant. "That explains why I never got spring sickness."

"How so?" Dr Taylor asked.

"I stole me an orange almost every day. From the markets. I went to a different one every day, so I wouldn't get caught," she bragged.

Dismay surged through Temple. Didn't she realize she'd admitted to being a thief? The charade as his wife had hardly begun and already it teetered on the edge of disaster.

"Simone!" He tapped his finger on his mouth to shush her.

"Simone, really!" Mrs Featherstone exclaimed.

Simone looked at Temple. At the sight of his murderous expression, she switched her gaze to the captain's wife.

"I didn't mean to say that," she mumbled. "Sometimes I say things without thinking." A flush crept through her cheeks.

"Agreed," Temple growled. "So enough chatter and let us begin our meal." He couldn't decide whether his own embarrassment at Simone's behaviour or embarrassment on her behalf peppered his brow with beads of sweat. He swiped his forehead with his napkin, frantically shaking his head when he noticed Simone about to copy him. Bloody hell, how would they survive this meal without looking like a pair of buffoons? He groaned inwardly and looked at the clock.

She blinked and replaced her napkin on her lap.

Mrs Featherstone served the soup from a chipped tureen, carefully passing out the bowls one by one. Simone immediately grabbed her bowl and slurped its contents.

Temple gave her a ferocious kick under the table.

At another time, the sight of two piercing blue eyes glowering at him over the rim of her bowl might have amused him but not tonight, not now. He rolled his eyes skyward. The evening promised to be interminable. Somehow they must get through it without drawing more attention. No, he corrected himself. Without *Simone* drawing any more attention.

He shook his head slightly. "Watch me first," he whispered. "Do as I do."

She put down her bowl, flashing him an indignant glance in the process. *How else am I supposed to eat soup,* she seemed to say.

He picked up his spoon in his right hand; so did she. He dipped it into his bowl and raised it to his lips. She did too although it was plain to see she had overfilled the spoon for a trail of amber broth dripped off of it and onto the table cloth. Not too bad, considering the motion of the ship. He gave her an encouraging smile.

Simone took it as permission to go ahead and finish the bowl for she lowered her eyes and bent her head down closer to the bowl, shuttling the liquid between it and her lips without looking up once.

He contemplated giving her another kick but decided against it, opting instead to eat his own soup while it was still hot. A quick glance around the table confirmed the others were occupied with the tricky liquid as well. Perhaps they wouldn't notice her struggle with the soup.

Of course, she finished long before he did. Soup dripped from her chin and he paused long enough to pat his napkin to his lips. Her expression brightened with understanding and she did the same.

After that she fidgeted while he finished his soup. She tapped her fork on the edge of her plate before tapping it on her glass.

The conversation died away. Temple swivelled his head to find the doctor, clerk and first mate gaping at Simone with a mixture of surprise and amusement. A sympathetic Mrs Featherstone cast an apprehensive glance at the captain, who regarded Simone with blatant dislike.

Bloody hell, they'd only finished the soup course and already things had become undone. Perhaps an explanation would be in order.

"Lady Wellington comes from rather unusual circumstances," he began in his most pompous voice.

"What is unusual, Lord Wellington, is that you think you can teach the chit table manners." Captain Featherstone leaned back in his chair and crossed his arms. "I fear you're wasting your time."

Temple's hackles rose at the captain's haughty manner. "That sounds like a challenge to me. Perhaps you are up for a wager?"

The captain shrugged. "Perhaps."

"I shall teach Simone proper table manners." He ignored her sudden gasp and focused on the captain.

The captain shook his head. "We have a good five weeks ahead of us. A monkey could learn to eat during that time. You must up the stakes."

"I shall turn her into a proper lady. Speech, comportment, everything." Inspiration struck as he thought of his limited supply of coins. "If I do, you return our fares."

"And if you do not?"

"We pay you double." The brash words slipped out before he realized the consequences. They had better win—he took pride in the fact he always covered his wagers but the sad truth was, he didn't have double the fare.

"You have yourself a wager, my lord." The captain leaned forward and held out his hand for Temple to shake. "Our last dinner on board will be the test and Mrs Featherstone shall judge."

"Agreed," Temple said as he shook the proffered hand. "Please go on with your meal and do not pay us any attention." He inclined his head to the others at the table and turned his regard to Simone, who sat there scowling with bottom lip jutted out, plainly not pleased with the wager.

He flashed a reassuring smile and picked up his knife and fork. "The utensils are there for a purpose, Simone. The fork goes in your left hand and the knife in your right."

Reluctantly, she complied with Temple's instructions, holding the utensils awkwardly upright before her. Her lip still jutted out and for a crazy instant, he wanted to kiss it back into place. He shook his head at the ridiculous notion. Concentrate on the task at hand, he told himself.

"Good." He nodded his approval at her death grip on the utensils. At least she wasn't arguing with him, which he had been expecting when he saw her rebellious expression.

She continued to scowl.

"Now watch me." Temple placed his fork in his own slice of beef and neatly cut off a morsel with the knife. Again he waited for her.

Silent, she glared at him and her left hand quivered as if she would rather stab him with the fork than her own piece of meat.

Nonetheless, she followed his instructions.

"Oy," she grunted. "It ain't as easy as it looks."

The meat slid about on her plate as she struggled with it. She managed to cut off a chunk, holding it triumphantly in the air. Unfortunately, the piece she had cut was too large and she chewed for some time before choking it down. "It takes so much longer to eat," she complained.

"Yes, nevertheless dining is an activity meant to be enjoyed."

"This ain't very enjoyable," Simone muttered as she tackled the beef again. After fumbling with it a minute or two more, her face flushed and she gave up, piling her knife and fork with a clatter on the plate before pushing the plate aside.

She stood then and, paying no heed to the startled glances of her dinner companions, stalked off, a perfect picture of frustration.

Temple excused himself and caught up to her in the hall outside their cabin. She had her hand on the latch and at the sound of his footsteps she tipped her nose in the air in an apparent ploy to ignore him.

"Simone, wait." He grabbed her elbow and turned her about.

"Don't ye think ye should have asked me?" The words exploded from her as if from a fermenting keg left in the sun too long.

"About what?"

"About the bet with the captain. About making me into a lady." She swallowed hard.

"How could I? The opportunity presented itself and I took it. You've been looking for a way to pay me back. It seemed a reasonable solution."

"Reasonable ta ye, maybe." She pulled her elbow free to frown at him. "Not ta me."

He recognized her belligerence for what it was: apprehension and self-doubt. "Why are you afraid? I vow, I shall shape you into a lady of quality in no time."

She looked at him, disbelief shining in her eyes.

"Use your wits. You learned to pickpocket, the best in London if I recall your boastful words. Now use your talents for something else. Look upon it as a dare."

"But what if I can't do it?" she whispered, eyes wide. Her gaze held his for an instant before she looked away.

"Nonsense. You'll be an apt pupil, you'll see."

With a start, he realized he meant every word. He had been in her company enough to know real intelligence hid beneath those distracting blue eyes.

Too, there was nothing he enjoyed more than a challenge and this promised to be a good one. He pulled open the cabin door. "After you."

"Thank ye." She marched in ahead of him, ducking behind the sail that had been tacked to the ceiling to serve as curtain.

He could hear the creak as she sat down on her bunk.

"Simone?"

"Aye?"

"Don't worry, you'll get it mastered in no time."

"Aye."

"Simone?"

"Aye?" Her voice was muffled, as if she were trying to stifle sobs.

"Are you all right?" He reached over and swiped aside the curtain, hooking it behind a nail.

As he suspected, tears streamed down her cheeks. His heart squeezed at the sight and then squeezed again when she managed to pull herself together enough to glare at him.

"Can I have me privacy please?" She wiped her nose on the back of her hand. "Good night."

"Of course. I shall spend my evening elsewhere. Good night to you."

Simone watched the door close behind him. Golly, he confused her, difficult but kind too, to offer to teach her even though he knew of her dubious background.

But how could he possibly turn her, Mona Dougherty, late of Bishopsgate Street, into Lady Wellington, a lady of quality? Ladies of quality weren't found in the workhouses and busy streets of Houndsditch and Spitalfields.

Genteel ladies were born that way, born into a life of privilege and protection. They didn't become ladies as the result of a frivolous wager so how could he expect that of her?

She drooped forward, propping her elbows on her knees to cup her chin in her hands. Two tears balled and slid down her cheeks to drop unnoticed in her lap. She wanted him to be proud of her, wanted him to smile at her in that dark-eyed way that turned her knees into jelly. In short, she wanted to be the very thing she wasn't: a lady of quality.

She considered what he had said, about using her wits. Although it seemed a Herculean task, he had said she could learn. She sat up and wiped her cheeks.

Learn she would.

And if I don't?

Chapter Six

Several days later, on the foredeck of the *Annabelle*, Simone wondered if she had made a serious mistake.

"Ee-ewe," she said, face screwed in concentration. Her lips refused to form the word properly and it felt like she had chestnuts tucked in her cheeks.

"No, like this," Temple prompted. "You." He said it slowly. "Watch my mouth. You."

"That's what I said," she retorted before trying it again. "Ee-ewe." Oy, how many times would she have to repeat it before he was satisfied?

As many times as it would take, she vowed. *I don't want to disappoint him.*

"Well, actually, it's not quite what you said. But you're getting closer," he encouraged.

The two sat side by side on the plank bench behind the foremast. Above them, the sails strained against the overcast sky and the lack of sun turned the ocean around them to dull pewter.

The dreary sight didn't dampen Simone's spirits for she sat with Temple, basking in his undivided attention. Plus, she wore a new dress made from the periwinkle blue seersucker that Mrs Featherstone had given her. She ran her hands appreciatively across her lap before hugging her borrowed shawl closer against the chill in the air. She turned her head to look Temple square in the face.

"Why can't I just say ye like I always done? And who makes up the rules anyway," she added mischievously, wanting to see his reaction to her impertinence. Darkening eyes and a frown flashing across his face rewarded her.

"Hundreds of English scholars before you made up the rules," he said stiffly, holding up the grammar book discovered in the ship's library only this morning. "You are not one to argue."

"Ye," she said defiantly. Then she smiled at him. "Ye."

"I'm just telling you how it's pronounced properly." Exasperation tinged his voice. "To be a lady of quality, one must sound like a lady of quality."

"Yer no fun." She stuck out her tongue at him. "EE-you. You."

"Better, much better."

"You." She said it again. "You."

"Very good." He smiled at her. "How was your sewing lesson this morning? Mind you answer me with proper diction."

She liked it when he smiled at her, it turned her insides to mush, like pease pudding. Her gaze lingered on his lips, at the even white teeth they framed. Her breath caught in her throat. How would it feel to brush her lips against his? Highly improper, she knew, but oh, so very, very tempting. Without realizing it, she leaned toward him a little.

"Simone?"

His voice penetrated her reverie. With an effort, she straightened and pulled her thoughts back to his question, but not before one last, regretful look at his mouth.

"The lesson went well, thank ye, no, thank you, my lord. I learned how ta—er, to finish a button hole."

"Again," he commanded. "Speak slowly if it helps."

"The lesson went well, thank you, my lord. I learned how to finish a button hole." She clapped her hands. "I did it, didn't I?"

"Yes, you did. On that note today's lesson is finished. Shall we take a turn about the deck before supper?" He stood up and held out his hand to her.

"That would be lovely, my lord." Simone said it slowly, carefully.

She was learning but oh my, what a challenge. Her mind always raced a sentence or two ahead of her mouth so she had a tendency to mangle the words even more. But Temple was unfailingly patient with her. Fun to be with, too, with always an amusing anecdote or observation to break the tedium of her instruction.

She put her hand in his and stood. His warm fingers clasped her cold ones and she felt the vigour pulsing through him. She looked down, mesmerized by the sight of her small fist clasped within his large, very masculine one. Reluctantly she pulled her fingers free.

"Simone, I should put the book away. Carry on without me, I'll join you."

It had become their habit over the past few days to take a stroll up and down the deck and she looked forward to it every day for it marked the end of the daily lesson.

And she also looked forward to how he pulled her fingers through his elbow as if she were a real lady walking through London proper. Sometimes she would even let herself think fanciful thoughts about being his real lady. Not for long, though, only a few minutes. She didn't belong in his world and well she knew it.

"Yes, my lord." She answered him promptly. That phrase had been easy to master. She liked to fall back on it as much as she could to build her confidence.

She made her way to the bow to wait for Temple and gripped the rail, looking down at the skirts swaying about her legs.

The pretty seersucker dress was the first item of new clothing she had ever owned. What a lovely sensation it had been this morning to slide the stylish gown over her head, over her arms, smoothing it down past her hips until it fell to her ankles. The stateroom had only a small cracked mirror and in vain she had pirouetted in front of it, trying to see as much of herself as possible.

"Now here be a pretty piece, just the thing for a lonely sailor."

A raspy voice interrupted her thoughts and an arm draped boldly about her shoulders, trapping her.

"Wh—what?" Simone tried to free herself but pressed against the railing by the sailor, she didn't have room to manoeuvre.

"Give Petey a kiss, cutie." The sailor leaned toward her, wet lips mere inches from her face. She almost gagged on his rancid breath.

"No!" She struggled against the man, pulling on the rail in an effort to lean away as far as she could.

"Oho, I like 'em with a little fight." Petey grinned and tried to kiss her again.

Frantic, she managed to gain enough space to kick him in the ankle. At the blow, the sailor loosened his grip a fraction, giving her the opportunity she needed. A swift knee to the soft flesh at the apex of his legs and Petey doubled over with a grunt.

"That'll teach ye to bother me." Satisfied with her handiwork, she stepped back.

"Ye'll rue the day you crossed Petey Malone," he gasped, still hunched over. He swiped at her with one hand. The other arm he still held protectively over his middle.

"I kin take care of meself." She took another step back, out of the sailor's reach. "Next time, it shan't be such an easy blow."

Her warning must have worked, for Petey's eyes widened and he dropped his arm.

It took her a second or two to realize that Petey's eyes were not on her, but rather focused behind her, over her left shoulder. Surprised, Simone turned around.

Disbelief surged through her, followed by joy at the sight of Temple, stone-faced and with murderous intent in his eyes. He had come to her rescue, as if she were a real lady.

Temple reached forward and grabbed the man by the throat, holding him at arm's length. "I suggest you apologize to Lady Wellington."

"She ain't no lady. She ain't nothing but street trash. Ye can't blame a sailor for taking a little fun when he can have it," the man whined.

"Apologize or else." Temple's threat took tangible form and hung in the air between them like a sinister shadow. The two eyed each other until finally, Petey looked away.

"Beggin' yer pardon, my lady," he spat out, a dull flush staining his weathered cheeks. It was obvious the man was not happy about the apology.

"I accept your apology on, er, my wife's behalf," Temple growled. "Now take yourself off and be about your business."

The sailor couldn't resist a parting shot as he limped away. "Yer a fine one to talk. She ain't yer wife. Ye've been sharing her bed for days now, when are ye going to share with the rest of us?"

Temple said nothing, although the sudden clench of his jaw showed the other man had hit a nerve. He waited until Petey disappeared from view, then swung about to face Simone.

"Are you all right?" The anxiety in Temple's eyes warmed Simone like the sun peeking through on a chilly spring day. No man had been concerned about her before. No woman either for that matter, although occasionally Mrs Dougherty would fuss about Simone's comings and goings.

"Aye, it were nothing," she replied.

"It was nothing," he corrected gently.

"It was nothing," she repeated. "Nothing I haven't managed before."

Stern-faced and silent, he nodded.

His harsh features daunted her. Had she done something wrong? "I didn't really hurt him." Her voice trailed away and she clasped her hands together.

Unexpectedly, a grin split his face. "I daresay you handled yourself like nobody's business. Where did you learn that little trick?"

"I saw a thing or two out and about on the streets. But Mrs Dougherty taught me that one. She were, no—was—worried about me. She didn't like me being a pickpocket."

"Oh?"

"Aye. She said with my looks I should try and better myself. I tried, really, I tried but…." She stopped and shrugged her shoulders. "Beggar woman? Bar maid? Whore? None of that appeals to me. Kitchen help? Housemaid? I don't come from your world, my lord. Growing up in a workhouse and with no references, do ye think I could find myself a position in a fancy house? And if I did, then find myself with a bun in the oven because I caught the eye of the master?" She looked Temple full in the eyes. "It didn't take me long to figure I could do much better at going after the careless ones. It ain't, isn't," she corrected herself, "respectable, but at least I got me dignity."

Or I did have until I started sharing your cabin.

Simone looked away to the distant horizon. Did she imagine it, or had the sky become a little darker? She sucked in a breath of air and exhaled it slowly. It served no purpose to voice her doubts. Temple had been nothing but kind to her and she must try harder if she wanted to confirm his faith in her abilities. It was just so difficult sometimes.

"You do," Temple nodded. Yes, he thought, she had her dignity but at what price?

Furthermore, his reaction to the sailor accosting Simone had surprised him. Rage had overtaken him and his first thought had been to throttle the man.

Plainly, other than Mrs Featherstone who was perhaps too nice to voice her disbelief, no one on the ship believed they were married. Petey provided ample testament to that. Feeling a dolt, Temple began to understand Simone's delicate situation. Her virtue may be intact but who in their right mind would believe that of her? She wanted nothing more than to earn a decent living with dignity and respect, taking what the fates had handed her and making the best of it.

He studied her profile closely. Her nose was straight but pert, the jaw delicate, and the eyelashes long and lush. Her neck where it disappeared into the ruffled collar of her dress was creamy smooth. By looks alone, if he had met her at any society function rather than on the docks one foggy evening, he would never doubt her background. Intriguing, really, for she did not fit his idea of a street urchin in the slightest. She was too, too—his mind grasped for the proper word—patrician.

Nonetheless she was what she was and for the wager to be successful, she would have to accustom herself to being his social equal, with all the rules and restrictions of the ton. It was up to him to see it happened.

"Simone, you must be chaperoned from now on."

"Why," she asked him sarcastically. "Everyone knows we are not married."

"Everyone knows you share my cabin but we know it's a matter of convenience only. Just because everyone thinks the worst doesn't mean it's true. A lady of quality would be chaperoned." He shook his head. "Why didn't I think of that before?"

Because, he answered himself mentally, she had never looked as attractive before as she did in her new blue dress. He took another long, appraising look at her. Blood rushed to his loins and he fought the urge to take her in his arms, to taste the luscious lips beneath his own, to kiss her repeatedly until they both were senseless.

"Lady of quality? No one believes that of me," she scoffed.

At her sarcastic voice, he was brought back to the conversation with a jolt. Regretfully, he tucked away the pleasant image of her in his arms.

"I do," he replied stoutly. "Being chaperoned is really for your own protection."

"I kin protect meself," she announced. "And I could have run away. I'm quick on my feet."

"Run?" He looked pointedly about them. "To where? There?" He pointed his finger to the crow's nest on the main mast. "Or perhaps over there." He pointed over the railing. "Assuming you can swim, that is."

"Oh, all right," Simone grumped.

She hated to admit Temple was right. She stood on the deck of a ship, with nowhere to run. Here there were no alleys or alcoves to duck into, no doorjambs to press against, no crowds to disappear into. Here was a three mast wooden ship, insignificant against the vastness surrounding them. She couldn't run if she wanted to.

"When do we start, then, with the chaperoning?" Voice resigned, she slumped against the railing.

More rules, apparently. Her previous life, so restricted due to the circumstances of her birth, was nothing but freedom in comparison to a lady of quality. Before, short of running foul of the law, she had no one to answer to. She could come and go as she pleased, say what she pleased, behave as she pleased. No one expected anything of her.

Now, her entire day was planned, all because of a silly wager. At first, it had been easy enough but now Temple told her how to eat, how to talk, how to walk, with nary a minute to herself.

How she had once envied the ladies as they visited the shops, so perfect, so carefree, while she stood cold, dirty and shivering in the street.

However, ladies of quality paid a price. For all intents and purposes, they lived in a prison. Not a prison of bars and stone but an invisible prison imposed on them by the society in which they lived.

Sighing, she pulled out from beneath her dress the gold medallion hanging about her neck. It usually lay hidden beneath the floor boards beside her cot in the workhouse but she had been wearing it the day she met Temple. She rubbed her thumb over it, taking comfort in the familiar grooves that formed the image of a crest.

She wanted Temple to be proud of her, to repay the faith he had in her. If it meant more rules, then so be it.

The wager had not been made by her, but she would honour it.

* * *

Simone cheered up at dinner. Temple had not noticed her new dress but Gordon Dixon, the young clerk, couldn't keep his eyes off her. Only it wasn't Mr Dixon's admiring eyes she wanted, but Temple's.

Truthfully, she wanted Temple to find her attractive, to see her as a woman and not an obligation. Impossible, of course, considering the difference in their stations but that thought crept in her mind every now and then to tease her with its ridiculousness.

She turned her attention back to the young man. "You may seat me," she murmured.

"Of course," he stammered, beet red. He held out his elbow and Simone lightly placed her hand on it. "Lady Wellington, you look particularly lovely this evening,"

"Why, thank you, Mr Dixon." She replied slowly, carefully forming her words as Temple had taught her. She batted her eyelashes and almost laughed out loud at the result it had on the poor fellow. Beads of sweat popped out on his forehead and he almost fell over in his attempt to pull out the chair for her.

Really, this was too easy. The young man had turned to putty in her hands. She pretended not to notice the scowl on Temple's face as she smiled at the clerk, enjoying the influence she had over the smitten fellow.

How lovely to have the clerk's attention and so delicious for her ego. For once, she looked forward to the evening.

* * *

"Your display at dinner appalled me," Temple snarled as he shut the cabin door before turning around to face her. "A married lady of quality never carries on in such a blatant manner."

She looked at him, amazed. He had ignored her all evening, so why this reaction?

Realization cascaded through her.

"Why, you are jealous," she said in her very best lady of quality of voice.

"I am not," he growled back at her.

"Oh, but you are." She clapped her hands in delight.

"Don't be ridiculous." He pushed past her to stand in front of the porthole. He stared out into the blackness for a moment before turning around, displeasure evident in the set of his face. "It's disappointing to spend time in your instruction only to see you disregard everything you have been taught the minute some bleeder looks your way."

Anger spurted through her at his hurtful words. Just this afternoon, he had wanted to chaperone her for her protection and now he verbally attacked her over her behaviour at dinner?

"What do ye mean, disregard everything." She glared at him, hands on her hips. "I let a gentleman seat me. I didn't slurp. I used me knife and fork properly. I watched me diction."

"That's not what I'm talking about and you know it," he interrupted. "You practically threw yourself at Mr Dixon for all to see."

"So what if I did," she snapped. "For the first time in me life, a man looked at me, really looked at me."

"After such an exhibition, you want me to believe your virtue is intact?" His voice dripped with disgust.

"Believe it or no, it's true," she retorted. "Besides, where's the harm in talking to Mr Dixon?"

"Dinner chit chat is one thing, monopolizing the man is another." Temple shook his head. "What was I thinking? You can take the girl from the street but you can't take the street from the girl." He meant the nasty remark to wound her.

Simone felt it as purely as if he had slipped a blade between her ribs. She stared at him, speechless. This unpleasant side to Temple she had not seen before. Moisture began to gather on her lashes and she swallowed hard, not wanting to dissolve into tears in front of him. She looked down at the beautiful dress, sick at heart.

It seemed as if she would never get it right.

Only one thing gave her a glimmer of hope. Temple's jealousy had to mean something. She peeped up at him but he had turned back to the porthole and all she could see was his back, stiff with disapproval.

"I am sorry if I disappointed you," she whispered, hoping he noticed how proper she sounded.

He didn't respond.

Temple's anger surprised her. He never got angry with her, no matter how many mistakes or mispronunciations she made. Perhaps he had a point. Perhaps her behaviour had been unacceptable. She would ask Mrs Featherstone about it later.

In the meantime, she would try and smooth things over.

"I'll do better, really I will." She vowed to try harder for she wanted his praise not the derisive words he had just flung at her.

He turned around, still glowering, eyes full of misgiving. He ran both hands through his hair, leaving it tousled and unkempt, and heaved a sigh before speaking. "Perhaps we should cancel the wager. The captain has asked me to join him for an after dinner brandy. I shall discuss it."

"No!" Her cry pierced the heavy wooden beams. She plucked at his sleeve. "We can't cancel it. I can do it, my lord."

He brushed past her again and lifted the latch on the door before turning to her. "If you would excuse me," he said, resignation heavy in his voice.

Dismayed, Simone watched him leave. Her heart splintered at the regret etched in his face. Plainly, she had failed him.

* * *

Temple strode down the corridor toward the dining room, baffled by his reaction. Aye, he had been angry when Petey had accosted Simone but it had been nothing compared to the rage flooding through him when watching her play the coquette with the smitten Gordon Dixon earlier this evening.

At the door to the dining room, he poked his head in to discover the captain had gone, doubtless not expecting Temple's return. Ah well, that suited him just fine, he needed air to sort his thoughts. He made his way above board and proceeded to pace the deck, from bow to stern.

He paused to chat to the first mate whose knobby hands deftly manned the wheel.

"Petey has complained to the captain regarding Miss Dougherty. He's accused her of unwarranted fisticuffs." Allan McCabe's voice was apologetic. "I find Miss Dougherty charming and I don't believe him."

Temple's mind reeled with the news and he tightened his fists. "It's not true. He was fit to be tied for she rebuffed his advances."

"Aye, Petey's a vengeful one." McCabe leaned against the wheel, holding course into the wind. "I thought to warn you so perhaps you could smooth things with the captain."

"I do thank you. I'll meet with Captain Featherstone tomorrow as I have another item to discuss with him." He bowed slightly and paced anew, weaving figure eights between the masts. Petey's allegation didn't concern him—one word from Temple as witness and that would be put to rights.

Nevertheless, there was still the matter of Simone's behaviour earlier this evening.

By his fifth pass, the crisp air had cleansed his mind and cooled his rage. Rueful, he realized Simone had been right—he had been jealous. He wanted her teasing eyes and dazzling smile focused only on him. Each day, he enjoyed her company more for her keen wit and saucy attitude pleased him.

However, the more time he spent with her, the more he realized the enormity of the wager he had made with the captain. To put it succinctly, her shortcomings were many: her language, her manners, her lack of training in the womanly arts, her lack of appropriate clothing. The list could go on and on.

He had seen her horrified face when he had told her he would cancel the wager but in truth, he thought to cancel it to spare her feelings. As much progress as she had made, it was simply not possible for her to transform in the few remaining weeks at sea.

He leaned over the stern, watching the ship's wake foam and glisten in the moonlight. It would mean going back on his promise to himself that he always covered his bets. That didn't sit well with him either but his impetuous words had instigated the whole escapade and he bore the responsibility to deal with it and Petey's allegation.

A vision of the captain's sharp features arose in Temple's mind; his curt voice echoed in Temple's ears. The captain, used to giving orders and having them obeyed, would be a formidable opponent.

Chapter Seven

The following morning, a thoughtful Temple emerged from the meeting with Captain Featherstone and went in search of Simone. He didn't find her in the cabin, nor in the dining room, nor at her favourite spot by the bowsprit.

Puzzled at her disappearance, he turned toward the sounds of hilarity swirling on the stiff breeze, nipping at Temple's ears. What the devil?

Rounding the bulwark, he found the source: Simone had found herself a card game with two of the crew members and was doing very well at it, judging by the coins in front of her.

He stifled the urge to join in. No matter how much he enjoyed a brisk round of cards, he couldn't waste time gaming—Simone must hear of the captain's decision.

So instead, he stood and watched, silently applauding Simone's prowess.

"That's mine!" crowed Simone, throwing down her final card, the ace of hearts, onto the crate that served as makeshift table.

"I'm out." A disgusted Thomas Becker tossed down the rest of his cards at the squeal of the bosun's whistle. "It's coming up to my watch."

"Saved by the bell," laughed Samuel, exposing gapped teeth beneath a fierce black moustache.

"Aye, I had no luck today." A muttering Thomas Becker stood and stalked away, patting his empty pockets as he disappeared from sight.

"Shall we play?" Simone asked of Samuel as she gathered the cards.

"No, Lady Wellington, I've sails to mend."

"Coward."

"Aye, I know when I'm out of my league." He laughed again. "But count me in for the next game." He groped for his crutch and hauled himself up, adjusting the red bandanna about his neck before stumping away on one wooden leg.

"May I?" Temple pointed to the keg vacated by Samuel. At her nod, he settled himself. "Whatever possessed you to play at cards?"

Surprised at her apparent good humour, he gazed at her. Childlike blue eyes sparkled back at him. Clearly, the game had agreed with her although he wondered at the too-taut face and brittle smile.

"Because of what you told me last night." She shuffled the cards. "We shall lose the wager." She paused, holding the cards in one hand. "If that is so, I believe we owe double our fares. And," she put down the deck, "we don't have enough money for that." She leaned back and crossed her arms. "I thought to help."

"How do you know I'm not able to pay the wager?"

"I watched you count out the coins to pay the captain that night we came on board. Your money sack was almost empty when you put it back in your pocket."

Wonder at her acuity rushed through him. But why would it? As a thief she knew very well the value of money.

"Not to worry about the wager, it is off without penalty." He deliberately made his voice casual.

"What?" She gaped at him. Was that disappointment or relief he saw in her eyes?

He nodded. "Evidently, the captain's wife has taken a shine to you. She's been scolding him nonstop over what she perceives is his ill treatment of you. He was only too glad to let it go to spare himself. There is, however, one stipulation."

She cocked her head and looked at him.

Relief, he decided, for she appeared much happier, the previous tautness of her face relaxed.

"You must avoid the crew. Ladies of quality mingle with their peers, not with others not of their station."

She flushed and nodded. "I understand. No more card games. But what shall I do instead?"

"You still have your sewing lessons with the captain's wife. Besides, I should like to continue your instruction."

He meant every word. The wager may be over but that didn't mean he couldn't live up to his vow to teach her to become a lady of quality.

Astonishment flooded her eyes. "But the wager is over."

"I am bored silly." He lifted his hands. "I've nothing to do. I've read all the books in the ship's rather limited library. Besides, I detest unfinished business."

A few splatters of rain sprinkled the deck, the breeze stiffened. The *Annabelle* bucked the growing swells and around them, crew members ran in organized pandemonium to furl the snapping sails. A storm brewed.

"Shall we go below deck?" He held out his arm.

"Aye, but you go ahead. I've things to tidy." Cards fluttered in the breeze and she pounced on them, slipping them into her pocket. Then she gathered up the coins and palms cupped, held them out to him. "For you."

Sudden suspicion nudged him. "Where did you get the ante?"

She coloured. "I, ah, I borrowed a shilling. From you."

"Bloody hell." The oath erupted from his very core. He should have realized she knew where he had hidden his money pouch. They did, after all, share a cabin.

He didn't know whether to paddle her bottom or congratulate her on her success.

He did neither. Rather, he did the one thing he had wanted to do since Petey had accosted her on deck.

He kissed her.

Buffeted by the wind and pelting rain, he pulled her close, wrapping one arm about her shoulder and tilting her head back with his free hand. Dimly, he heard coins bounce and roll away as her hands tried to push him away, fluttering uselessly against his strength.

His mouth landed on hers, forceful, teasing her lips, nipping them until they parted.

It was as if he had never kissed anyone before.

The second his lips touched hers, serenity washed through him like dairy cream pouring from a pitcher, thick and sensuous and frothy. Awareness of his surroundings receded until there was only the feel of Simone in his arms. He lost himself in her essence, in her warmth.

More. He wanted more.

With a groan, he thrust his tongue into her mouth to tease hers, sucking, on and on until that cadence was matched by the cadence throbbing in his loins.

Simone didn't try to resist, couldn't fight the attraction he had for her. With a whimper, she wrapped her arms around his neck and stood on tiptoes to get closer. Of their own volition, her eyes closed and she melted into him, drawn into his heat, his strength. She wanted to hold him forever, to feel his lithe body this close to hers forever. Time ceased to exist. All that existed was her and Temple, locked in an ageless battle. It was a heady sensation and she wished the moment would last forever. She moaned.

Her moan was lost among the hoots, applause and catcalls of the watching crew. The sound must have distracted Temple for he pulled his lips away to look down at her with hooded eyes. A smile ghosted across his lips. "That wasn't so bad, was it," he whispered before stepping back.

He looked down and, suddenly business-like, squatted on his haunches to collect the coins.

She gazed down at his bent head and lifted trembling fingers to her mouth to touch her lips, lips still tingling with the feel of him. It had been magical, transporting her to another world, another time.

Yet somehow she sensed there was more, for her woman's place pounded and hot dampness spread there, between her thighs. Try as she might, she couldn't stop the disconcerting reaction of her body.

Coins collected in his palm, he picked out a shilling, tucking it into his vest pocket before handing her the rest with a conspiratorial wink. "Keep these. You earned them."

Simone looked down at the coins in her hand and from the corner of her eye watched him swagger off, soon to disappear behind the bulwark.

A grin tugged at the corners of her mouth and she tucked the coins into her pocket. Hugging herself, she marched back to the tiny cabin.

It was empty when she arrived there. Grateful for the opportunity to steady herself, she poured some water from the tin pitcher on the trunk that served as nightstand into its matching basin and splashed her face and neck. After wiping her face on the cloth that hung from a peg above the nightstand, she lay down on her cot to ponder what had passed between them just now.

Her air of insouciance when he had found her playing cards had been just that, an air. Inside, she was bitterly disappointed over losing the wager. She had wanted to please him and prove him right for believing in her ability to transform herself. As well, she had come to realize that she could build a better life for herself with a bit of education. Maybe even open a gaming house. And with the proceeds of the gaming house, make things a little bit better for Mrs Dougherty.

Now she yet had a chance, for Temple had said he would continue the lessons. She'd have to find a way to repay him for that.

Oy, her debts toward him were piling up.

Then there was the matter of his kiss.

The light from the oil lamp glowed through the curtain. She studied the wall beside her, counting all the knotholes she could see, then all the planks, and then all the nail heads. She even resorted to counting backwards from one hundred, not once, but several times.

Anything to avoid thinking about the kiss because she wished for him to kiss her again and that was an entirely improper wish.

* * *

Simone slept when Temple finally returned.

He had spent the last couple of hours prowling the deck, trying to scrub the desire that Simone had inadvertently evoked in him. It was just a kiss, he had scoffed to himself. Snatching a kiss was not something that caused him remorse. On the contrary, it had been good sport that had a time or two led to the adrenalin rush of a sunrise duel, which had made it even better.

No, this kiss had been different. True, he liked her, in fact, liked her very much. But there was more to it than that.

Simone aroused feelings in him he didn't want to face. Not yet.

He undressed quickly and climbed into his bunk. Her even breaths bathed the cabin in tranquillity but the thought of her behind the sailcloth tortured him. Her proximity had never bothered him before but now he paid for his folly. Tonight, this very moment, his loins ached. Manners battled with desire.

Why not take her? She was an urchin, a disreputable ragamuffin.

Because she trusted him, and he couldn't betray her trust like that.

With a groan, he pulled the bedclothes over his head in a futile attempt to block out the gentle sigh of her breath.

* * *

Gentry Ted threaded his way through the boisterous crowd filling his favourite pub in London's east end, the Pint and Platter, until he found a spot at the scarred counter. Signalling the barkeep, he waited until the man came over with a pint of ale before he posed the question that had plagued him for the past few weeks.

"Have ye seen Mona?"

The barkeep stopped and, with a surprised look, glanced around the room as if he could spot the missing girl there. "No," he replied. "No, I ain't. Now that ye mention it, I ain't seen her for at least a month."

"Nobody's seen her, it's like she's dropped from the face of the earth." Gentry Ted's voice was puzzled.

The barkeep shrugged. "Like as not she's found greener pastures. She'll come around."

"I ain't so sure," muttered Ted before lifting the foaming mug to his lips. Mona, that one, what a peach, had her hands in and out of a pocket in a twinkling, so smooth that the bloody nobs she picked had no idea.

He well remembered the day he had dropped her off at Mrs Dougherty's workhouse. Somehow, those blue eyes had stuck with him and he had made it a habit to check in on her regularly, sometimes even throwing a coin or two Mrs Dougherty's way to help out. It had given him great pleasure to see her success on the streets, particularly after being told she was not suitable for that kind of work.

He drained his mug, slapped down a coin, and stood to leave. He turned to scan the room as if Mona had somehow miraculously appeared in the past few moments but of course she had not.

Adjusting his cravat, he made his way to the door and out into the street. He shook his head as he walked. Maybe Mona were just lying low because the constables were after her.

Chapter Eight

Temple and Simone did not talk of their kiss and after a while, it seemed as if it had never happened. The days sailed by as smoothly as the *Annabelle* sliced through the Atlantic Ocean. Two weeks flew by, then three, then four.

The at times tedious morning sewing lessons had produced another dress, this one a sprigged muslin, as well as several shifts and a nightgown. Simone thanked Mrs Featherstone repeatedly and the kindly woman would always give an airy wave of her hand. "I say do unto others as you would have them do unto you. There's nothing to thank me for. You making something of yourself and making your lord proud is all the thanks I need."

Her afternoons with Temple, however, were golden. She concentrated on every word and every phrase, wanting to do her best for then he would reward her with a smile or a curt "Well done." She memorized endlessly, practicing the pronunciation over and over until Temple was satisfied she got it right. Then they would move on to the next.

Nay, her afternoons were never boring, they were exhilarating.

Bit by bit, she began to believe, she, Simone Dougherty could become a lady of quality and have a better life for herself.

And bit by bit, she found herself falling in love with the darkly handsome Lord Temple Wellington, a man above her in station.

A man who could never be hers.

* * *

"No!"

Simone threw off the bedclothes and sat bolt upright. Perspiration drenched her nightgown and clotted her hair. Panting hard, she held her wet face in shaking hands. "No, please no."

Again.

It had happened again.

The nightmare where she was drowning, sinking into the murk of unfathomable depths. It had visited her with unfailing regularity when she was younger, less as she grew older, perhaps once every year or so. But now the familiar nightmare had returned and it still held a horror she couldn't shake.

"Temple? Did I wake you?"

She pulled back the sail curtain to look over at his empty bed, the bedclothes still rumpled. She listened for a moment. Silence. There were no footsteps or shouts from without.

She scrambled out of her bed and dressed quickly and, stumbling down the hallway, rammed the last few pins into her hair. It may not be tidy, but it would have to do.

By the time she made her way above deck, she found Temple, flanked on one side by Dr Taylor and on the other by Gordon Dixon, leaning against the starboard railing.

"What is it?" She moved to stand beside the young clerk.

"Look!" Dr Taylor pointed. "Land ho. That's North America."

"I must beg pardon?" Simone followed the doctor's finger. "I don't see anything. The horizon's a bit blurred, nothing else."

"This might help." Gordon gave her the looking glass that he had tucked against his side.

"Thank you." Squinting, she peered through the lens. "Are you sure that's land?" she asked as she handed the glass back to him.

"Oh, yes. You should have heard Robert sing at breakfast this morning."

"Who? Oh, Robert." Of course, the captain's bird, how could she have forgotten? Every morning she passed a few crumbs into the cage hanging from the corner beam in the dining room.

Gordon's mention of breakfast reminded her of her own hunger.

"There's a scone for you on the sideboard," Temple drawled, as if he had read her mind. He leaned around the clerk to look at her. His eyebrows lifted at her dishevelled appearance. "Is something the matter?"

The concern in his voice warmed her right to the very tips of her toes. "Just a dream I have every now and then."

"I daresay a nightmare, judging by the looks of you."

She didn't want to talk about it. "It's over now. If you gentlemen would excuse me, I'll go find my breakfast."

She found the scone on a plate covered with a linen towel. After spooning some preserves on it, she selected an orange from the ever present basket on the sideboard and returned to stand by the railing.

She finished the scone, licking the stickiness from her fingers, then dug a finger nail into the dimpled peel of the fruit to pull off a chunk. One bit at a time, she threw the peels to the sea gulls and watched them swarm.

He loves me, he loves me not. He loves me, he loves me not. As the peel dwindled, the pieces got smaller until she ended on he loves me. A childish, fanciful thought but one she yearned for. The reason being?

The answer leapt into her mind like a soldier joining the fray.

She loved him.

Totally, irrevocably, loved him.

She shook her head. Nay, that wasn't possible. He attracted her, yes, but it was a doomed attraction for they were of disparate worlds.

Perhaps she mistook gratitude for love.

Yes, that was it, she was grateful to him for taking her along, giving her a chance to improve her life.

"Oy," she sighed, watching the gulls circling about much like her thoughts.

Thankfully, the voyage was almost over. They had all been cooped up for weeks now and the prospect of setting foot on land enticed her. Too, once on land, she wouldn't be in constant contact with Temple.

She pried the fruit apart and sucked on the first bit, the flavour reminding her of the flavour of Temple's mouth. Sweet yet tangy.

The prospect of accompanying Temple to New Caledonia teased her. Her desire to be with him, to see the journey finished, warred with her sense of self preservation.

How hellish would it be to be in his company day in and day out? All the while realizing the futility of her growing feelings toward him and the impossibility of her future twining with his?

However, she couldn't see a way out for only she knew where his package was and she doubted he would journey on without her. Perhaps if she simply told him of its location, she could persuade him to let her stay in Montreal.

It seemed her only solution if she thought to save her sanity.

Chapter Nine

It was almost too easy, Simone thought, pulling from her shawl several leather pouches and a crocheted reticule and placing them on the little writing desk by the window of their room in one of Montreal's quaint hotels.

Satisfaction filled her at the realization the long weeks at sea had not diminished her talent. It had been no idle boast she'd made to Temple the night he found her in his trunk.

Montreal proved to be fertile ground. At this rate, she would soon be able to repay Temple for her passage. And whatever remained would help her on her dream to start her own gaming house and help Mrs Dougherty.

She picked up the reticule and emptied the contents on the desk: a lace handkerchief, a small pot of powder, a fan and several coins.

The clack of the door knob and the screech of hinges in want of grease interrupted her.

"What have you there?" Temple demanded as he entered the room.

Surprise held her and she froze. The heels of his boots clicked on the polished floorboards, stopping only when he was directly behind her. His breath tickled her cheek and she dropped the reticule and whirled about, leaning back against the table to hide the pile of booty.

"You startled me," she bleated. Damn, couldn't he have been a few moments more, long enough for her to count the money?

Temple bent around her to look then let loose an oath. "Are you trying to get us thrown in jail?"

"It's money to repay you for my passage," she blustered. He had caught her by surprise so she went on the verbal attack. "And just keeping me hand in."

"My hand," he corrected her automatically.

"We're not getting thrown in jail," she reassured him, trying to ignore the ominous frown on Temple's face. "The bleeders didn't notice a thing. I told you, I'm the best there is," she finished lamely.

Perhaps it had not been such a good idea after all. He didn't look at all pleased with her. She rocked back on her heels, contemplating how to appease his anger over her thievery.

He spoke before she could think of anything.

"The best there was." He ground out the words between gritted teeth. "You don't need to be doing that anymore, remember?"

"Really?" Simone stared at him. "Who would suspect me?" She clasped her hands primly under the bosom of the high-waisted sprigged muslin dress and batted her eyelashes.

"It doesn't matter if you're suspected or not. One does not behave in that manner when it is not necessary to do so." He glared at her.

"I think it is necessary. I should like to repay you for my passage for I wish to stay here." She dropped her gaze. "In Montreal."

"Out of the question." The authoritarian tone of his voice unnerved her and she snapped her gaze back to him. His lips were clamped firmly together and his eyes were darkened with disapproval at her suggestion.

Oy, she hadn't expected this reaction. What could it mean? Did he care about her behaviour more than he cared about her debt to him? Did that mean he cared about her?

At the thought, hope spurted through her, only to be quashed at his next words.

"You took something of value to me," he declared. "I should like it returned and until it is, you will remain with me."

Of course. He only kept her because of the package she'd hidden back in London. She had best not forget that to him, she was a pickpocket, a street urchin, nothing more.

She swallowed hard against the disappointment welling in her throat.

"I'll make a map for you," she countered, hating the wobble in her voice. She swallowed hard once more to steady it. "Where to find your packet. I can't write the street names but you can if I tell ye—er, you. Then you can get it when you return to London."

"Which I should like to remind you shan't be for quite some time. Besides," he pointed at the pile of stolen goods behind her, "you could find yourself locked up soon enough."

"They'll not catch me."

Temple narrowed his eyes at her boastful words. "Enough nonsense, Simone. I will not leave you alone in a strange country."

Her bottom lip jutted out, along with her chin. Before she could say any more, he held up his hand.

"Now get your shawl. I'll buy you the boots I promised you."

She gazed at him suspiciously for a moment before she turned away

A rueful little grin zigzagged across Temple's lips as he watched her ready herself; when at last she turned to him, he was quick to stifle it.

At her inquiring gaze, he pulled open the door. "After you."

His thoughts wandered as he followed her down the rather narrow hall. He should have known she wouldn't stay in the hotel while he attended to errands for the upcoming journey.

She was a child of the streets, comfortable with that life and more than capable of taking care of herself regardless of which city they were in. In her own fashion she had attempted to be honest and repay him for the favour he'd done her.

He couldn't really fault her for that. However, she did engage in risky business which would have unpleasant consequences for her if she got caught.

Why should I care what happens to her?

He did care about her, he told himself, but only because she knows where the package is.

He would have to keep a closer eye on her or he could forget any hope of a future as a genteel landowner with a genteel wife. Preferably one from an adjoining estate.

Not one with golden curls and sparkling blue eyes and an adorable mutinous lower lip.

* * *

Later that evening, Temple sat in the one and only chair in their room and watched a slumbering Simone, curled up on her side with one fist tucked beneath her chin. A contented expression suffused her face—the earlier shopping expedition had been successful.

Her new boots were lined up neatly beneath her bed. As well, they had passed a modiste's shop by happenstance and he had felt obliged to buy her a heavy woollen dress with a matching fur-lined spencer, something with a little more substance than the two lightweight dresses she had made on board the *Annabelle*. The spencer she had spread over the foot of her bed to admire.

The sight of her angelic face, relaxed in repose, forced him to face the unavoidable truth.

His stowaway thief, the ragamuffin pickpocket and keen witted product of the streets, was stealing his heart one sorry chunk at a time. Oh, it wasn't blatant theft but it was happening, slowly and surely.

He shook his head. Nay, it couldn't be. He had simply spent too much time with her. A trip to the nearest brothel would cure him and put things in their proper perspective. He stood, taking one last glance at her sleeping figure before stalking to the door.

Once outside the hotel, he held his hand over the remaining coins in his vest pocket to stop them from clinking. They were heavy, almost as heavy as the night was dark, and his pocket sagged a little. He hoped no one would notice and take him for an easy mark.

Gliding through shadowed lanes, he found his way back toward the river, back toward the brothels and gambling dens he knew he would find there. He stopped at the first one, just beyond the glow of light spilling from the open door, lifting his nose and flaring his nostrils as he drew in a breath to test the air, seeking a familiar scent.

There it was, just a tinge but enough to trap him and pull him in, shadowed hands that plucked and pushed at him—the fumes of cheap gin and opium. No need to walk further, for he had found what he sought.

He stepped through the doorway and paused to look about before walking over to the planked bar running down one side of the room. A slew of sounds— ribald comments, hoots of laughter and rowdy conversation—surrounded him. It had been quiet on the ship and he had forgotten how noisy an ale house could be. It gave him the sensation of pushing his way through a dense curtain of noise.

"Gin," he said to the woman with drooping features tending the bar. He tossed her a coin then, eschewing the generous glass she poured for him, grabbed the neck of the bottle instead and raised it to his lips, tilting his head back to suck back the contents.

It burned in his throat, a satisfying sting that he knew from experience would dull his mind and veil unwanted thoughts. He slammed down the empty bottle with a bang that rattled the planks.

His face must have said what his words didn't, for the woman gestured him up the stairs that leaned haphazardly against the back wall. Fearing they would collapse beneath his weight, he nonetheless climbed up to find several curtained partitions.

A brassy head popped out from behind one and beckoned to him. "Ooh, yer a fine one," she cooed through crudely rouged lips. "Let Sally take care of yer troubles."

"Please do," he choked out as the woman—he hardly dared refer to her as such—fumbled with his waistband.

He tried to lose himself in the harlot's willing flesh but the solace he sought escaped him. An image of blonde hair and angelic blue eyes stuck in his mind and try as he might, he could not dislodge it. "Sorry," he mumbled as he pulled his trousers back on.

"That's not what ye want, is it then," the whore said shrewdly. She pulled out a bottle of gin from the chest beside her bed and passed it to him.

Defeated in his attempt to convince himself Simone meant nothing to him, he sat on the edge of the cot and held out shivering hands to the beckoning bottle of sweet oblivion.

The sun pushed up feathering rays of pink and gold by the time he stumbled back up the hill toward the hotel.

Much to his disgust, the trip to the brothel had done nothing to settle his thoughts; it had only succeeded in making him feel ill.

Bloody hell, the only way to find peace of mind again would be to part ways with the alluring Simone Dougherty. He would take her up on the offer of a map for his missing package and then send her on her way.

* * *

Through slitted eyes, Simone watched Temple flounder with his boots, barely managing to pull them off before flopping, fully clothed, onto the patchwork quilt-covered iron bed that was his. He lay on his back, arms tucked behind his head, staring at the ceiling through red-rimmed eyes.

"I know you're awake," he said at length. His voice was indistinct, rough, as if he hadn't spoken in some time.

"How did you know?" Simone sat up, pulling the bedding up under her chin to lean against the headboard.

"By the sounds of your breathing. It's different when you sleep. And after six weeks together," he rolled on his side, head cradled on one arm to look at her, "I know exactly how you sound."

The torment in his eyes frightened her. She knew he had private demons for at times he would cry out in his sleep, but it looked as if he had given them full battle.

And lost. His gin-laden breath filled the room. The gin. That had to be it. Cheap gin changed a man.

"What happened to you, you look…." She stopped, trying to find the right words. She couldn't so she changed her tack. "What's the matter?"

"Nothing." His voice was curt. He rolled back onto his back before next he spoke. "I shall take you up on your offer of a map. And," his chest heaved as he said it, "I think it best to send you back to London."

Her head reeled at his words. London? What notion was that? She couldn't return to London.

"I should like to stay here," she said defiantly. She must try and dissuade him, even if it meant telling him the real reason she had taken refuge in his trunk that long ago evening.

"No. You will return to England. I could give you a letter of reference. That should help you find another form of employment."

"I can't go back."

"Why not?" His voice was weary, as if he had expected an argument from her.

"Because I wasn't entirely honest with you. About why you found me in your trunk."

"Would you care to enlighten me then?"

How would he react if he knew the truth? Her heart started to pound; her mouth grew dry.

"I was on my way to Newgate prison. Constable Miller had me collared. Davy and the boys distracted him and I managed to slip away. I chose your trunk because I knew the constable would never look in the trunk of a lord." She stopped to look at him, gauging his reaction. She couldn't tell for he still lay on his back staring at the cracked plaster ceiling. "Constable

Carstairs is one of Miller's mates. He'll not be pleased knowing he had me and let me get away because of you. They'll both be looking for me. I can't go back or it's certain prison and the hangman."

Her hands started to tremble as she waited for his answer. She wanted more than anything to stay with Temple, to revel in his company as long as she could, to face the consequences of shattered dreams later rather than sooner.

She studied his profile, looking for a clue, anything to indicate his thoughts.

The silence stretched out to one minute, then two and still she waited, nervous and uncertain.

Bloody hell, Temple thought. In all good conscience, he couldn't send her back to certain incarceration, death even. She'd become a pickpocket for survival. Survival, the most basic human instinct.

His gentlemanly upbringing wouldn't allow her to stay alone in Montreal—she'd already displayed she would revert to what she knew best. Sooner or later it would be her downfall.

His pilfered heart be damned, she would have to stay with him still. And, he consoled himself weakly, if she stayed with him, at least he wouldn't have to renege on his vow to teach her to be a lady.

He rolled over at last to face her. "Well then, it seems you continue to be my companion." Resignation sat heavy in his voice. "Companion, mind you, not wife. We are no longer on the *Annabelle* and I see no need to present you as Lady Wellington. I'll ensure in future we each have our own accommodation."

He couldn't see her reaction in the grey light. He hoped his words had not been too harsh.

Truth be told, continued close contact with her would, quite simply, drive him mad.

Chapter Ten

That afternoon, while Temple visited the offices of the North West Company, a relieved Simone strolled further up the slopes of Mount Royal. Relieved because her role as Lady Wellington had come to an end and she no longer had to live a lie. Relieved she would no longer be in his company every waking moment.

And relieved she no longer had to worry about disappointing Temple with her shortcomings.

The busy street churned with finely dressed men and women, as fine as any in London, along with roughly clad tradesmen, sailors, and even men dressed in furs. A wagon rumbled past, piled high with roughly hewn logs and she stopped to watch it, smiling so brightly at the driver that he almost toppled from his seat.

When she returned to the hotel, she encountered a dour-faced Temple in the lobby, top hat in one hand, leather folder in the other. He didn't wait for her to speak but led her outside and pointed to the weathered straight bench on the veranda of the hotel.

"Sit." His sombre voice brooked no argument. He jammed the hat on his head and tucked the folder under his arm.

Filled with apprehension, she sat, stomach roiling at his stern visage.

"I spoke with the gentlemen of the North West Company. They informed me unmarried women are not allowed on trading expeditions."

"Oh." Panic swept through her. She wouldn't be able to accompany Temple after all. But that was best for her wilful heart, wasn't it? She sucked in a breath of air, filling her lungs all the way to her stomach. "Then I shall stay here," she answered bravely.

"No, you shall not. The French Canadian voyageurs bring their women. We'll continue the charade." He eluded her gaze as if he was unwilling to witness her true reaction.

"What?" Incredulity cascaded through her breast and her jaw dropped. "The charade is over." She made her voice firm. "You told me only this morning that Lady Wellington is no more."

"I've changed my mind." He swivelled his head to pierce her with his gaze. "If you wish to remain with me, you must agree to continue as Lady Wellington. If not—" He shrugged.

She tried to gauge his mood but his face was immobile, his mouth a thin line, his eyes evasive. The relief that had made her light-hearted earlier today dissipated in a "poof". She frowned. It would seem she must maintain the role of his wife, whether she liked it or not.

"Very well." She felt lightheaded as she said it. The sham marriage continued. The question was, would she be able to convince herself her growing love for him was a sham as well?

"It's not an easy journey," he warned her. "There are no roads. No inns. None of the creature comforts of civilization."

"Then why should I go with you? I already said I could stay here. In Montreal."

"Out of the question, Simone. Your talents will only find you swinging from the gallows." He scowled. "You wouldn't evade capture here. Montreal is simply too small a city for you to hide. And if I could remind you." He slanted a serious glance her way. "Unmarried ladies of quality are never without a chaperone."

The serious look on his face worried her. She hadn't given much thought to the journey itself and what lay in store for her.

"Tell me about the North West Company," she said suddenly. "I should like to know more about it."

"It's a fur trading company. I've agreed to be a wintering partner at Stuart Lake Outpost. It's a relatively new fort, in an area still rich with beaver. However, it is isolated." Enthusiasm coloured his words; apparently, Temple Wellington's new position excited him.

"Perhaps I could start an ale house there." She ignored the surprised look on his face and nodded. "You've said you're going to New Caledonia to find your fortune. Well, couldn't I find mine there?"

Yes, that would make worthwhile any difficulties encountered on the trip. Once in New Caledonia, she could help him with the map to his package and then they could go their separate ways, she to run her ale house and he to work in the fur trade.

Best of all, she need not return to London any time soon.

An animated Simone jumped to her feet to pirouette in front of him. Her skirt lifted with the motion, exposing two shapely calves before it fell into place again.

Temple licked his suddenly dry lips and ignored the pounding heat of his arousal. How would he keep his mind off her delectable attributes? The six weeks in her company on board the *Annabelle* had been one thing, but the trip ahead loomed long and arduous.

"It won't be easy, Simone. We'll be travelling by canoe and horseback and sleeping under the stars for months." Bloody hell, it also wouldn't be easy trying to keep intact his heart from the lovely "Lady Wellington".

He groaned inwardly. His idea to continue the sham perhaps wasn't the wisest for his peace of mind, however he couldn't renege now.

What in blazes had he agreed to?

* * *

Simone held herself erect on the edge of Stuart Lake and fought the disappointment threatening to burst forth in a torrent of tears.

This was it? Stuart Lake Outpost? The administrative centre of the Northwest Company in New Caledonia? The perfect place for her ale house?

The bustling village she had expected hadn't materialized. Instead, situated on the shores of a vast lake, another wooden palisade greeted her. Inside, several small houses, a store and a warehouse.

She stripped off her boots, throwing them aside to let her bare feet sink into the tiny line of sand and gravel that passed for a beach. Cold and crystalline clear, the water lapped at her toes, refreshing them after being jammed into boots night and day.

She leaned down to splash some water on her face then lifted her gaze to look ahead over the shimmering, tranquil water, surrounded by verdant mountains cascading into its very shores. So vast the lake, the mountains at the far end were misty and indistinct.

Oy, there was a lot of water in this country. The roads of the fur traders, she had been told, rivers and such being much easier to navigate than fighting through impenetrable woodlands.

What lay in store for her now? Would they even have a roof over their heads and a place to call their own? How would she pass the days, for plainly there was no call for an ale house there. What a silly notion that had been.

She swiped her fingers across her cheeks to dry them and then sucked in a huge breath of sparkling fresh air to steady herself.

"Why are we here?" she blurted when Temple moved to stand beside her.

He tapped her on the tip of the nose. "You're here to hide, remember? From the constables. And I'm here to earn a living."

"Couldn't we have found somewhere closer?" A wave of homesickness rolled over her and she squeezed shut her eyes. "How long do we have to stay here? I want to go back."

"Not long, Simone. I'll fulfil my obligations to the North West Company then we'll go." He dropped a hand on her shoulder.

A brotherly gesture, nothing more, but she took comfort in it and lifted her hand to her shoulder to cover his. They stood silent for a moment, gazing out over the silken water reflecting the pristine clouds and blue June sky.

"I can see why this land is called New Caledonia," he remarked. "I visited the Scottish highlands once. It looks very similar."

"Wouldn't the Scottish highlands have more people?" An inane comment but at least it gave her a chance to collect herself. She dropped her hand and stepped away. No use thinking he meant anything by the gesture.

"I daresay yes," Temple grinned. "Anywhere would have more people than here." He tilted his head back to watch an eagle circle high over them, a scrap of feathers against the soaring sky. "Magnificent birds, aren't they?"

"It's just as well there are so few people here." Her voice trembled. Blinking hard against the still threatening tears, she pointed first to her heavy woollen dress, soiled and stained from the journey, sleeves rolled up against the heat, then to her discarded boots, muddied and worn at the heels.

"Our attire would turn more than a few heads in London," he hooted. "Fashion pariahs we are."

"If nothing else, it's practical." A strange voice interrupted them.

They both whirled about to see a dark-haired white man on horseback drawing to halt. He slid off his mount and threw the reins over a bush before approaching them, hand extended.

Intelligent eyes peered at them from beneath quizzical eyebrows and a receding hairline, and long sideburns feathered away along his clean-shaven jaw. His clothing was European in fashion: trousers, jacket and high-collared shirt. In short, a welcome breath of civilization.

"Daniel Harmon," he said. "And you are the new partner sent by the North West Company? Your travelling companions told me," he added.

"Yes, Temple Wellington." The men shook hands, eyeing each other up and down like bulldogs. Apparently satisfied with what they saw, they broke apart.

"But who are you?" Daniel pointed at Simone.

"Mrs Wellington," she answered. Temple had instructed her not to use his title so as not to arouse too much curiosity and by now "Mrs" slipped off her tongue naturally. "I'm very pleased to meet you, Mr Harmon." She bobbed a stiff curtsy, the first one in a long while and a welcome reminder of refined manners.

Daniel stared at Simone, clearly amazed but too courteous to say anything.

"I couldn't bear to part with my darling wife. Simone agreed to accompany me," Temple interjected, correctly interpreting the expression on the other man's face. "I know it's rather unusual."

"Yes," Daniel replied. "Some of the French Canadian traders travel with their wives, but they're native women. You are the first European woman I've seen this far in the wilderness. How very brave and adventurous of you."

"Yes, my wife is an extraordinary woman." A half-smile curled Temple's lips.

Simone felt Temple's gaze on her, warm and admiring. She blushed. His wife. It never failed to astound her how much she liked the sound of that. If only it were true. She looked away to hide her discomfort.

"Is this all there is," she blurted out, waving an arm toward the few buildings she could see.

"There's an Indian village a short distance away, where the river joins the lake. But yes," the other man said ruefully, "this is all there is."

"I see." Simone drooped at his words then glanced over to Temple. A barely concealed air of excitement emanated from him and there was no doubt he embraced the challenge of this wilderness. He seemed happy to be here and she didn't want to spoil it for him. Hiding her lingering disappointment, she pulled herself upright.

"Lisette, my woman, will be pleased to meet you. It can be a little lonely here. Come, there's a cabin ready for you." Daniel grabbed the reins of his horse and without looking back, started toward the fort on foot. "Follow me."

"Come, my dear." Temple waited while she collected her boots and slipped them on then held out an arm to her as if they were strolling through London's Hyde Park and not clambering up a slight bluff toward their new home.

Simone clung to Temple's elbow. One question had been answered—it appeared as if they would have a place to call home.

She kept her gaze focused on the horse's rump. At least it was a familiar sight—there were horses in London too. The homesickness receded. And, she reminded herself, she remained here with Temple.

"Here ye be." Daniel showed them a tiny bark-roofed log cabin within the palisade. "I'll leave you to freshen up then come find me in the warehouse." He pointed to the largest building.

"I thank you, Mr Harmon, I'm certain we'll be comfortable here," Temple said.

Daniel waved then climbed on his horse and rode off.

Temple stood back to let Simone enter first. She took a few steps inside then stopped, dismayed.

So newly built, patches of grass dotted the dirt floor within and gaps of light shone between the poorly chinked log walls. The cabin contained not a stick of furniture and sported only one window. Rather, she supposed it to be a window for it was covered in parchment rather than glass.

A stone fireplace dominated one wall but for the rest, the tiny cabin scarcely had room for them and their belongings, thrown haphazardly on the ground.

"Where are we going to sit? And sleep?" She clapped her hands to her face, covering her mouth to hide the trembling lips. True, their accommodations on the journey here had not always been the best, in fact, a lot of nights had been spent curled up on the ground under a tipped over canoe. However, she had kept in mind their destination which had made the discomforts bearable.

Ale house, bah. What a fanciful fool she had been. She should have realized Stuart Lake Outpost would be just as the other fur trading forts they had passed through, should have realized that Temple's aspirations were so much different than hers.

She gave way to the disappointment that had hovered over her shoulders since their arrival. She couldn't deny she had expected much, much more. A few tears slipped out of her eyes and rolled cool and wet down her cheeks.

"It will be fun, Simone, just give it a chance." Temple made his voice hearty to bolster Simone's obviously sagging spirits. Prudently, he kept his thoughts to himself.

He, too, had expected a flourishing settlement. During the journey, he had attributed the warning comments about the outpost as tiresome meddling from those jealous of his plans and had disregarded them. Who had known finding one's fortune in the wilderness would be such a crude endeavour? Nevertheless, he was here and determined to make it a go of it.

However, there was the matter of Simone. Spending each and every day in her company, although delightful, was driving him to distraction. Ever since leaving Montreal, he had avoided being alone with her. Easy enough to do when surrounded at all times by voyageurs and traders with no privacy whatsoever but it hadn't stopped his thoughts from turning to her. Often.

The enticing thought of finally being alone with her during the night drifted through his mind.

Her tears surprised him. She had been a stalwart companion during the long trek overland. At first, there had been raised eyebrows over her sex but she proved to be as tough and resilient as any of the men. Nothing fazed her, nothing upset her, not the long portages when they had helped carry the canoes and goods, not the lack of decent accommodation, nor consuming strange foods such as pemmican and bannock. Yes, as long as she was warm and dry, she was happy.

Thankfully, she was not accustomed to luxury.

That was it. That was how he could coax her around and restore her good humour. Surely the little cabin was much better than a pallet in the workhouse?

"Simone," he began.

She turned reddened eyes and tear stained cheeks toward him. His heart twisted at the pathetic sight. With clenched fists, he held his arms firm at his side, resisting the urge to take her in his arms to comfort her.

Memories of that long ago afternoon he had kissed her surged in his mind, making it doubly difficult to hold himself back. With all his will, he controlled himself. He couldn't, however, control his traitorous desire. He turned away to hide the sudden bulge in his pants.

"How long must we stay here, my lord?" She sniffled as she said it.

He glanced back at her over his shoulder and shrugged. "As long as it takes." Relieved, he felt his erection begin to dissipate. He turned back to her.

"For what?" She wiped her nose on her elbow.

"To find my fortune."

"You don't need a fortune, you have one." Her voice was accusing.

"Well, actually, I do not. May I remind you I'm the younger son." Bloody hell, why was she asking about this now? She'd never mentioned it before, therefore he had assumed it was of no consequence to her. Evidently, her distress was genuine and guilt stabbed him that he had put her in this situation. He must make it up to her somehow.

"Couldn't you have found your fortune back in England?"

"No." How could he tell her the truth? He had tried to make his own way but had only succeeded in digging himself in even deeper. That was why he had left England—not to seek his fortune, but to save his skin.

She looked at him long and hard. He schooled his face to remain expressionless.

"Well," she said at last, pulling her shoulders back and stiffening her back. "If I help, we could go home sooner, couldn't we? If I help, we would be two to share the load."

"And how do you think you can help?" Amused, he watched as she poked through the bags and bundles piled around them as if determined to do something that very instant. "What of your ale house?"

"There is no call for an ale house here," she said sternly, as if to convince herself as much as him. "I don't know, there must be something I can do." She straightened up, apparently discarding the notion of unpacking. "Where did Mr Harmon go? I'll ask him."

She had recovered her good humour although he was sure she was saddened over the loss of her idea. He admired her resiliency. "Shall we check in with Mr Harmon? We can set up our bed rolls later."

"What a wonderful suggestion," she said. "I would like to see more of the outpost." He frowned at the bright tone in her voice but she returned his look without a hint of guile, even flashing him a little smile.

They stepped outside and started across the yard through a fog of mosquitoes.

"Wretched things," Simone muttered, swatting at the insects. "I shall never get used to them."

"I know," Temple groaned. "My arms are a mass of welts. Let's walk faster, shall we?" He picked up the pace.

"Very well." Simone ignored his outstretched hand and picked up her skirts in one hand, leaving the other free to wave about her face. "Phew."

"Hello!" Temple shouted once they reached the warehouse.

"In here, come in, come in." A man's voice drifted through the door.

They stepped inside to find Daniel sitting behind a table, open ledger, quill and ink pot in front of him.

"Oh, my." Simone looked about her. Speechless, she let her gaze wander.

A hodgepodge of goods surrounded them: stacks of furs of all sizes and shapes, blankets, rifles, powder, iron pots and even bolts of cloth. The faint odour of smoke mixed with the musky smell of the furs and the acrid bite of gun powder. Not unpleasant, but a raw, savage odour much like the land they were in. She took a deep breath, releasing it slowly to better catch Daniels' words.

"This is what drives the North West Company," Daniel explained. "Furs." He pointed to different piles as he as he spoke. "Wolf, mink, otter, fox, bear. But particularly beaver, and the more, the better. That's why we've set up here. It's a central location for a very large area." He showed them a map pinned on the wall. "See? We are on the edge of Stuart Lake which connects to many other waterways."

Temple strolled over and peered at the map. With one grimy finger, he traced several of the rivers shown. "This is a commercial enterprise of good size, is it not? That's what I was told."

"Yes." Daniel nodded. "We trade our goods for furs, pure and simple. You won't be that busy. Our duties only take a few hours a day. For the rest, it is up to you to while away the time." Daniel turned toward Simone. "Will you excuse us while I go over what's expected of your husband?"

"Yes, of course, Mr Harmon, but I would really like to help. Have you something for me to do?" Simone asked.

"You would be too much of a distraction here or in the store. But if you are amenable, I'd like you to speak English with my wife. She speaks French and Cree but I have been teaching her English. I'll take her with me when I return to my home in the United States and she's going to need English."

"I may not be the best choice," Simone began, looking Daniel Harmon full in the face. How could she possibly teach Mrs Harmon when she had only just learned proper English herself? The idea daunted her.

"Nonsense," Temple interrupted her. "You'll do just fine. What better way to reinforce what you have learned from me than by teaching someone else?"

"Lisette wants to practice her English," Daniel said. "I'm not always the most patient with her."

Simone doubted her ability to be a teacher, especially if teaching required patience. Surely she could do something else. She opened her mouth to reply but Daniel spoke before she had a chance to say anything.

"I will not take no for an answer."

Drat, it seemed he had read her mind. She frowned.

Daniel leaned back in his chair and stretched his arms overhead. "Besides, I've already mentioned to her that you would be teaching her." The chair legs landed back on the ground with a solid thump.

"Oh, all right then," Simone said, hoping her voice didn't sound too cross. "When would you like us to start?"

"She's waiting for you. In the garden plot."

"It'll give you something to do, Simone." Temple's voice was bland. "Mr Harmon and I have accounts to review."

"Of course," Simone said with as much grace as she could muster. It appeared the role of teacher had been thrust upon her, wanted or not. "If you would excuse me."

The look she threw Temple as she left could have stopped a bear at thirty paces. He let loose the grin that he had stifled at her indignation and watched her march away, back rigid.

He couldn't wait to discover how she made out.

Chapter Eleven

Simone let her shoulders sag as soon as she was out of sight. Teach English? It hadn't been quite what she had in mind when she had suggested to Temple that she could help. However, she welcomed the prospect of feminine chit chat. It reminded her of Mrs Featherstone and her time on board the *Annabelle*.

She found the garden plot easily enough and from within the roughly fenced area drifted a woman's voice and a toddler's babble.

"Hello?" She raised her voice.

"Hello!" Lisette Harmon popped up from behind the uneven timbers. Her welcoming smile put Simone at ease immediately. About her own height, Lisette was sturdily built, with silken black hair plaited in two and smooth skin the colour of burnt sugar. A serviceable apron well spotted with dirt covered her gaily striped cotton dress. "Mrs Wellington? Daniel told me you and your husband had arrived." The woman's voice was low, guttural, her words spoken with a lyrical accent that Simone recognized as French with a hint of something else. That must be the Cree influence Daniel had mentioned.

"Yes." Out of habit, Simone curtsied. Temple had taught her—curtsey begat courtesy. "Mrs Harmon?"

"Please, call me Lisette. And this is Polly." She held up a dark haired little girl perhaps fourteen or sixteen months old.

"Simone, then, please call me Simone."

"I am so happy you are here. It can be lonely as we are only ten here in the fort."

"You speak English. Your husband wanted me to teach you."

"I do not need teaching, I need practice."

"What have you planted?" Interested, Simone leaned over to look on the other side of the enclosure. She had never seen a garden before. To her, vegetables were found in market stalls.

"Potatoes, turnips, carrots, onions. It is the second year we try." Lisette's velvet brown eyes gazed at her appraisingly. "But you do not want to hear about my garden. Look, the sun is high. Go to the water and wash."

Simone gaped at her. "How did you know?"

"It is in your face. The miles must be washed away. Go." Lisette pointed to the lake. "You will find a good place. It is safe, the men work and the Indians are away today. We will talk later when we cook the food."

Simone didn't need to be told twice. With a hasty "thank you", she twirled about and darted toward their little cabin. Ducking inside, she scrabbled through the packs until she found what she sought: a precious bar of rose scented soap. Temple had bought it for her in Montreal and sadly, she had not had the opportunity to use it. It was still in its wrapper, a square of coarse paper.

She picked her way down the little bluff, stopping to pluck a pink wild flower to tuck in her bodice. Following the direction Lisette had pointed, she continued along until a curve in the beach hid her from the fort.

The prospect of a bath was too tempting to allow for false modesty. A quick glance proved her to be alone and within seconds she had stripped off her clothing, leaving it in a little pile on the beach save her shift. That she could wash with her. If she wrung it out thoroughly, it would dry quickly in the hot summer sun.

Her inhibitions were stripped away with her clothes. Lifting her face to the sun, she raised her arms and inhaled deeply, once, twice, as if the unsullied air could wash her inside as the water would wash her skin outside. Picking up her shift and the soap, she waded thigh deep into the water.

"Oh, how lovely," she sighed, tossing the shift aside to unwrap the soap. The paper stuck and she dunked it beneath the surface of the lake to loosen it, marvelling at the clear water that allowed her to see her hands perfectly. Her nails were chipped and dirty, the skin brown and weathered against the ivory of the soap bar. She caught sight of her face, mirrored on the water's surface.

"You're as brown as the Indians," she murmured to her rippled reflection.

Oh my, her tan would fade, wouldn't it? Ladies of quality had pale, pale skin. Perhaps plenty of lather would lighten her face.

She dunked the soap and rubbed it briskly between her hands, working up a handful of froth that she applied to her face. Eyes squished, she dunked beneath the water to rinse then worked up another handful of bubbles for her hair. Again she dunked below the surface of the water, placing the soap on the sandy bottom to free both hands to massage her scalp. She stood and lifted her face again to the sun, pulling her hair over one shoulder to wring it out. How blissful to be clean.

"Simone."

She froze at the husky growl that crawled through the air.

Temple.

Panic seared her. What was he doing here? She had thought him busy with Daniel. She sank down until her shoulders were covered then crossed her arms before turning around to look.

"If you please, my lord, I would like to finish bathing. Alone." She made her voice frosty. Her words died in her throat when she caught his eyes.

They were ravenous eyes, avid, the eyes of a predator. And she was the prey.

"Simone." Temple whispered her name again. Glorious in her nakedness, he had seen her worship the sun with arms outstretched. The sight of her, wet skin satin shiny and nipples pebbled with cold, snared his gaze, captivated him. She had become one with the wilderness, a pagan nymph.

He wanted her.

Now.

"I thought you were busy in the warehouse," Simone said, dread limning her words. She cast a frantic glance toward her clothes before remembering she had brought her shift with her to be washed. Where was it? She tried to find it beneath the water, kicking out a foot first one way then the other.

"We saw you walk toward the beach. Daniel thought I should watch over you. " Temple left the shelter of the woods and started across the beach. His footsteps crunched on the gravel, an ominous sound that alarmed her even more than the look in his eyes.

"Go away. Please." Her whispered words mingled with the soughing breeze high in the trees.

"No." He ignored her plea, taking a step closer before slowly, deliberately, beginning to remove his clothes.

"Please, my lord. Mr Wellington. Temple." She made her voice stern. "Please leave me." Again, she searched for her shift. It wouldn't provide much protection against him but it was better than nothing.

"I want you," Temple said, stripping off his trousers. "I want you as I've never wanted another." As he spoke the words, he realized it was the truth. Simone, the street urchin, the unknown one, had become an integral part of him. He wanted, nay, needed to make love to her, needed to surrender to the ache of stifled desire. He knew from prior experience that women derived as much pleasure from the sexual act as men and he would show her, now, in this very moment. There may indeed be consequences but he would deal with them in time.

"No, please." Simone started to shiver, whether from cold or his presence, she couldn't say. She forgot about the shift, just stared at him, mesmerized by the expanse of rippling skin that grew with each piece of clothing removed.

"Simone. My love." Naked, Temple stood at the water's edge, sensibilities swayed by the savage surroundings. His erect penis pounded with a life blood of its own, a life blood he could no longer ignore. He waded toward his quarry.

Simone was not so easily intimidated. Fury leant an edge to her tongue.

"I beg you, my lord, please reconsider," she snapped, shifting away. "If you think calling me your love is going to win me, you can think again."

"Oh, Simone," he sighed, shaking his head. "How can you think you can escape?" He was now waist deep, only a step or two away from her.

"By appealing to you as a gentleman."

"I think not." Temple lunged forward with a splash and grabbed her wrist. "Furthermore, it's high time I disabuse you of the notion that I am a gentleman." He exerted just enough pressure to pull her closer, a relentless force she couldn't fight. "Come to me, Simone. Let me show you the pleasure to be had between a man and a woman." His last words were whispered, his dark eyes earnest.

"Don't," she pleaded. "You'll ruin me." She leaned away in an effort to resist, digging her feet into the sandy bottom, slapping the water with her free hand. Her attempt to escape him came to naught for his hold on her was steely. Another tug and her body glided into his.

"I'll not ruin you against your will." With a growl, he pulled her up to hold her tight against him, tipping her head back with one rough hand to look down at her. "Command me to stop and I shall."

Her skin where it touched his burned while the rest of her was cool, soothed by the water. Of a sudden, Simone knew she could not resist him, could not resist the heady sensations prickling her insides.

Wicked, so very wicked, to be naked. But right, so very right to be with him.

Aye, she would lose her virginity today but she would lose it willingly and not dwell on the outcome. Yet.

She trembled and her hands crept up to rest on his shoulders. They were alone in the wilds and Temple had become as savage and untamed as the country around them.

Helpless with surrender, she looked into his dark and brooding eyes. As he continued to hold her captive in his gaze, her arms, of their own volition, wound about his neck and she raised her mouth to his. His lips swooped down on hers. They were hot too, as hot as the rest of him. She drew in a deep shuddering sigh and yielded.

Temple savoured the feel of her in his arms, savoured the craving she aroused in him that he knew would soon be assuaged. He wooed her with his lips, willing her to accept him, to want him as much as he wanted her.

He tore his lips away to lose himself in her remarkable sapphire eyes, eyes as limitless as the soaring skies above them, eyes of time without end.

She made as if to pull her arms away from his neck. "No, don't," he murmured, sliding his hands over her shoulders and down her back. "Don't let go of me."

Grabbing her legs, he wrapped them about his hips. It was exquisite torture, knowing the cleft he sought was right there, a prize ripe for the taking. "Feel me, Simone, feel how much I want you." He cupped her buttocks in his hands and moved her up and down against him, making ripples in the water that fanned out around them.

"Oh," Simone gasped. Sensations tumbled through her like dice in a cup, rattling and slamming against her ribcage. Desire. Trepidation. Desire. Hesitation. Desire. Desire as she had never before desired in her life.

She reached up to his head, to wind her fingers in his hair and pull his lips back to hers. Beneath her mouth, she felt him moan, a rumble that coursed through her, filling her with exultation. She had power over him, the age-old power of a woman over a man.

Beneath her thighs, she could feel his muscles flex and release as he manoeuvred them through the water, back toward the beach. Water cascaded from them like the fountain of desire they were as he stepped free of the lake.

She clung to him, ankles hooked behind his taut bum, arms clasped around his neck. Each step he took rubbed her mound against the velvet steel of him. Her breasts flattened against his chest as he leaned over to pick up his shirt, a delightful sensation twining with the pleasure boiling between her thighs.

"A bower for a lady," he breathed as he tossed his shirt to the ground in a semblance of a blanket.

Effortlessly, he lowered himself to his knees, clasping her tight with one sinewy arm and leaning forward onto the other one. "Drop your legs," he commanded and wrapped his arms around her to kiss her again, playful kisses that nipped her collarbone, tugging kisses that pulled at her ear lobes, fairy kisses that trailed up and down her neck.

"Temple," she moaned, squirming against him, searching for surcease against the feelings that pummelled her. "More, I want more," she pleaded, digging her nails into his back before sliding her hands down to his flanks to grasp the strength there.

"Aye, Simone, and you shall have it. Now." And he plunged deep into her slick flesh, holding still for an instant before finding a timeless rhythm she instinctively knew.

Thrust for thrust, they danced and parried until Simone spiralled with the birds on the air currents, searching for a pinnacle that had to exist, only where? Frantic, she arched her back, rooting her heels in the ground to push herself ever closer to Temple, to his maleness, the very essence of him that washed over and through her.

When it came, her climax was violent, shattering in its power. A piercing scream ripped from her throat at the intensity of awareness that surged through her, to subside to a golden glow radiating from her belly.

Without a doubt, she had reached womanhood.

Now she understood the attraction between a man and a woman, why the baker's wife down the street looked at her husband with eager eyes, why Marianne would creep back into her own cot late at night after a secret tryst despite the risk of raising the ire (and fist) of Mrs Dougherty.

Above her, she felt Temple pump once, twice before he tilted his head back and let loose an animal howl that startled the crows playing in the breezes above.

He sagged into her, dropping a kiss on her forehead before pulling himself free. Rolling over to prop himself on one elbow, he gazed down at her, his face gentle. With one finger, he began to trace the outline of her collarbone, back and forth, back and forth, a mindless gesture, and intimate.

Her heartbeat slowed and she snuggled closer, relishing his strength. She closed her eyes and leaned into him, his chest hair crinkling into her cheek. His scent, and hers too, filled her nostrils and she inhaled. She liked the odour, a trace of her but mostly him, untamed and a bit smoky, and she took another breath.

Languid, she lay there, feeling him beside her, feeling his chest rise and fall. Oy, if she could only capture this moment, capture the contentment and security, to be taken out and savoured at another time.

The seconds stretched into one minute, then two before he spoke.

"The sun sets," he remarked in a conversational tone. "We had better get dressed." He sat up.

Feeling suddenly exposed and embarrassed at her nakedness, she rolled over onto her stomach, hugging his shirt to her.

"Yes, of course," she replied in what she hoped was a normal voice, as if lying with a man on a beach in the New Caledonian wilderness was a normal occurrence. "Will you fetch my shift? It's in the lake somewhere."

"You bathed with your shift?" It sounded silly when he said it and she blushed.

"Yes. I wanted to wash it."

"Happy to oblige." Temple grinned at her and in an easy motion, rolled to his feet. As he strode back toward the lake, she watched him for a few seconds.

Muscles rippled his buttocks and thighs as he walked and the setting sun outlined his shadowy figure with molten gold.

Reluctantly peeling her gaze away, she scrambled to her feet and dove for her clothes. She managed to arrange her dress around her shoulders as a makeshift shawl by the time he turned around.

"I have it," he said, holding it up to show her. "At least I think it's yours."

A tide of heat crossed her cheeks at the sight of him, striding toward her without a trace of shame.

"Oh, my," she murmured. How odd to see him naked while her dress covered her. Another tide of heat flushed her entire body.

"Here." He wrung out the shift before he gave it to her. "It's wet, are you sure you want to put it on?"

"It will dry," Simone stammered, jerking it away and trying desperately not to look at him. Looking down the beach, she feigned interest in the crows circling in the breeze.

"Why don't you wear my shirt instead of your shift? It's dry."

His chivalrous offer stunned her, as if she really was the lady of quality he always spoke about and not the street urchin.

And that's when uncertainty and dismay crept in. As neatly as if she had handed him a silver tray, she had just given him more proof of her street upbringing. What had she done, allowing him to take her with nary a struggle? What must he think of her wanton behaviour? She felt ill.

"Go away," she whispered, turning around to avoid seeing the censure she was sure she would find in his eyes. With shaking fingers, she donned her wet shift. Cold and clammy, it matched the feeling in the pit of her stomach. She tried to pull on her dress but it clung to the wet shift and she struggled with it.

What had she done? She had given him the only thing she had of value, that's what.

The beauty of the afternoon, the passion they had just shared, spluttered away like a candle that had finally guttered itself out. Behind her, she could hear him getting dressed. Swallowing hard against the bile rising in her throat, she at last managed to pull down her dress.

"You can turn around now," he drawled.

"I don't want to," she said. "I—" Her voice died away. What could she say?

"Now we are man and wife in deed, if not words." He sounded pleased, unaware of her distress.

His words stung her to the core. She had become the one thing she had vowed she would never be.

A whore.

The sick feeling in the pit of her stomach welled up and smothered any charitable thoughts she had had toward him.

"You're just like the rest," she snapped, looking at him over her shoulder. "Take what you want with nary a thought."

"Simone?" His jaw dropped and confusion filled his eyes. Confusion, she knew, at her sudden change in mood.

She bolted so he couldn't see the tears. They dribbled down her cheek, falling from her chin to disappear into the woollen cloth of her dress.

"I'll look after you, Simone," he shouted behind her. "I'll not cast you aside despite what just passed between us."

Simone pretended not to hear, tried not to notice his bewildered tone.

He had ruined her utterly. Thanks to him, she could never become the lady of quality he had vowed she would be. Ever.

Numb with shock, she marched on, back straight, shoulders back, stumbling over the rocky ground. Only one thing roiled through her mind: she had lost her virginity, symbol of her independence. Her virtue, the one thing she swore would never happen to her, the whole reason why she had become a pickpocket in the first place.

Damn Temple. Damn him all to hell.

* * *

Temple wasn't sorry. He watched her stalk away, admiring her at every step, at the determined tilt of her head, the vigour in her shoulders. Making love with Simone had been glorious. How could something so right be wrong?

That thought bothered him—how right she had felt in his arms. She shouldn't even be in his life but by fate's hand, their paths had crossed.

Recently, it had occurred to him on more than one occasion that he could quite happily have Simone at his side for the rest of his life.

Easy enough to do in this country where a man and a women were judged by their character and not by their station. But he knew they wouldn't be staying in this remote fort forever.

He knew one day, when he deemed enough time had passed for Mortimer-Rae to forget all about him, he would return to England with hopefully a bit of extra coin in his pocket. Dare he take her home as his wife? Oh, how tongues would wag. An enticing thought.

One he would let simmer in his mind for a while.

Chapter Twelve

"Please, Simone," Temple pleaded. "Please talk to me."

"We have nothing to say." Arms crossed, Simone kept her back to him.

"I assure you it won't happen again."

"What." She whirled around, glad the interior of their cabin was dim enough so he couldn't see the tear stains on her cheeks and bosom. "What won't happen again." Some devil inside her wanted to hear him say the words, wanted him to acknowledge what had passed between them a scant hour ago. "What won't happen again," she repeated.

"What I perceived to be a very enjoyable pastime." He gave her a sardonic smile and lifted one eyebrow.

"At my expense." She made her voice haughty. Enjoyable pastime, perhaps, but she would pay the piper for it, not he.

"What did you expect?"

"What did I expect?" His question infuriated her. "What did I expect? I expected to be treated as a lady of quality, that's what. Remember that's what you were going to teach me," she added sarcastically.

"Yes." Temple shrugged. "I am teaching you." He leaned toward her and lowered his voice. "If you want to know the truth, you still have a few things to learn." He gave her a devilish wink, as if he was trying to tease her into better humour.

The insult and his casual manner wounded her to the quick. She drew her hand back and slapped him, a slap powered by hurt and anguish. With grim satisfaction, she saw him flinch.

"You're abominable." Her voice, and eyes, spat venom.

"So I've been told. I've never given it much consequence, though." Simone's words appeared not to ruffle him in the slightest. He rubbed the red mark on his cheek. "Nicely done, by the way, you pack quite a wallop. Something else you learned on the streets?"

"At least I learned to stand on my own two feet and not mistreat others."

"Mistreat others? Is that what I just did on the beach, mistreat you?" The sardonic smile flitted across his mouth again. "I thought it was just another lesson in your, ahem, education."

"An education I can do without, thank you very much."

Temple chuckled at Simone's prim words. "Ah, what a pity," he said. "You were a very apt pupil. Very well, let me assure you for a second time, it won't happen again."

Speechless, she glared at him. What did the man not understand? He had ruined her.

But ruined what? The little question wormed itself insidiously in her mind. Nothing, really.

She was a child of the workhouse, thought to be a lady of easy virtue. Worthless in the eyes of many, and, in the eyes of many others, long past a date with the hangman.

He was a lord of the upper class and as such lived by his own rules.

What foolish notions had she harboured, that he was cut of a different cloth and would grow to love her, take her with him when he returned to England? He had treated her exactly as the rest of the world expected. The miracle was it had taken him this long to have his way with her.

Her shoulders sagged under the weight of crumbling disillusionment. He wasn't her knight in shining armour, not hers to dream about. A sense of loss washed through her. Only one thing could make things worse right now—if his seed took hold within her.

"What if I am with child?" She posed the question, heart lurching at the thought.

A child. How could she possibly raise a child in this wilderness? What would Temple do? Would he claim it as his own? Or cast her from his life forever? A hurtful, dreadful thought.

He recoiled as if the words were stones she had thrown at him. "Oh, that."

"Yes, that." Nerves boiled in her stomach in anticipation of his answer.

"Well, I expect we will cope." His voice and demeanour were calm, reassuring.

"Do you really care so little?" she asked, bewildered at his sudden change in manner.

"On the contrary, Simone, I care very much." Temple reached over to clasp her hand. "However, there's no point in worrying about a child until the matter is clear one way or the other."

"Oh." Simone could feel her cheeks redden as she realized his meaning. "Of course."

Nonetheless, his response gave her some comfort. He hadn't dismissed the notion summarily.

"What we should be worrying about is setting the place to rights before it gets too dark to see." Temple's voice was brisk. "And finding something to eat."

Obviously, the conversation was over. By his matter of fact air, Simone knew Temple intended to carry on as if nothing had happened.

Well, if he could, then so could she, at least outwardly.

"Very well, my lord." Simone deliberately used the salutation. She would do well to remember he was not of her station and what better way to do that than use his title.

With a heavy heart, she pulled her bedroll from the jumble on the floor and spread it out.

* * *

Temple lay on his back, arms clasped under his head, staring into the blackness. A child. The gift of life, sprung from his loins. A consequence he hadn't thought about before taking Simone.

His conscience troubled him—he had taken advantage of her, abused her trust. He fought the feeling; he had done nothing wrong, had only acted on nature's creed. It was not like she didn't know what went on between a man and a woman. She had enjoyed it, he had felt that in every fibre of his being.

But a child. Not just any child, but his child. Hardly anything to worry about, considering her background, and certainly not his concern. A guinea or two a month should put things to rights.

Somehow the idea of his child being a bastard didn't sit right with him. He inhaled, filling his lungs with as much air as he could before letting it out slowly with a hissing sound. He had learned this trick to calm himself whilst duelling, to keep his hand steady and his mind clear.

There was, however, another solution. The babe would not be a bastard if he married the mother. Marry Simone? Odd how often that thought crossed his mind lately. Simone wasn't the genteel woman he had always pictured, but did it matter?

A child. Well, he would abide by his own counsel. It was pointless to speculate until it was actual fact.

Beside him, scant feet away behind one of his chests, slept Simone, oblivious to his churning thoughts. He listened to her breathe, concentrating on the sound, letting it soothe him as it always did.

* * *

As Simone had surmised, Temple carried on as if their encounter on the beach several days ago had never happened. On this particular day, his duties in the warehouse over, he had sought her out in their cabin where she knelt organizing one of the trunks to hold her clothing.

He stood before her now, face illuminated by the glow of sunlight through the parchment window. Her heart bounded at the sight—the radiance infused his face, making his mocha eyes tar black, enigmatic.

"I beg your pardon?" His announcement astonished her.

"I am going to teach you to shoot a pistol," Temple said, matter of fact. "Pistol shooting is one thing ladies of quality do, particularly at country house parties. Besides," he leaned closer with a glint in his eye and a grin lurking on the corners of his mouth, "it's a useful skill to have in these surroundings, don't you think?" He held both arms out as if to prove his point. "You must keep the animals at bay."

He said it in such a way that Simone knew he referred to himself. Somehow she doubted that knowing how to shoot would have saved her that day on the beach. "If you say so."

"I do. So put aside what you're doing. I've already set up some targets." His demeanour was light-hearted, infectious.

Simone regarded him through dubious eyes. What, shooting pistols? Needlework, yes. Watercolours, yes. Playing the pianoforte, yes. But shooting? Nonetheless, he must be sincere in his offer, for he had a pistol jammed in the waist of his trousers, the same pistol she had found in his trunk that night they left London.

"I agree with your husband." Lisette interrupted, poking her head through the door. "You must do as your man tells you."

"Now you can't say no. I have an ally." Temple gestured toward Lisette.

"I shoot too," Lisette said. "It is only good to protect yourself and those you love." She placed a hand on Polly's tousled head.

Oy, a shooting lesson would put Simone in Temple's company, something she had been avoiding, but Lisette's reasoning was sound. Simone threw her hands in the air. "Very well, I surrender. Pistol shooting it is."

"Jolly fun, let's go then. Will you be joining us?" Temple asked Lisette.

"Oh no." Lisette shook her head. "I came by to ask Simone to come with me to the Indian village later."

"I should like nothing better," Simone said. "Shall I find you when my shooting lesson is over?"

"Aye," Lisette nodded. "I will be in my garden. Come, Polly." She took her little daughter by the hand and walked away with the graceful stride that reminded Simone of the grand ladies attending the Royal Opera House in Covent Garden.

"I'm ready," Simone declared, throwing away her apprehension and she followed Temple with a light step as he headed out the door. The brilliant sun matched her mood and she started to hum, a little ditty sung to her a hundred times by Mrs Dougherty.

"Oranges and lemons," she hummed.

"Say the bells of St. Clemons." To her amazement, Temple finished the first line.

"You owe me five farthings," she sang, heartened by his participation.

"Say the bells of St. Martins." He stopped walking and turned around. A grin lifted one corner of his mouth. With a start, Simone realized he grinned more often these days. Life at Stuart Lake suited him. She liked his new, light hearted manner; it charmed her.

"When will you pay me?" She stopped a step or two away from him, just out of arm's reach. Golly, he was so appealing right now. If she even so much as brushed against him, she would throw herself into his arms unabashedly. Definitely not the behaviour of a lady of quality. Best to keep back and let only her eyes consume him.

"Say the bells of St. Bailey." He sang back.

"When I grow rich."

"Say the bells of Shoreditch."

Together they sang the last two lines: "When will that be, say the bells of Stepney, I do not know, say the great bells of Bow." They broke out in laughter at the absurdity of singing about the bells of London's churches thousands of miles away.

"You have a lovely voice," Temple remarked, "another accomplishment for your list."

"Th—thank you," Simone stammered. His admiring gaze warmed her. If only she could capture that admiration forever. But she couldn't. He belonged to polite society and a position she could never share.

However, one thing she could do capture was his company for the present. This time in New Caledonia would be all she would ever have of him.

And she would enjoy every precious second.

The realization swelled within her, bursting forth in an overwhelming smile that took him somewhat aback for he raised an inquiring eyebrow.

"So singing is one thing I have mastered already," she exclaimed.

"Oh, yes," he answered. "Learn a few songs and you would fit in quite nicely at the musical salons."

His praise bolstered her confidence. "Then let's begin the pistol shooting. I should like to add that to my accomplishments."

This time Temple gave her his arm and together they passed through the gate of the palisade.

"Over there." He pointed toward a fallen log at the edge of the clearing. Several items were lined up on it: a large stone, a small branch, a battered pewter mug.

"We'll stand here." He paused, swinging off a leather bag from one shoulder and leaning it against a stump. "This will be our base." He yanked the flintlock pistol out of his waistband and handed it to her. "It's ready and loaded."

She grasped the cool ivory handle firmly in one hand, fitting her index finger into the trigger. The pistol was heavy but she liked the feel of it, liked the sensation of power.

"First, move the hammer from half-cock to full-cock to release the safety lock." Temple demonstrated for her. "Now, lift it up and point toward your target." He stood beside her, positioning her body, pulling a shoulder one way, pushing her arm away just so. "The stone is your first target. Sight down the barrel and line it up."

Simone followed his instructions. It was awkward to hold the pistol at arm's length but she did her best, looking down the silver barrel toward her target some thirty paces away.

It was awkward, too, to keep her thoughts on the pistol because all she wanted to do was luxuriate in his proximity, luxuriate in his heat burning through the fabric of her dress. It distracted her.

"Now pull the trigger."

The first shot rang out. Her arm swung up wildly and she dropped the pistol. The ball disappeared in a flutter of leaves behind the target.

"I wasn't even close," she said ruefully, looking back over her shoulder to him.

"Not bad for a first effort but this time steady your shooting hand with your other hand. Like this." He picked the pistol up off the ground and showed her what he meant. "Watch me load it then try it again."

"I have to learn how to load it too," she groaned.

"It's easy. Watch." He poured powder in the upright barrel then jammed the paper wrapped ball on top. "Finish with more powder in the flash pan." He handed her the loaded pistol.

She took it from him and resumed her position, lifting up her arm and pointing the pistol toward the targets. Her hand shook a little and she lowered the pistol.

"Simone, you're holding it like a boiled potato. It's a weapon. You are the master and you must be firm with it. Now, try again." He patted her shoulder. "Support your hand with the other hand and sight down the barrel."

She did as he instructed. Although this time prepared for the recoil, it still jarred her shoulder. Again, the ball whistled past the target.

"See, you're getting closer. Try again because we're not going to stop until you hit at least the stone. Load the pistol."

"You like to order people around, don't you?" Smiling, Simone turned around to reach over to the bag. Her arm halted in mid-air.

She had an audience from the fort, among them Daniel. More disturbingly, several Indian men also watched in silence from the edge of the forest.

"Who are they," she squeaked, pointing toward the Indian men.

"Don't be alarmed. They mean no harm," Daniel said. "They're more interested in the colour of your hair than in your abilities as a marksman."

"Yes, pay them no mind," Temple added. "They are indeed harmless. I've met them at the warehouse." He lifted a hand in greeting.

"That's all very well for you to say," grumbled Simone. "You're not the one with an audience."

"Ignore them and load the pistol. I've already shown you how to do it." His voice was brisk, authoritarian.

"Very well," she pouted. "I still think you like to order people around, though. Were you in the army?"

He hesitated before answering. "Yes. But only a very short time. The military life did not suit me."

She turned her focus back to loading the pistol. Her fingers shook under the attention of the watching men and she spilled a little powder but eventually she held up the pistol in triumph.

"Well done, Simone."

Heartened at his encouraging words, she turned to smile at him. And froze.

The Indians had moved closer and stood silent, with hands on the hilts of their knives, charcoal eyes filled with curiosity. They formed an unyielding barrier, blocking their way to the palisade.

"Don't move." Temple hissed to Simone, pulling her behind him. "And don't say anything."

Tension settled heavily around them, so thick that it stilled even the whispering leaves.

Sweat trickled into Temple's eyes, dripped off his nose, oozed down his neck. He longed to brush it away but he kept his palms up in plain sight for he did not want to make any threatening movements. The seconds ticked by and still no one moved.

Shouts tumbled over the spiked wall of the fort; a crow, startled from its perch on the gate, squawked then flew off.

Two figures burst through the opening, the welcome shapes of Daniel and Baptiste, both carrying rifles. They pelted toward them. Simone moaned once, more a sigh than a sob and her fingers clutched his midriff, knife-edged nails digging into his skin.

Daniel and the interpreter, Baptiste Bouche, slowed to a walk, waving their rifles over their heads. They sidled around the human wall and positioned themselves one on either side of Temple and Simone.

Immediately Baptiste started talking. A few animated minutes of discussion ensued punctuated by the show of rifles.

In unison, the Indians backed away a few steps,

Temple heaved a sigh of relief. "I thank you both. I don't know what would have become of us without your aid."

"We're not out of danger yet," Daniel cautioned, still holding the rifle like a shield cocked and primed for action.

"We are saved," Simone whispered. Her head itched with sweat and she pulled her hands from Temple's waist to loosen the scarf from her head, letting it fall onto her shoulders. Her golden curls tumbled free.

Gasps of awe filled the air and gnarled brown fingers pointed to Simone's head, followed by a torrent of unknown syllables. Baptiste listened intently, offering a comment or two of his own before turning to Simone.

"They want to touch your hair," Baptiste explained. He turned to Daniel. "They say they want to touch the sun. They want to touch Simone's hair."

"Touch her hair?" Temple was sceptical. "Do you think that's a good idea?"

"I can't see the harm," Daniel mused. "We're armed, they're not. It should be safe. With the others within the fort, we outnumber them."

"She's the first white women they've ever seen", Baptiste interjected. "She fascinates them."

"Why would they want to touch my hair?" Simone asked, puzzled.

"For luck, superstition, you name it. If you would oblige, that is. I know it is an odd request, but—" He stopped. "It's your choice, really."

"I see." Simone stood silent for a moment, thoughts roiling. She'd attracted a lot of attention on their journey here, if not for the colour of her hair, which she had taken to covering, but also for the colour of her eyes. Until now, that attention had always been at a distance. The thought of having her hair stroked was a trifle odd.

"Why, I can do better," she exclaimed as a solution presented itself. "I could give them a lock of my hair."

She reached into her pocket for a length of blue satin ribbon that she had promised to Lisette. Surely Lisette would understand. She separated a lock of her hair then tied the precious bit around it. "Does anyone have a knife?"

"Aye." Baptiste pulled a shiny blade from his boot top and hilt first, handed it to her.

"Thank you." She hacked away at the lock of hair, holding it up triumphantly. "Done."

"Good." Daniel nodded, satisfied. "Step forward slowly and present it to Chief Kwah." He pointed to the Indian who stood slightly behind.

Simone nodded, wiped a sweaty palm on her skirt then dragged an arm across her forehead to blot the perspiration there.

Quivering like an aspen in the wind, she took a tentative step forward. She held out the lock of her hair.

"For you," she said.

After he took her offering, she sank into the deepest curtsy she could manage, holding her skirts out as far as they could stretch, dipping her head so that all she could see was the ground beneath her.

She heard the murmur of Baptiste's voice as he translated her words yet still she kept her head lowered. To his people, the chief was the leader, much like the king was to her and thus deserved her total respect.

"He is pleased," she heard Baptiste say. "He tells you to rise. He has heard tales of your eyes. He wants to see them.

Simone stood, keeping her eyes on the ground until the very last minute. She let her gaze travel up over the muscled, bronzed body until she looked the man full in the face.

She startled him as much as he did her; she could tell by the way his obsidian eyes first widened then narrowed. A smile split his face, teeth standing stark white against his leathered skin and he began to gesture, pointing first at her hair, then his, then from her eyes to his. A curtain of shiny black hair rippled down his back when he tilted his head to look at the sky.

He stared at the sky for a few seconds then looked Simone full in the eyes again. Amazement shrouded his face. A sound erupted from him, a rough bark that startled Simone until she realized the man laughed. He said something to Baptiste, who began to translate again.

"He is called Kwah, Chief of the Aghelh Ne, or Carrier Indians. He thanks you for the lock of hair. He will treasure it and put it in his medicine bag."

"Tell him I am happy he likes the gift."

As Baptiste translated, she lowered her gaze again. Kwah's moccasins caught her eye and she inspected them, admiring the stitches, much neater than her own sorry attempts on leather.

"Kwah wants you to look at him. He has a question."

Startled, she jerked her head up. Kwah's eyes were on her, intense, searching, his mouth stern. Feeling much like a fly caught in a spiders' web, she clasped her hands in front of her, trying to still the turmoil in her guts.

"He wishes to take you to wife."

"I must beg pardon?" She whirled about to look at Baptiste. "You must be mistaken."

"No, Mrs Wellington." Baptiste grinned at her, revealing a row of rotting teeth beneath his shaggy moustache. "He is dead serious."

"She is already married," Temple snarled. "To me."

Simone turned the other way to see Temple looking daggers at the other man, chest straining against the fabric of his shirt, fists clenched tight around his rifle. It was an obvious territorial display.

Over her. Delight cascaded through her at the sight.

Over her.

Embracing that thought, she turned back to look at Kwah, careful to school her features.

The aggressive stance and tone of Temple's voice were not lost on the chief. He spat out a few words then turned away, patently ignoring them all.

"He apologizes. He did not realize the woman with sun in her hair and sky in her eyes belonged to you."

"Apology accepted." Daniel interrupted, taking control of the situation. "I have blankets and some pots to show the chief if those are of interest to him and his men."

While Baptiste completed the translation, Simone felt Temple's hand drop on her shoulder for an instant. She risked a quick glance at him but he watched the Indians intently.

At Baptiste's words, the Indians smiled and nodded and followed Daniel to the warehouse.

Temple watched until they disappeared into the palisade. "That was an interesting situation, don't you think?" Temple's casual remark belied the tension in the fingers clutching the stock of the rifle. The index finger of his right hand brushed the trigger repeatedly.

"Flattering, I suppose. It's not every day one receives an offer of marriage." Simone tried to make light of the circumstances.

"Your bearing impressed me." Temple meant every word.

Her natural grace had shone through, so much so that even Chief Kwah had noticed. The gesture of giving a lock of her hair showed a generosity of spirit not usually seen in the women of his acquaintance.

Not for the first time, he wondered about her background. The way she carried herself was at odds with the environment she had grown up in. The cream rises to the top, his schoolmaster always said. Surely it could apply to a woman as well as a man.

A gust of wind rattled the tree tops, breaking the mood.

"Shall we go?" Temple noticed Simone shiver. "The wind has chilled you."

"Aye, I'm damp. I'd like my shawl."

"Come." He draped a solicitous arm over her shoulder to shepherd her back to their cabin, loving the feel of her as she walked beside him.

He made sure they passed the open warehouse door so they could be seen by Chief Kwah. The chief had better realize Simone was his woman in more than just words. Simone.

His woman. He loved the raw, primitive sound of that. His woman.

Certainly his woman as long as they stayed here.

Then what?

Chapter Thirteen

"I have something to show you," Temple leaned on the fence to look down into the garden where Simone, on her knees, weeded the turnip rows. A month had passed since the incident with Chief Kwah's son and it neared the end of July.

"Phew, your timing is perfect," Simone answered, squinting up at him before rocking back on her heels. Perspiration beaded her hairline and she used a corner of her apron to swipe at her forehead. "I've just now finished up. Lisette asked me to take over because Polly needed a nap and wouldn't settle here like she usually does. I think it's too warm for the little one."

"It is hot," Temple agreed, "the perfect day for a surprise."

"A surprise? For me?" She tried to read his expression but the late August sun sat behind him and all she could see was the dark outline of his head.

"I daresay it's a surprise for me, too."

"How can it be a surprise for you? You know what it is." She got to her feet then bent over to massage the ache in her knees. "Do we have far to go?"

"A surprise in that I didn't know I could do it." A self-deprecating smile crooked his lips. "Doubtless a few other people would be surprised, too. And no," he added, "it isn't far. Just down to the beach below the trading post."

"Stop teasing me and tell me what it is," Simone pouted, hands on her hips.

"No, you have to see it. Come along." Without waiting for her, he spun around on his heel and strode away.

"Temple! Wait!"

"You'll just need to walk a little faster, Simone. The faster we get there, the sooner you'll know what it is." The words tumbled over his rapidly receding shoulder. Within mere seconds, he passed through the gate and disappeared from her view. Even though out of sight, his whistled tune hung on the breeze—a ribald ditty usually heard in the ale houses at home.

"Oh, you," she muttered before picking up her skirts to scurry after him.

Temple was headed straight to the water's edge, toward what looked no more than a skinned log. Not until she got closer could she see it was hollowed out.

"It's a canoe," he said proudly when she reached him.

"I can see that. Where did it come from?"

"I made it. With the help of Baptiste and Musdoos."

"You made it?" She stared at him, dumbstruck. "You? But when?"

"Yes, me." He scowled at her obvious amazement. "It's where I've been every afternoon after finishing in the warehouse."

She had offended him so she hastened to make amends. "It's beautiful. Are you going to take me for a paddle?" She flashed him her sweetest, most winsome smile. "It's a lovely afternoon."

"After that reaction, I'm not sure you deserve a paddle." He grumbled but Simone could see him softening.

"Oh, please, Temple, please. You took me by surprise, is all. Gentlemen aren't usually caught up in the pursuit of making canoes."

"I loved it, Simone." Excitement exploded from his very pores. "With every pull of the blade, every blow of the chisel, a thing of beauty came to life beneath my hands. Feel how smooth." He tugged on her hand, placing it on the forward lip. "And here." He moved her hand to feel inside.

"It is beautiful," she breathed. "I love how you can see every stroke in the wood. You did this?" She touched the outside of the canoe, feeling the ridges left by the blade. The ridges made a pattern that resembled feathers on a bird.

Temple had built this. Pride at his ability filled her. Her man.

"Well, Musdoos started it but once I got the hang of it, he left it to me. Baptiste came along to interpret for me."

"Musdoos?"

"He's one of the Indians I meet regularly at the warehouse."

"Have you tried it out yet?"

"I have." His chest swelled with satisfaction. "I had to paddle it over from the village."

"Take me out on the lake, Temple. It's too warm here." She fanned herself with both hands so as to prove her point.

"Precisely my thought, Simone. That's my surprise—a paddle on the lake. Get in." He held his hand out to help her in. "You must sit facing forward so you can see where we go."

Once she settled herself, he shoved off, wading through the water a few steps before stepping in. The canoe rocked a little while he manoeuvred to his knees then he grabbed a paddle.

"Are you certain you know how to do this?" Doubtful, she looked over her shoulder at him as he dipped the paddle in the water first on one side, then the other. In no time, it dipped and flashed in rhythm and they were gliding over the water.

"Nothing to it," he replied. "I've practiced a bit. Musdoos gave me some tips."

Simone sat for a few moments, fists so tightly clutching the edge of the canoe that the fingers were white. Gradually, however, she relaxed, letting loose her grip to lean over and trail one hand through the cool liquid.

"How lovely." She lifted her hand, watching the drips roll off her fingers and hit the water like so many crystal beads.

"Yes, very lovely." Temple said pleasantly, to all intents and purposes agreeing with Simone, but in reality commenting on the pleasing sight of her in her periwinkle blue seersucker frock. "Now sit still or you shall tip us over."

"Aye aye, captain." She twisted around to throw him a saucy look but her motion caused the canoe to rock side to side. With a squawk, she grabbed for the canoe gunnels, holding on with both hands.

Behind her, she could hear Temple's throaty chuckle. Thankful he couldn't see her face for certainly it must be beet red, she kept her back stiff, nose tipped in the air.

At first they followed the shore but as Temple grew more confident, he began to traverse their little craft across the rocky points marking each little indent in the shoreline. They rounded one promontory and saw a bear gorging itself on berries; another time, a flash of rusty red as they disturbed a fox drinking from the water's edge.

"Look!" Temple pointed at an osprey hovering overhead.

"Oh!" With wide eyes and open mouth, Simone watched as it dove at breakneck speed, plunging into the water before emerging with a wriggling silver fish clutched in its talons. It flew off into the blue brilliance of the sky, disappearing behind some tree tops, fish still struggling valiantly to escape.

A doomed endeavour, Simone thought. "Poor fish," she murmured.

"That's the law of nature," Temple shrugged, voice matter of fact. "Kill or be killed, eat or be eaten. Sink or swim."

"Be that as it may, it's still a horrid end."

"Speaking of a horrid end, it's time we turn back. The sun is getting low."

"I'm ready to go back, too. I'm getting hungry." As if to emphasize her words, her stomach rumbled. "Lisette has a fresh salmon and invited us to eat along with them."

"Well, double the reason to hurry back, then." And with a few strokes, Temple turned the canoe. "I think we can cut across the lake to save some time."

"Will it be safe so far away from shore?" But even as she asked the question, she could see the lake resembled a looking glass, with nary a ripple to mar its surface. There would be no danger in traversing that water. Besides, she was with Temple. He would keep her safe.

"As long as you sit still," he teased. "You almost swamped us once already."

"Well, you didn't warn me how easy it was to tip," she retorted.

"True," he acknowledged. "But now I have."

"Having no desire to get wet," she said loftily, "I shall sit as still as can be. If we tip, it shall be on your conscience." Simone squared her shoulders to the bow of the canoe and shifted to a more comfortable position.

Even with a short cut, she surmised it would still be at least an hour before they were back at the outpost and her back was already stiff thanks to the hours spent earlier in the garden.

Behind her, she could hear an occasional grunt from Temple and the peaceful, cadenced slap of the paddle. The late afternoon sun warmed her shoulders and content, she began to drowse.

* * *

Temple cast a worried glance forward past the sleeping Simone, to the ruffle of wind speeding across the surface of the lake, tipping the water with white foam. The cheerful sunlight of a scant few minutes before had disappeared, and an ominous shadow chased the ripples.

"Bloody hell," he snarled. Cursing his lack of attention, for in truth, the calm waters and late afternoon heat had lulled him too, he tried to manoeuvre the canoe to hit the onslaught head on. "Simone, wake up! Hold on!" He watched her just long enough to see her head jerk before turning his attention back to the stormy lake.

Regrettably, his lacked prowess with the paddle and the first waves hit them broadside, rocking them with ferocious intensity.

An idyllic afternoon outing had turned into a fight against nature. That grim thought had no sooner crossed his mind than the canoe tipped in the heavy waves, sending a sprawling Temple into the lake. The water, chilled by undercurrents whipped up by the storm, fair took his breath away.

He surfaced, gasping for air, treading water frantically. He twisted his head, first one way, then the other, searching the waves for Simone. Dread clutched at him with bony fingers, sending shivers through him that had nothing to do with the icy water.

"Simone!" No sooner did he open his mouth to shout than a wave slammed into his face, filling his nostrils, shoving him down.

He struggled to the surface again, in the process kicking off first one boot, then the other. He burst through and sucked in precious air, one heaving breath, another one, life-giving breaths that cleared his mind and focused his thoughts.

Simone, where is Simone? Cursing the waves, he heaved himself out of the water as far as he could, scissoring his legs in an attempt to give himself as much leverage as he could. "Simone! Simone!"

She was nowhere to be seen.

Taking a desperate gulp of air, he dove beneath the waves, searching the watery depths.

Nothing.

Panic chilled his heart much as the water chilled his body. He must find her, had to find her, for he couldn't bear to lose her. He surfaced only long enough to grab another desperate breath then dove again.

There.

There, directly below him.

Blue skirts billowed, golden hair glinted, bright against the murk. Kicking strong and hard, he swam down toward her, grabbing her by the hair to pull her up. Her eyes were closed, her body limp. Dragging his precious cargo, he kicked hard, hard, up toward the light. Lungs bursting, he broke through the surface.

"Simone! Can you hear me?" Turning her on her back, he slapped her face once, twice, before cradling her chin in one elbow. No response. He had to get her to dry land, had to start pumping her lungs.

Fighting the waves, he swam toward shore, towing her lifeless form behind him. His progress was agonizingly slow, every second that passed adding to the mounting fear. His feet touched the rocky bottom and he waded toward the shore, throwing her before him on the sandy strip of beach.

"Simone, breathe," he pleaded, thumping her chest then pausing to listen for breaths. Raw, naked fear gripped him, a terror so total, so complete, it drove all else from his mind. He couldn't lose her, not now. She meant too much to him.

"Simone, Simone!" He began to shout, willing his voice to rouse her. He pounded on her chest again.

She coughed, and water splashed out of her mouth. When she coughed again, he turned her head so she wouldn't choke.

"Thank god, Simone, can you hear me," he demanded.

"Papa?" Her voice was weak, childlike. "Papa, what happened?" Her eyelids fluttered briefly, but her eyes remained closed.

"No, not your papa, Simone, it's me. Temple." He grabbed her chin. "Look at me, Simone, it's Temple." Still, her eyes remained shut.

"Papa, where are you? Where's Mama?"

Bloody hell, she'd lost her wits.

"Simone! Open your eyes, it's Temple." He leaned forward and gathered her into his arms, pulling her into his lap before brushing wet tendrils away from her forehead to plant a kiss there. "Simone, look at me, I'm not your papa, I'm Temple."

Your man, he thought. For an instant, Lisette's face rose before him. *Your man*. That's what Lisette always said to Simone when talking about him.

Simone coughed one more time, retching hard to expel the last of the water before her eyes opened fully. With relief he saw recognition flood through them.

"Temple. What happened? Why are you wet?"

"I dare say you're wet too, Simone. The canoe tipped. You almost drowned but I was able to snag you before you sank to the bottom of the lake."

"Oh." Her eyes closed and she sagged against him. A second later, her eyes shot open. "It's happened before, Temple. In my dream. Only in my dream, no one saves me." Sorrow passed across her features, a brief shadow clouded her sapphire eyes then she smiled at him. "But you did. Thank you, Temple."

"No need to thank me." He brushed it off. "I'm not really the hero type."

"You are to me," she whispered, looking up at him, blatant adoration pouring from her eyes. "This is the second time you've saved me. First from a dreary life in London and now this."

"Yes, yes, I know." Bloody hell, now he knew for certain her wits were addled—she thought him heroic. Embarrassed, he changed the subject.

"I can't possibly fathom what your dream means." He looked at her, eyes narrowed. "Dreams are, I believe, one's mind clearing out memories and thoughts. Is it possible you almost drowned before?"

"I don't know." She shook her head. "I don't see how. We always stayed away from the river. I can't swim," she added.

"I know," Temple said wryly.

"I never thought it was something I needed to know," she blurted out, defensive. "Don't tell me ladies of quality need to know how to swim, too."

"No, no, of course not." He rubbed his finger along her jaw. "You're an orphan, aren't you? Isn't that why you grew up in the workhouse? Do you know anything of your life before then?"

"No." She shook her head. "No. The only thing I know is that Gentry Ted brought me to the workhouse. I only have this chain." She pulled it out of her blouse to show him.

"Yes, I've noticed it before. Simone." He leaned forward to gaze into her eyes. "Do you think it's happened to you before? Do you think that's why you keep having the dream?"

"I don't know." She shrugged. "I never thought about it at all. But I always wanted to find out about the chain. See, it has a medallion with a crest on it. I just never knew how to go about it."

"Let me see."

Obedient, she pulled the chain off over her head and handed it to him.

He inspected the medallion carefully.

It was the size of her thumb nail. Although worn, it apparently held a family crest—a boar's head and a stag rampant facing each other with a fleur de lis below. The fleur de lis intrigued him—it would imply French ancestry. Simone was a French name, so it was plausible.

Fool, he chided himself. Why didn't he think to ask to see it before? It definitely offered a clue as to her identity.

"Were you named by Mrs Dougherty?" He handed back the medallion.

"No." She shook her head before slipping the chain back over her head. "Mrs Dougherty told me I knew my name and that I was this old." She held up three fingers.

He nodded thoughtfully. "When we get back to London, we can make some inquiries."

"Of course." Simone didn't want to remind him she couldn't go back to London. She would be doing the dance upon nothing if Constable Carstairs saw her face again.

"In the meantime, it appears as if we'll be spending the night here. It'll be dark soon, too dark too travel for it is new moon." He looked behind them to the wild jumble of trees crowding the little beach and then out to the lake. "We may as well stay where we are. We're more visible here." He gestured toward the sky. "The storm seems to have passed us by so we won't need shelter."

"Shall we have a fire?" Simone's voice quavered a little. Still chilled from the fall in the lake, fear from her recent ordeal had not left her yet.

"I can try, Simone, but my flint's wet."

"Let me help you." She pulled herself out of his grasp. "I need to move about before I collapse with cold. Surely if we can find dry moss, it won't need much of a spark." She picked her way into the forest and returned in a matter of minutes with hands full of moss and twigs to add to the pile of dead branches Temple had gathered in her absence.

"Put it here." Temple pointed down at the rough fire ring he had cobbled together with a few larger rocks picked from the edge of the beach. He broke a few branches over his knee and placed them beside him within easy reach. "Let's have a go, shall we?"

With a nod, she set the moss and twigs in the centre of the rocks and he began to strike the flint.

Luck smiled on them for with a tap or two, sparks flew. In no time, the smouldering moss turned into a cheerful blaze that brightened the evening.

They sat close to each other, close to the flames, savouring the warmth now that the air had turned cool with the sun's disappearance.

"Your socks are steaming," Simone said suddenly. "Where are your boots?"

"I lost them in the lake."

"It will be difficult to walk back to the outpost."

"Difficult," he shrugged. "Not impossible."

"Lisette and Daniel will be worried for us."

"Aye," Temple agreed. "But perhaps they will see our little fire and know we are safe."

I am safe, Simone thought. *I am with you*. She kept those thoughts to herself for to voice them would only make him uncomfortable, she was sure. "Yes, the fire will keep us safe," she said instead.

"You sleep, Simone, you've had quite the ordeal. I'll keep watch."

The offer was gallant but then, she wouldn't expect anything else from him. She said nothing, just collapsed against him as he pulled her close. The shelter of his arm calmed her, the fire warmed her and soon her head tipped sideways against his chest.

After she fell asleep, Temple shifted carefully, placing her head on his lap so he could better see her face.

Simone's face, the face of the woman he loved.

The events of the afternoon had opened his eyes to that outrageous realization. Somehow she, with her cocky bravado and optimistic outlook on life and outrageous comments, had wormed her way into his very soul. And more, she belonged there.

How absurd, for he had never expected to find love and now that he had, he had no idea if she reciprocated his feelings.

Throughout the night, Temple threw wood on the fire. He couldn't tear his eyes from her, glad every time he added a stick or two for the flames would leap up and he could see her more clearly. She had drawn her clenched fists up beneath her chin and her knuckles were sharp against her jaw line. With coal dark lashes fanned over her cheeks, and face slack with repose, innocence radiated from her.

A protective urge swelled through him. *I'll see you safe through the night, Simone. I'll see you safe back to the outpost.*

And, when the time came, he would see her safe to London.

The question remained: what the devil would he do with her then?

Chapter Fourteen

"Ahoy!"

Hoarse shouts roused Simone. She opened her eyes to see Temple standing on the shoreline, waving at Daniel and Baptiste gliding in by canoe, paddles upraised in salutation. She sat up and waved back.

"How did you know where to look for us?" Temple asked, face scored with relief as the two men crunched into the beach, pulling their craft behind them.

"We saw the fire last night and assumed it was you. We waited for daylight so we could come by canoe," Daniel said. "Lisette worried about you but I told her not to fret, that the evil spirits didn't want you quite yet." He joked but his face was serious. "I trust both of you are well?"

"Yes," Temple nodded, "but the canoe is gone. Swamped in yesterday's squall. Jolly good you're here, though, I've lost my boots and didn't fancy the trek back in my stocking feet." His voice was rueful and Simone could tell he was upset over losing them—they would be difficult to replace. Not to mention the canoe he had worked so hard to build. In some way, she knew it had been a symbol to him, of what a man could achieve with his own bare hands.

She took her time getting up, yawning and stretching before lurching to her feet. She brushed away the sand clinging to her cheek and stretched once more.

"I don't suppose you brought something to eat?" She flashed the three a saucy smile. "I'm starving." A lady of quality, she knew, would never admit to such a base instinct as hunger but surely she could be excused just this once.

"Here, Lisette sent this along." Daniel handed her a small leather bag. "There should be enough for both of you."

"Thank you." Eagerly, Simone grabbed it and pulled open the flap to find a handful of soap berries and several slabs of what looked like wrinkled leather.

"Dried salmon," Daniel explained at her questioning look, "the first harvest of the season. You had better get used to it," he added, "winters here are long. Fresh food is hard to come by but thanks to the natives, we'll have an abundant supply of dried salmon and we shan't starve."

"I'm sure it's lovely." Although her words were brave, Simone was dubious as she took one of the pieces. She handed it over to Temple before taking one for herself, flipping it over to inspect both sides before taking a suspicious nibble. She chewed slowly, finding the flavour strong and she popped a berry in her mouth to counteract it. It was palatable, to be sure, and although she had gotten used to eating dried meat on the journey here, she hoped Daniel was wrong about subsisting on nothing else for the winter.

In a few minutes they had finished eating and the four set off for the outpost, Simone and Temple seated in the middle of the canoe, and Daniel and Baptiste manning the paddles. The water was choppy, the morning breeze stiff, so the two paddlers kept the canoe close to shore.

"Supplies came late yesterday," Daniel remarked after a while, seemingly unaffected by the exertion of paddling against the waves. "With them came a letter for you, Temple."

"Oh?" Temple said. "That's odd." His words came out strangled, as if he had to physically force them past a constriction in his throat.

At the peculiar tone in his voice, Simone turned around to see a scowl on his face, his jaw clenched and brows drawn together so tightly they resembled a bristled charcoal awning over his eyes.

And his eyes. She caught only a glimpse before he looked away but his scorched mocha eyes seethed with anger, with bitterness, with loathing. In a flash she knew—his family had found him, had somehow tracked him here to a wilderness on the very edge of the world.

"Temple?" Nerves boiled in her stomach at his obvious upset. It was all she could do to clutch the gunwales and not vomit over the side.

Thankfully, neither Daniel nor Baptiste noticed her distress, or Temple's frown, or if they did, they politely ignored it. Diligent to their task, the canoe fair flew over the water.

The sun shone well and high by the time they arrived at the fort, where a smiling, visibly relieved Lisette waited for them in the doorway of the Harmon cabin.

"We worried about you," she scolded gently as they trudged in, Temple and Simone trailing Daniel and Baptiste.

"Now, Lisette, I told you we would find them safe and sound." Daniel leaned his paddle against the wall.

"I know, but there are many dangers in the forest." She peeked around Daniel to look at Simone. "You are unhurt?"

Simone nodded. She didn't trust herself to speak. Lisette's obvious worry for their wellbeing was almost more than she could bear and she was afraid if she opened her mouth, she would collapse into a sobbing, wailing heap. Yesterday's events had left her on edge.

"Good," Lisette said. "Go rest for a while and come back for lunch. We have fresh bear meat today."

Simone nodded again and turned to go.

"Wait, Temple," Daniel said. "Let me get your letter."

His words stopped Simone in her tracks. The letter.

She sucked in a deep breath of air and waited for her world to stop whirling.

The letter that could or would change everything.

"Go ahead, Simone." Temple gave her a little nudge. "I'll follow you shortly."

"Very well," she said faintly. Swallowing hard against the lump in her throat, she waved at Lisette and walked away. She held her head up proudly, resisting the urge to run, not sinking to her knees until the door of their little cabin swung closed behind her.

And there she stayed, arms clasped about her middle, rocking back and forth, as if the motion could keep her apprehension at bay.

It couldn't.

She tried to keep her thoughts under control, to not jump to any wild conclusions as to the contents of the missive but it was futile. Various scenarios crowded her mind, each more ridiculous than the last, but all with one thread in common: Temple would move on with his life and leave her behind. She knew it had to happen sooner or later but somehow had thought the vast New Caledonian wilderness would hide them forever. Apparently not. Now all she could do was to wait for Temple and hear his news.

Dry-eyed, refusing to give in to tears, she continued to rock.

* * *

"Thank you." Temple took the letter from Daniel's hand, recognizing his mother's carefully formed lettering on the envelope.

"If you would excuse me?" At Daniel's nod, he walked away, out of the fort, back down to the beach. His clothes stuck against his skin, rocks jabbed his feet through his stocking feet, but he could not wait to read the letter.

He sat down cross legged and gazed appreciatively at the distant, tree-mantled mountains fringing Stuart Lake before looking down at the envelope in his hands.

How foreign, to see his mother's handwriting in this setting. Usually, her cards and notes would find their way to the silver tray in the entry hall of his town house. It had been, what, a year since he had left London? Regardless of the elapsed time, the sight of her handwriting stirred the familiar sensation—resentment.

An image floated through his mind—of him, his ear in the firm grip of whichever hapless governess was in charge at the time, the smug face of Richard, his older brother standing before him, and the entire scene laced with the detached voice of his mother saying, "Whatever you do, Richard, do not emulate your brother."

And he, Temple, would be punished and ostracized over the escapade that inevitably had been Richard's doing. Not once had his mother believed Temple when he had protested his innocence. "Temple, remove yourself this instant. Shame on you for placing the blame on Richard." Then she would turn away, her disapproval a solid block of ice that he could not melt, no matter how hard he tried.

Temple sighed and shook his head before turning over the letter in his hands to pry open the wax seal. What was the news from home this time? That his father's prize bull had taken first prize? That Boney was marching on London, leaving a wake of destruction? That his oh-so-proper sister-in-law had finally whelped the squalling brat that would be heir to the duchy?

He scanned the lines then in disbelief, scanned them again and again before crumpling the letter into a plum-sized mass and pitching it into the water. It floated there for a minute or two before sinking slowly leaving only a series of ever expanding circles as the only evidence it had ever existed. Eventually they too, disappeared.

He raked his fingers through his hair. None of his guesses had been correct—who would have foreseen that both his father and brother had died?

Deep in thought, he sat with fingers steepled for some time, staring blankly at the wavelets lapping at his feet. At length he stood up and pulled a vial of laudanum from his pocket. He hefted it in his hand a few times before heaving it as far as he could. It, too, disappeared into ever expanding circles.

Relief rolled over him, lightening his mood. It was over. It wasn't that he had been addicted to the substance but the vial had been a symbol of the pointless mess his life had become. He had carried it with him, knowing that one day he would toss it in a figurative gesture.

He laughed aloud, savouring his newfound freedom. Truly, this land had given him what he had sought: a new start and a new life. He was ready, nay, anxious to return and carve a responsible niche for himself. And his first responsible act? To help Simone find a respectable position.

As his countess.

At a dead gallop, he returned to the cabin.

* * *

He found her on her knees. At first glance, it appeared as if she prayed but then he noticed her hands were not clasped in front of her but instead, were gripping her middle as if battling a great inner pain.

"Simone?"

Large, hollow eyes turned his way, anguish fading the usually lively blue to pale grey.

"Simone, what's wrong?"

She just shook her head, once, twice, a tiny motion barely moving the curls framing her face. She opened her mouth to speak then closed it again. Two large tears balled in her eyes before spilling over and trickling down her cheeks.

He moved over to squat down in front of her, elbows propped on wide spread knees. "It's the letter, isn't it?"

"How did they find you?" she gasped before two more tears followed the first two down her cheeks. "I thought nobody knew where you were going to?"

"I left word with my solicitor." He fumbled in his pocket for his handkerchief. Wadding it in his right hand, he gently brushed away the moisture from her cheeks. "Don't you think I should tell you what it's about before you become distraught over the blasted thing?"

She swallowed hard before answering. "It can only be bad news, can it not?" Her voice was thin, reedy, as if all the spirit within her had shrivelled away.

"Perhaps for me it is. It all depends on how you look at it." He reached over and pried one hand away from beneath her rib cage. Tenderly, he pulled it up to rub her knuckles against his cheek then turned it over to drop a kiss in it. He placed it palm side against his cheek, effectively trapping the kiss there.

Her fingers were cold against his flesh. It truly seemed as if all the life had been sucked out of her.

"You're going away." Her words were stark, emotionless as she drew her hand away.

"Not necessarily," he shrugged. "Not until I discuss it with you."

She turned startled eyes to him. Good, he got a reaction—she had a bit of life left in her after all. He continued. "The letter was from my mother."

"And?" It came out as a puff of air as if she had been holding her breath.

"My father died in a fit of apoplexy, and sadly, several weeks later, my eldest brother, Richard, was thrown from his horse and broke his neck. He leaves behind a grieving widow but no heir," he added.

"Sadly for your brother but not your father?"

"Yes, well, I say sadly … for now it appears I am the next Earl of Leavenby and have been requested to return to fulfil my familial duties."

"Earl? You?" She gaped at him. Chuckling, he reached over to tap her chin. She closed her mouth with a resounding little snap.

"I daresay it's a bit of a stretch, isn't it?" A self-deprecating grin lingered on his lips and he inclined his head toward her in a caricature of a little bow.

"And what about me?" She lowered her face as she said it as if to avoid reading the truth in his eyes.

"I shall take you back to London."

"You know if I return it is straight to Newgate." Her voice was bitter. "And the hangman's noose."

"Not if you're the Countess of Leavenby." An outrageous suggestion, he knew, but one which made eminent sense to him.

"What did you say?" Her head jerked up as if she were a marionette on strings.

"I'm saying all your problems would be solved by marrying me. Constable Carstairs would not clap a countess in jail. Particularly if he has no proof you are Mona Dougherty."

"You want to marry me?" An array of emotions paraded across her face. Confusion, incredulity, doubt, and, he was pleased to note, hope.

Splendid. That meant she had some feelings for him. For now, however, he would leave that matter alone. He would have to use the other weapons in his arsenal to convince her to accept his proposal.

"Yes. It wouldn't do to see you dangling from the gallows."

She frowned at him.

"Besides, we wouldn't want to let all your lessons go to waste now, would we?" he continued cheerfully. "And what better way to thumb your nose at everyone who ever pulled their cloak aside as they walked past you or pretended you didn't exist as they rode by in their carriage while you stood shivering on the street? It's your chance, Simone, your chance to make something of yourself."

"But what's in it for you?" she said shrewdly.

"The occasion to bring home a woman of my choosing." *And to assert myself.* The look on his mother's face when he introduced Simone as his wife would be entertaining, to say the least. He leaned over and tapped her on the collarbone. "What do you say, Simone, shall we make it a partnership?"

He sat back on his heels and waited for her response. Nothing would give him more pleasure than to bring her to wife and the vehemence of his conviction surprised him. Of course his desire to wed Simone had everything to do with annoying his mother and less so with his feelings for her. Hadn't it?

"Are you certain I'm who you want?" Her voice was puzzled. "As an earl, you can have your pick of eligible women and—"

"Any of them would bore me to tears in no time," he interjected.

"What if they find out I'm nothing but a workhouse sod, a pickpocket? Does that not concern you?"

"The power of an earl is substantial," he answered glibly. "A few well-placed words here and there, a few timely introductions and numerous denials if need be. No one would dare dispute me. Besides, it would be a bit of a lark, don't you think? To play the part of countess?"

Face expressionless, she gazed at him, firstly perusing his features before letting her eyes wander up and down his body. It discomfited him a little, as if she were inspecting him for purchase rather than considering him for marriage. Much to his surprise, he found himself anxiously waiting her reply although, really, why would she turn him down?

"Very well," she said at last. "I will marry you."

"Splendid!" The word shot out of his mouth, propelled by the breath of air he had been holding while waiting for her answer. He reached over and raised her hand to his lips. "You won't regret it, I promise you."

"Regret? I scarce think I shall be the one to regret this preposterous arrangement. Now you, on the other hand." Simone's voice trailed away but he was glad to see a familiar twinkle in her cerulean eyes.

"Yes?" He lifted an autocratic eyebrow.

"You may come to regret it. I intend to play the role fully." A brilliant smile swept across her mouth. "And to the best of my ability."

He laughed but that didn't stop his loins from thickening at the image of her playing the part fully. Unclothed. In his bed.

"When? Everyone here already thinks we're married." Her question interrupted his pleasant thoughts.

"On board ship."

"Oh, how romantic." Simone clapped her hands.

"Er, of course." Bloody hell, romantic. How did that signify? This was a partnership. In return for his protection, she would become his countess, no more, no less. Nonetheless he was pleased to see her mood had changed and he didn't want to disabuse her of any notion that cast a happy glow on her face.

"Romantic," he muttered. "Right."

* * *

How had it happened? An incredulous Simone leaned against the door frame of the cabin she shared with Temple and looked out over the mundane, everyday activities in the yard of the outpost.

Baptiste gutted fish over by the gate, and Daniel was standing in the door of the warehouse while Musdoos and several other Indians walked away from him with their arms full of blankets. Lisette wrung out linens by the garden with a grubby faced Polly hanging onto her skirts. Out of sight, the crack of tortured timber rent the air as Temple chopped wood.

And she, Simone Dougherty, was going to become a countess. And not just any countess, but Temple's countess. The thought stunned her. How had she, a workhouse orphan, come to this? What had compelled her to take refuge in Temple's trunk? What had compelled her to offer the whereabouts of his package in return for him taking her with him to North America? Stranger still, what had compelled him to agree? And now, to offer her, a nobody, nay, worse than nobody, his name in marriage?

An unwelcome thought niggled its way into her mind. A lark, he had called it.

What if he had offered her marriage in order to disturb his family and disrupt their social circle? He would not stoop to something so low as to use her as a pawn? Would he? Nay, she decided, shoving away the unwanted idea, it could not be.

Oy, Simone, ye be the luckiest chit on this bloody earth.

A giggle burst loose from her chest and drifted away on the air. Temple would be appalled at the diction of her thoughts after all his hard work. But they were her thoughts and couldn't be heard by him or anybody. Furthermore, she would keep it that way. She may well be street rubbish but she vowed to do him proud.

And, dare she say it, she would be free to love him and earn his love back. There. She wanted his love and she would do all in her power to earn it.

She swept her deepest, very best curtsy to an imaginary Temple before going back inside to shake out the bed furs.

* * *

Darkness shadowed the cabin by the time Temple returned. Simone had lit the one and only oil lamp while she mended a pair of his breeches at the table and the insignificant flame barely conquered the shadowed corners of the room. It was a warm, homely little tableau and with a contented heart, he sat down across from her.

"Thanks to the voyageurs that came in yesterday, we are able to leave in several days. I must thank Daniel somehow for it's his doing that we're able to depart so quickly and avoid a long and tedious winter here."

"It's going to be a long journey," she sighed, before biting off the thread.

"Well, actually, no. We're not going through Montreal. We'll head west, travelling down the Fraser River then over to the Columbia River to follow that to Fort Astoria, on the Pacific Ocean. Then we'll sail to England around Cape Horn. We'll be home by early summer."

"Still a long journey, just not so much by land. Which suits me," she added airily. "I don't have a problem with sea sickness." Oy, did she just tease him? How does one speak to an earl, anyway? Even a soon-to-be-her-husband earl.

"Right." He shuddered. "Terrible stuff. Incidentally, I've changed my mind about marrying." He stopped to lean over and brush a wood chip from his leg.

"Oh," she squeaked.

The bottom dropped out of her heart. It hadn't taken him long to change his mind. Of course, he had gotten his wits about him. Of course it had been a jest at her expense. Her face must have betrayed her because he jumped in right away with an explanation.

"On board ship. Rather, I believe we'll be able to find an Anglican priest in Fort Astoria."

Her heart started beating again. She sucked in a huge, life-giving breath and fanned her face.

"You thought I was going to change my mind? Not on your life. I may be a scoundrel but I do keep my word." He chuckled, a humourless sound sending chills up her back. "No, Mother will have far less quarrel with my marriage if it's actually performed in the Church of England. I am taking secure measures, is all."

Simone nodded as she took a long appraising look at his shadowed face. With the fire light dancing on it, he looked saturnine, cold, a creature of the night. It was as if his impending return to civilization brought out the wild beast in him rather than the other way around. She shivered. This was a part of Temple she hadn't seen at all.

She wasn't sure she liked it.

Chapter Fifteen

True to his word, upon their arrival in Fort Astoria six weeks later, Temple tracked down a Vicar Williams.

Within a matter of hours, Simone found herself standing, clad in her rumpled, soiled dress and muddy boots, in the common room of a local inn that doubled as a church. The only thing remotely clean about her was her shawl, which she draped over her shoulders in an effort to hide as much of the travel stains as she could. Two of the six voyageurs who had travelled with them from Stuart Lake Outpost, Alain and Guillaume, acted as witnesses, while the others stood behind. All in all, a bedraggled little group but sincere nonetheless.

"Dearly beloved," began the vicar, "we are gathered here in the sight of God."

She focused her gaze on the man, trying to follow the ceremony but the dreamlike situation, not his words, held her attention. While Vicar Williams droned on about the responsibilities of marriage through thick lips and stained teeth, all she could think was that this was some kind of joke and that Temple would call a halt to the proceedings once he came to his senses.

She peeked at Temple, standing so solemnly beside her. His face was a stone mask, as if he listened intently to every word and took them to heart. At the movement of her head, he glanced down at her. The corners of his mouth lifted slightly and his eyes crinkled in the beginnings of a smile but his sombre expression returned at the priest's next words.

"Do you, er," the man fumbled with the prayer book in his hand, searching for the paper with their names, "er, Temple Wellington, take this woman to be your wife,"

Simone held her breath. This was his chance to deny her and to walk away. Would he?

"I do."

The simple declaration shattered the air and her doubts. The conviction with which Temple said the words boosted her confidence and she turned back to face the priest.

"Do you, Simone Dougherty, take this man to be your husband."

"I do," she whispered. "I do," she repeated, louder this time so that all within the little inn could hear her. Her lips quivered and she tried to still them, squeezing them tightly together.

The vicar began droning on again. Simone had difficulty following him, so full of disbelief was she over the phrase she had just uttered. *I do.* Two small words yet enormous in their implication.

"Do you have the ring?" Vicar Williams asked, the abrupt question bringing Simone back to the proceedings at hand.

The ring. Simone cast a horrified look to Temple only to see him pull a gold signet ring out of his pocket.

He slid it on her finger. It was big and heavy and no sooner had he placed it than it swivelled around so that it hung upside down. She squeezed her fingers around it, a solid and reassuring lump nestled in the crease between her palm and fingers.

"I now pronounce you man and wife. You may kiss your bride."

To the cheers and whistles of their companions, Temple leaned over and placed a chaste little kiss on her cheek. Bemused, Simone gazed around the rough room with its hand hewn flooring and log walls, plank tables and backless benches. It certainly didn't resemble the churches at home, but then had she ever expected to be married in a church.

Or married, period.

She looked back up to her groom. Much to her astonishment, he radiated happiness. It swirled about him in an ever-increasing cloud that soon enveloped her too. Her heart swelled and her lips broke into a smile.

Grinning like an idiot, she stood there and lost herself in the endless depths of his eyes. Eyes beckoning to her, promising her a lifetime together. Fanciful thoughts, to be sure, but marriage was forever, was it not? Had those words not crawled through her consciousness during Vicar Williams' ramblings—until death do you part?

They stood for what felt an eternity although in reality perhaps only one or two moments passed before Alain poked Temple in the ribs.

"Monsieur, you devour your wife with your eyes but may I suggest you save that for later? The inn keeper's wife comes now with your wedding feast, and we are hungry, oui?"

Temple held her gaze for one last second before he turned away to shout, "Ale to all! Come, Madame Innkeeper, come with your finest ale. Fill the cups and keep them full until not one man is left standing."

Cheers filled the rafters and the wedding feast began.

* * *

"Come," Temple whispered in Simone's ear several hours later. "I tire of these rapscallions, charming though they be." He squeezed her hand. "Come, Madame Innkeeper assures me our room is ready and a bath awaits."

"A bath?" Simone echoed stupidly, glancing down at the unusual sight of her small head grasped within his very large one.

"Aye, a bath. You know, a tub filled with warm water accompanied by soap and towels?" Temple's droll voice made her giggle. "Oh, and usually a maid or some such helpmeet but sadly, I will have to suffice," he added.

"A bath," she repeated.

"I assure you, a bath can be a pleasant diversion."

"Of course." It wasn't the idea of a bath filling her with apprehension. It was what would follow. Don't be silly, she chided herself. He's had you already. Despite her nervousness, she thrilled with the thought of feeling him again, of feeling him plunge into her, taking her to the very precipice of wonder.

"You go ahead. We have the room on the left." He gave her a gentle nudge toward the steep staircase leading up to the sleeping quarters. "I'll divert our guests so no one will take note of your departure."

Alas, a quiet exit wasn't to be. To a chorus of masculine voices singing a ribald tune interspersed with whistles and cat calls, Simone climbed the stairs. Certain her face flamed so that it could almost light her way in the dark, she thankfully reached the second floor to find that Temple hadn't lied—they had the room on the left, in fact the only room.

To her right, an open loft littered with furs, bed rolls and several sleeping bodies. Against the back wall stood a few barrels and crates and what she now recognized as beaver pelts draped over the crates. Sibilant snores resonated, reminding her of the shared sleeping accommodations at the workhouse and it brought a twinge of wistfulness to her breast.

An image of Mrs Dougherty rose and she could almost hear her reproving voice, "Now, we'll have no fightin'—this be a place to sleep." And the pushing and shoving would continue amongst the giggling girls until, at length, the woman would threaten to withhold their breakfasts. A slight smile at the memory ghosted across her lips before she pushed open the door to the room she and Temple would share that night.

All thoughts cleared her mind when she saw the tub, steaming lazily, in the middle of the floor. Actually, it was the floor—the tub barely fit between the bed and the wall of the tiny room.

The flame from the candle stub jammed into a bottle swathed with the wax of countless candles fluttered briefly on the upended keg that served as bedside table as the door creaked shut behind her. It fluttered again as the door creaked open again. She felt the presence of Temple behind her, not even needing to turn around as his musky scent filled the room, knowing it was him.

"Simone?" His languid voice filled her ears and she could feel his breath brush against her cheek.

She turned to face him, keeping her features expressionless, hoping he couldn't see the pounding of her heart through her blouse. Though how could he not, for it thumped so hard it felt as if it might leap out of her very chest to lie exposed, still beating, on the floor at his feet.

"The inn keeper's wife pressed these upon me," he said, holding out two fluffy white towels, incongruous in the rustic surroundings. "She assures me they were not gotten by ill means. Something about payment for lodging from a ship's captain seeking a night away from his crew."

"They're lovely," she stammered, reaching out to stroke them. Inadvertently, her fingers touched his and she flinched.

He must have seen that, for he lifted his eyebrows before giving her a sensuous smile.

"Aye, and she gave me this to give to you." He reached into his pocket and pulled out a sliver of soap. "It's all she has but knowing it is our wedding night, she wanted something a little special for you." He handed it to her and she took it in trembling fingers.

"Thank you. I gave my soap to Lisette." She held it up to her nose, catching a faint scent of lemon verbena. "It's lovely." She balanced it carefully on the edge of the tub.

"If you say so," Temple shrugged. "But the scent of a pine forest clean and fresh after the rain is much more to my liking."

Simone blinked. Of course he had a favourite scent, everyone did, but it made her realize how little she actually knew about the man even after all the time spent in close quarters with him. Somehow favourite scents did not signify when battling to save one's life against the elements.

"Well, get on with it", he said. "Before the water grows cold."

"Of course," she stammered. "Will you turn your back?"

"No, Simone, I will not."

Of course he wouldn't, he was now her husband and as such, he took command of her life. She gritted her teeth. Very well, if he wanted to watch, then so be it. "Could you at least turn your back while I remove my clothes?"

He didn't answer, merely tipped his dark head in agreement before turning around.

She looked at his tall back, at the tanned skin peeking out between the collar of his loose fitting shirt and his queue. It wasn't the mode, she knew, rather, his hair should curl about his collar, but it had grown long and he had taken to tying it back.

If she stood on her tiptoes, perhaps, she could brush the queue aside and plant a kiss on his exposed neck. She took a half-step toward him before squashing the urge and turning back to the tub. Quickly, before she changed her mind, she stripped off her clothes down to her shift and stepped into the steaming water.

Ah, what heaven to feel the liquid warmth, to feel the waves of goose bumps rippling along her skin as she slowly immersed herself. She gripped the edge of the tub, sliding down, down, into the water. Her shift floated about her and she toyed with the idea of ripping it off.

"Take it off," a husky voice commanded from behind her.

He had read her thoughts. She froze but of their own volition, her hands crept to the hem and she pulled it off, bit by sticky bit until finally she sat naked, wet cloth dripping from her hands. Face hot with embarrassment, she lowered her eyes.

He reached over her shoulder and she could see his arm snake out to take the sodden fabric from her hands, tossing it carelessly aside. It landed with a soft slap.

"Temple," she whispered. Out of the corner of her eye, she saw him grab the soap. Seconds later, his hands caressed her shoulder blades, calloused yet strangely gentle, smoothing down her back only to trail back up to her neck. She shivered, hypnotized by the sensation of his fingers gliding along her skin.

"Simone." His breath fanned her shoulders. "Wet your hair. I'll wash it for you."

Nodding, she obeyed, smoothing her hair off her forehead with shaking fingers before tilting her head back and sliding a bit further down. Unfortunately, by the time her hair was submerged, her knees had shot out of the water and she felt a bit silly.

Not only had her knees emerged but so too had her breasts and she looked up to see a motionless Temple stare at them hungrily. A whoosh of air escaped his nose, the nostrils flaring with its passing. Then a slow, lazy smile spread across his face and he began to rub his hands briskly over the soap to work up lather.

"Sit up," he commanded and she obliged, his hands caressing her as he leaned closer into her back. She relaxed, more at ease because as long as he knelt behind her, she couldn't see his eyes and she felt less exposed.

"Oh," she sighed as he began to massage the bubbles through her hair, piling it on top of her head in one soapy mass. She let her head flop forward and he began to knead her neck, slowly, rubbing in ever increasing circles, over her shoulder blades, then her shoulders and upper arms, then her collar bone.

She looked down to see his hands slow, then stop just above her breasts. He was close behind her, his cheek almost nestled into hers. Ensnared by the sight of his tanned hands against the ivory of her skin, she said nothing, just watched, hypnotized as his hands moved again to curve around her breasts and cup them. Fascinated, she watched as her nipples hardened when his thumb and index fingers tweaked the rosy nubs.

"Oh," she sighed again, amazed by the sensation. Much to her surprise, her hands, as if separate from her mind, rose to curl around his. Suspended in time, she sat, mesmerized by the sight of her breasts cupped in his hands cupped again by hers. As if to break the spell, a dollop of soap fell from her hair and landed in the water between her knees. She shivered.

"You're cold," whispered Temple. "Let me rinse you off. That will warm you."

Beyond speech, Simone nodded, dropping her hands and feeling strangely bereft as he pulled his hands off her breasts. She risked a quick glance over her shoulder to see him lean over to pick up her shift. She lowered her eyes, peeking at him through her lashes, seeing him dip the shift into the water and wring it out experimentally.

Then he dipped the shift into the tub and wrung it out over her. He did it time and again, wringing out streams of water, rivulets that coursed down her hair, her body, over and over until the soap was rinsed from her.

"And I dare say your shift is clean, too," he quipped, draping it over the edge of the tub. He unfolded one of the towels and held it up. "A robe for my lady."

"Thank you, my lord." She made her voice flirtatious, teasing. Boldly, she stood up, daring him to chastise her, meeting his eyes and standing naked for an instant before he draped the towel around her.

"Minx," he muttered. "And it's high time you addressed me as your lord. As such, I expect you to aid in my bath."

"Very well, my lord." Simone wrapped the towel around her, tucking one end under beneath her arm. "Shall we begin?"

"Aye," Temple nodded.

Without another word, he began to strip, quickly and purposefully until he stood naked before her. She tried to avert her eyes, but her gaze was drawn to the burnished body. Simone gave up pretending modesty and instead stared at him, the broad shoulders and flat belly and the manhood that stood, pulsating with life, from the apex of his legs. He stepped into the tub.

"Sit down," she said, her voice hoarse with shyness and need.

He obliged and she giggled at the sight of him wedged into the tub. It had scarce been big enough for her—for him, it was ridiculous, and he sat with his knees jammed against his chest.

"You laugh at me, your lord and master?" His voice was light and she knew he teased her.

"Why, who better than your own wife?" His jesting mood relaxed her somewhat and she responded in kind, keeping her desire at bay.

He guffawed. "No one, I suppose."

"I would ask you to wet your hair but I fear it is a hopeless task. You're simply too big."

"I am sure if you put your mind to it, you could find a solution." He waggled his knees a bit side to side. "There is room."

"Hmmmm, let me see." She tugged on the leather lace binding his hair. She ran her fingers through the silky mass. "Lean forward, between your knees." And she gave him a little push.

He obliged, letting his head hang down. She plucked the shift and wet it, beginning the same routine. Over and over, dipping and wringing, watching the water's glistening tracks over his skin and his head until every inch of him was wet.

She started with his hair, rubbing the sliver soap directly onto it, working it with her hands before rinsing it. Dip, wring, dip, wring. Once his hair was clean, she used the shift as a sponge, rubbing soap into it before starting to wash his skin. The scent of lemon verbena mixed with the scent of him and she breathed deeply, all the while admiring the muscles rippling his back when he shifted position, the strong arms draped over the edge.

"Are you not going to wash the front of me?" His voice interrupted her. "I believe my back is most likely the cleanest it's ever been."

"Why yes, of course." Quaking, she manoeuvred around to kneel at the side of the tub, squeezing between it and the wall. Grabbing the shift and loading it up with soap again, she began to rub, smoothly, rhythmically, his arms, his legs, the sculpted, slightly furred chest. Everywhere but his groin.

"Simone." He whispered, grabbing the hand holding the shift and pulling it down between his legs. "Here. Wash here." He wrapped her hand around his penis, pulling it up and down the turgid shaft.

He was obviously very much at ease with her touching his private parts, totally oblivious to her discomfort and the waves of heat flowing across her face, down her neck and into her chest. Tilting his head, he let it lean back against the lip of the tub.

"Don't stop," he moaned, his lids heavy and almost closed. "I love your hand around me."

Astonished, she realized that he was literally hers, and the waves of embarrassment turned into waves of power.

He belonged to her and her alone, here and now in this little room, here and now in the palm of her hand. Simone squeezed harder, faster, relishing the hold she had over him. They were wrong, a man was not lord and master over his wife, nay, it was the other way around. A woman held sway over her husband if she but knew it.

And having gained that knowledge, the last vestiges of embarrassment faded away and Simone surrendered to the pleasure she knew would come, to the tingling in her groin and the thrills of excitement in her stomach.

She leaned forward to brush one breast against his chest, rubbing it up the furred skin, past his neck and up to his cheek. Like a suckling babe, he turned his head to take a rosy nipple into his mouth, nibbling it gently between his teeth. Pleasure pierced her, shocking bolts that resonated in the woman's place between her legs.

"Take me," she whispered. "Take me, Temple." An utterly shocking demand, she thought, but crazed with desire as she was, it was one she had to utter. Only he could give her the surcease her body craved. She leaned even harder into him, matching the strokes of her hand to the nibbles on her breast.

"Stop," Temple choked out the command, reluctantly letting loose the luscious morsel in his mouth to speak. No, he thought, he didn't want her to stop. But if she didn't, he would lose self-control and he meant to have her as a man had his wife on their wedding night.

He stood up suddenly, pulling her to her feet. "Dry me now," he whispered, grabbing the other towel where it lay on the bed.

She did as he bid, wiping every inch of skin dry, rubbing the towel through his hair. Everywhere she touched, every bit of his skin blazed, blazed with desire.

She knew the effect she had on him, the minx, for a half smile played around her lips and her eyes smouldered with triumph.

"Do you have a comb?" Her innocuous question must have struck her as silly for she began to giggle, a girlish tinkle that brought a smile to his lips.

"Later," he growled. "I want you now." He ripped her towel from her before picking her up and stepping out of the tub. He laid her on the bed and began to kiss her, every delectable inch of her, from her pert toes to her luscious legs to her satin neck and back down to nibble on her breasts.

"Ohhhh." Her whispered moan died away just as he claimed her mouth with his own, lying down over her soft body, wrapping his arms around her silken shoulders to hold her closer.

All self-control aside, he plunged into her, taking her with him, every stroke claiming her to be his wife, and only his alone. Exultation sang through his veins with the rhythmic thrusts. Below him, he could feel her tense and then her pleading voice filled his ears.

"Temple? Temple? Don't stop, Temple, I want more." He obeyed her whispered pleas until he felt the rush of liquid that signified she had reached her climax. With a snarl, he thrust once, twice, three times and then he reached his own climax, jerking his head back and letting loose a primal roar as his life seed spurted into her.

The ferocity of his orgasm stunned him. He relished the aftermath, relaxing into her for several moments, saying nothing yet loving how her chin nestled into his shoulder, how her arms wrapped around his neck. He rolled onto his side and, with head propped on one elbow, began to trace the profile of her face with one finger, grazing her lips a few times before continuing down to her determined little chin. Doubtless the satisfied expression on her face was reflected on his.

She turned toward him, giving him a tremulous smile. Love for him shone from her eyes and surprise at the sight smote him.

Bloody hell and come what may, it seemed he would quite enjoy married life after all.

And what better way to sample his wife's charms than a long ocean voyage?

Chapter Sixteen

London - 1813

Simone was astonished to see that London hadn't changed at all in the two years they had been away. Still the same hustle and bustle on the streets, the same cacophony of hawkers and drovers, the same smells of coal smoke and rotting garbage. Only now she rode through the city in a carriage, not pressing through the crowded streets on her own two legs. Excited, she recognized Bishopsgate Street and she plucked at Temple's sleeve to get his attention.

"I know where we are. This is home to me, we're home."

"Perhaps the east end of London was home to you at one time, but not anymore." He leaned forward and rapped against the carriage to get the coachman's attention. "Go by way of Fleet Street and the Strand through Charing Cross. I want to see the gas lights of Pall Mall before we head into Mayfair."

"Aye, m'lord." At the driver's acknowledgement, Temple relaxed back against the squabs.

"Why there?" Simone was curious.

"They had just been finished before we left for New Caledonia. It's nigh on evening, I wish to see them again."

"Oh." She had heard of the gas lights but hadn't actually seen them—they were out of her usual territory. The delay would be welcome, however—the closer they came to his townhouse, nay, the Leavenby townhouse, the bigger the butterflies in her stomach fluttered.

However, once in Pall Mall, they didn't stop. The coach merely slowed to a walk before resuming a brisk pace into Mayfair.

"Grosvener Square," shouted the coachman.

"Turn right at the corner," Temple instructed. "We want the second house."

"As you wish, m'lord." With a flourish, the coachman pulled up the carriage as directed. "This be the house ye want?"

"Yes," said Temple. He leaned over to glance out the window. He hesitated a few seconds as if uncertain about leaving the shelter of the carriage then decisively unlatched the door. The carriage creaked and sagged as he climbed out. He stood for a moment, gazing at the townhouse in front of which they were parked. A muscle twitched in his jaw but for the rest, his face carried no expression.

Simone didn't find the look on his face reassuring in the slightest and the butterflies in her stomach increased their cadence. Nonetheless, they were here and unless she wanted to spend the rest of her life sitting in the back seat of the carriage, she must exit. She prepared to climb out, pausing only to grab the handle by the door before placing one foot on the step.

She lifted her head.

And stopped dead in the doorway of the carriage.

"This is your home?" she gasped.

The London townhouse resembled so many others yet it stood a little higher, a little bigger, a little more intimidating. It loomed over the other homes lining the street like so many soldiers on parade.

"House," Temple corrected, one hand outstretched to help her down. "My mother's house. That doesn't make it a home."

"You don't care for your mother at all, do you?" She looked at him curiously.

"She is my mother only in that she gave birth to me." His voice was flat.

"How can you not like your own mother? You're lucky, I never had one," she said wistfully.

"Let's just say I disappointed her sorely and leave it at that, shall we?" He grabbed her hand and gave it a little tug. "Come on."

"If you like." She recognized his imperious tone and realized it would serve her better to accede to his wishes. She stepped down and turned her attention back to the house. "It is beautiful, though."

"I suppose." He shrugged, obviously unimpressed and gave her a little nudge in the small of her back toward the stairs leading up to the doors. "Up you go."

She nodded. Tentatively, she approached the house, trying not to be cowed by the grand entranceway.

And grand it was—marble steps and ornate wrought iron railings curving up to massive double doors carved with the same crest she recognized from Temple's signet ring. The house itself stood three stories, stately red brick with tall mullioned windows and a steep pitched slate roof edged with gutters and guarded by gargoyles.

Her apprehension must have showed, for Temple moved up, holding out a reassuring elbow. Gratefully she clutched it and together they climbed to the top of the landing.

No sooner had Temple raised his hand for the polished brass door knocker than the doors swung open inward. A tall, white haired man with a high shiny forehead and a permanent frown stood in the doorway, framed by the golden glow of lamplight.

"My lady is not expecting visitors," he grumped. "May I help you?"

"Stand aside, Tedham," Temple said. "It's the prodigal son come home at the Countess' command."

The man flinched as if he had been struck. He took a step forward, peering closely at Temple through myopic eyes then took several steps back. He pulled the doors open even wider then gestured stiffly with one black clad arm.

"Please come in, my lord," he groused. "My lady has been expecting you for quite some months now." He bowed, a grudging bow more insult than respect.

"Tedham, it must gall you to bow to me." Temple poked him in the midriff. "How refreshing you still can."

With a sniff, Tedham turned away then turned back. "I shall tell my lady you are here."

"Yes, do that, will you please, Tedham? Also, if you don't mind, a dram of father's finest whisky at your earliest convenience. That is, if there's any left."

"Of course, my lord," the butler said through lips that barely moved. "In the sitting room?"

"In the sitting room. I assume that's where I'll find my mother?"

The butler nodded, once, twice. He deigned to glance at Simone in her blue seersucker dress, well-worn and frayed along the cuffs and hem. He raised his eyebrows imperceptibly.

She shrivelled inside at his obvious distaste.

"I know the way, Tedham. The whisky, if you please."

With a last disapproving glance at Simone, Tedham shuffled away.

"Pay him no mind," Temple said, patting her hand. "He has grandiose ideas about his station but I shall set him to rights soon enough."

"He is rather a sour man," she commented, hoping against hope she wouldn't have to see too much of him. With his black suit and pale visage, he reminded her of a walking cadaver.

"Oh, bloody hell," Temple groaned. "Wait here for me, Simone, I forgot to instruct the coachman on the bags."

"Of course I'll wait," she declared. "I don't know the way to the sitting room."

Temple threw her a grin and disappeared down the entrance way stairs, bounding down energetically as if he had not just spent the past few hours in a cramped carriage.

She turned around to inspect the entrance hall, pivoting slowly on the parquet floor to take it all in. A massive chandelier hung overhead and although dark now, it hung with a hundred crystals she knew would shimmer and shine when lit with candles. Several life-size portraits lined the walls, family, she could only assume, and beneath these, an assortment of upholstered benches and stools.

However, the most imposing item was the staircase sweeping up to the second floor, a marvel of carved oak and wine coloured carpet. She remembered Mrs Featherstone's rug on the *Annabelle* and moved a little closer to admire the pattern. Yes, it did resemble the Persian carpet—

"Who let you in?" A cold voice lanced the air.

Simone whirled about. "Uh, oh, ah—" she stammered, intimidated by the grey-haired matron dressed in stark black silk who advanced on her, leaning heavily on an ivory walking stick.

"Out, out immediately," the woman ordered. "The servant's door is in the back." She raised her voice to a screech. "Tedham? Tedham?" She shook her head, disgust evident in every line of the rumpled face. "Where is that man when I need him?"

She looked down her nose at Simone. "Get out of my house." She lifted her cane and tapped Simone on one foot with it.

Alarmed and uncertain, Simone looked around. Surely this woman was not Temple's mother? Just before she made a dash for the door, she heard Temple's footsteps coming up the stairs and she swivelled her head to look for him, grateful for his timely arrival.

He came into the entrance hall, blatantly ignoring the older woman until he reached Simone's side. He took her elbow in his and together they faced the woman in black.

"Why hello, Mother," he said calmly, "I see you have met my wife. Mother, this is Simone. Simone, I give you my mother, Lady Frederica, Dowager Countess of Leavenby."

Stunned, Simone stared then remembered her manners and dropped a curtsy. "It is a pleasure to meet you, ma'am."

Frederica ignored her. "Your wife? This piece of baggage is your wife?" Her voice rose to a shriek. "What cruel joke is this, Temple."

"No joke at all, Mother. This is my wife. Shall we move to the sitting room? I'm afraid we're causing quite a scene." Temple pointed to two housemaids watching the proceedings from the second floor balcony. At his notice, they bobbed curtsies and fled.

As soon as they were out of sight, Simone could hear their peals of laughter, laughter which eventually echoed into silence. She shrivelled a little more inside.

"Very well," sniffed the countess. She stalked ahead, not stopping until she had reached the sanctuary of the sitting room with its gold brocade settee.

Plopping down in the very middle of it, she reached out with two veined and gnarled hands to pull the bolsters closer to drape her arms over them.

"Close the door," she commanded as Temple, dragging a very reluctant Simone, entered the room.

If Simone had had anything to say, she would have fled the house long ago. As a matter of fact, she would have fled at the first glimpse of Tedham. However, she took comfort in Temple's hand clasped tightly over hers in the crook of his elbow. He, apparently expecting her to bolt, was not letting go of her.

"Certainly, mother." He pulled the door shut with a "snick" that to Simone sounded like jail cell doors. Her knees shook and she was beginning to understand Temple's dislike of his mother. What a horrible, horrible woman. Sitting on the settee as she was, she rather resembled a malevolent queen perched on her throne.

Temple pried Simone's fingers out of the crook of his elbow and gave her a conspiratorial wink as if to say, "Don't let the old harridan intimidate you." He strolled over to stand in front of the settee.

"Where did she come from?" Lady Federica demanded, glaring up at Temple.

"What, no hello Temple, I am happy to see you? Or hello Temple how was your time in New Caledonia? Just an out-and-out attack on the woman I have taken to wife?"

Lady Frederica thrust out her bottom lip. "I demand you answer my question. Marriage from one of our station is not to be taken lightly. Where did she come from?" she repeated.

"Why, I found her in my luggage and she very kindly agreed to be my travelling companion." He twisted his head to wink at Simone again. She could see he was enjoying himself immensely which she found odd—it would never have occurred to her to deliberately bait the woman, no matter how nasty she was. He turned back to face his mother. "A most fine companion she was too."

"Please tell me the marriage is not consummated." The Countess' voice was ice cold and, frowning, she peered around Temple to take another look at Simone. Apparently, she was not going to challenge Temple on his explanation of Simone's appearance in his life.

"Oh, but it is, Mother." He leaned forward to whisper in her ear. "Very well, too, I might add."

"Oh!" Her gasp of outrage amused him. "To that—that hoyden?"

"Hoyden? I would thank you to please be careful as to how you address my wife. After all," he leaned forward again to whisper in her ear, as if to infuriate her further, "the walls have ears, do they not? We both know the upstairs maids have already informed any and all who will listen that the scoundrel, the ne'er-do-well, the black sheep of the family, has returned. With a wife, no less."

A glowering Lady Frederica said nothing.

"Oh, and Mother? I do believe she becomes the Countess of Leavenby which would make you the

Dowager Countess. May I suggest you be agreeable to her or she may banish you to the country house." He shook his head, clicking his tongue. "I know how difficult that would be for you, so far from London, the shops, the theatre, the opera."

"Stop it, Temple."

"No, Mother, I don't have to stop it. Are you starting to rue that you informed me of my position as Earl? You could have lived out your life with me never knowing about it. But wait." He tapped an index finger against his jaw. "I left my solicitor informed and in charge of my best interests, so you really couldn't avoid informing me, could you?"

"What of our agreement with the Earl of Dowbiggin? You are to wed his daughter, Lady Susannah." Lady Frederica fanned her face with one plump hand. "One can only imagine the scandal when people find out the Earl of Leavenby has reneged on a long standing arrangement."

"Your arrangement. Yours and father's. Not mine. If you recall, that is what set me on my wild ways. No wait. That happened when you sent me to Eton. Because I was—ahem—leading Richard astray." Bitterness filled his voice. "Always Richard, always Richard. Now he's dead. It is ironic, is it not, that I would take his place? "

His mother flushed, a crimson tide starting at the jet encrusted neckline and spreading upwards to end in the roots of her hair.

To Simone, it looked as if the woman was sinking into a red sea of chagrin. Or rage. She couldn't quite decide which.

"I think we've conversed enough for one evening," Temple continued pleasantly. "Simone and I will retire to the master bedroom. Please see that a tray is sent up to us, we shan't be down for dinner. Perhaps in a few days when you have recovered from the shock, we can start again and hopefully on a better foot. Because, Mother, for better or for worse and whether you like it or not—" He pulled Simone beside him. "—Simone is my wife."

Speechless, the Dowager Countess sat and watched as Temple and Simone left the room. Simone could feel her eyes, daggers in her back, as she walked away. Oy, what had she gotten into? She had had no illusions that Temple's family would welcome her with open arms but she hadn't expected open hostility.

* * *

"Well, I'm rather glad that's over, aren't you?" Temple remarked once they had reached the sanctuary of their room.

"She dislikes me, Temple. Doesn't that bother you?" Perhaps this wasn't going to be as easy as Simone had thought. Along with Lady Frederica and Tedham, every one, aye, every thing, every room, in this house intimated her. Even this room, Temple's haven, with its massive mahogany four poster bed draped in burgundy and framed by identical night stands, its matching burgundy and black brocade wingback chairs by the fireplace, and its massive mahogany wardrobe and chest.

"She would dislike anyone who was not of her choosing." He stalked over the window, fumbling through the curtain folds to find the draw cords. He pulled them shut then turned back to face Simone. "Mother has had her own way far too often. It's time she steps aside."

"She won't like that either, giving her place as Countess of Leavenby to me." Simone shook her head. "Perhaps we should leave straightaway."

"Mother is a bully. You must stand up to her. Don't worry, I'm behind you. And no," he added, striding back to her to take her hand to raise it to his lips for a kiss. "We shall not leave. This is our rightful home. If Mother cannot or will not accept you as my wife, then she shall be the one to leave."

Simone gave him a dubious nod. The idea of running this house daunted her, even more so if Lady Frederica was unhappy with Simone's position within it.

"Don't fret, Simone, the threat of banishment to the country house will be sufficient. Too, I suspect you'll find an ally in Joanna."

Ah yes, Joanna, Richard's widow. Temple had mentioned her to Simone on the voyage home one evening when he was instructing Simone on the intricacies of the Leavenby family tree.

"Of course," Simone murmured.

"I'll introduce the two of you tomorrow. She still lives here but I've seen no sign of her so one can only assume she is indisposed for the evening. I suspect she's still wearing widow's weeds and eschewing social contact. Joanna is one for proper convention although she has always had a soft spot for those less fortunate. I'm sure she'll be overjoyed to have you as company in this mausoleum that passes for a house. Don't let her angelic demeanour fool you—she knows how to handle Mother."

A knock sounded and at Temple's command, the door swung open. A housemaid stood there holding a covered tray, behind her stood another with a bucket of steaming water.

"I am Polly," chirped the one holding the tray. "Shall we light the fire for you, my lord? And turn down the bed?"

"Yes, yes, light the fire but leave the bed. We don't wish to retire just yet." He pointed to the maid with the water. "Fill the basin and then take my lady's bag. Wash and press her clothes for tomorrow."

"Of course, my lord," nodded the other. "I am called Anna."

After the two had left, Temple turned back to Simone. "Sit." He pointed to one of the wingback chairs. "Eat first then wash and ready yourself for bed. There will be a lady's maid for you but we've had quite enough for one evening. I'll help you. I've grown quite accustomed to being your maid." He waggled his black eyebrows at her, a silly yet engaging gesture.

Her heart swelled with love for him. He was going to stand by her. He was going to stand by her and show the world she was his wife in fact and not name only.

And she would do her best to stand by him and be the finest countess she could possibly be.

* * *

I never, silently fumed the former Countess of Leavenby as she sat alone on the settee in the sitting room, *never, ever expected any son of mine to treat me like trash. Me, in my own home. And to marry that—that woman. The shame, the scandal, once word gets out of Temple's ridiculous choice for wife. Never fear*, she promised herself, stamping her cane on the floor for emphasis, *she shall rue the day she married my son.*

Lady Frederica could easily use her position in polite society to make life difficult for the lowbred tart.

And she would.

Chapter Seventeen

"This is lovely," commented Simone the next morning, helping herself to the breakfast laid out on the side board in the dining room.

"What? Oh, yes," Temple replied, nose buried in the *London Times*. The morning paper, how he had missed that.

"What did you choose for your breakfast?" She seated herself to his right before pulling back the top corner of the paper. Two brilliant blue eyes sparkled at him.

"Has no one ever told you not to toy with a man's morning paper?" He made his voice gruff but he couldn't stop the smile curling over his lips. She was adorable and try as he might, he couldn't get angry with her.

"No, not until now. Let me see what you're having for breakfast." She pointed to her own plate. "I took a boiled egg, a slice of bread, two sausages and some orange wedges. I would have taken more," she lowered her voice and looked around, "but I don't want anyone to think I am greedy."

"Orange wedges." Temple had to grin despite himself. Of course she would take orange wedges. "Don't worry, Simone. You're the Countess of Leavenby, no one would dare think you're greedy."

"Oh." She seemed nonplussed by his answer.

"Really, Simone," he hastened to assure her. "In this house, you may well do as you please and no one will think the slightest bit of ill about you."

She looked at him, evidently puzzling over his answer. He could tell she wanted to say something but was obviously reluctant. She opened her mouth and shut it again. She glanced away as if to gather her courage then turned back to him.

"Why would you leave this?" She swept her arm around, encompassing the dining room with its table laid with crisp white linen and the food laden sideboard. "You are lord and master here. Why would you leave?"

Why indeed.

"My being the Earl of Leavenby wasn't in the cards," he began. "I only have it by default." He stopped. He didn't want to disillusion her. What could he say now?

Should he tell her about the things he abhorred, the petty mores of so-called polite society? Should he tell her he had planned to become a country gentleman, far from London's restrictions?

Or should he tell her he had not been able to stomach the thought of marriage to any of the eligible, mostly insipid, young ladies paraded every season? A parade which had culminated in the awkward match with Lady Susannah?

Or should he tell her the stifling boredom and the social expectations of the ton were what had pushed him into the unholy alliance with Peter Mortimer-Rae? A chilling thought, reminding Temple to be on his guard; knowing the man as well as he did, Mortimer-Rae would be on the lookout for him still.

The mantle clock chimed, nine strokes, pulling him out of his reverie. Simone's eyes bored into him. She wasn't going to let this go.

"I left because I was the younger son," he began. "Richard would inherit all and I, short of a monthly stipend, would have nothing."

Thankfully, his words were cut short by the arrival of an exuberant Joanna.

"Good morning," exclaimed his sister-in-law as she burst through the door. "The servants are all in a twitter about your homecoming."

She bee-lined toward Temple, a short, tubby bundle of grey flounce and ruffles, her pink rosebud mouth stretched into a welcoming smile beneath the button nose.

The first thought that crossed his mind was that she wore grey, not black. Of course, she would be in second mourning by now as it had been more than six months since his brother's death. His second thought was that her dressmaker should be shot—Joanna resembled a plump little blackcap, right down to the charcoal mobcap she wore over her brown curls and inquisitive grey eyes.

"Good to see you too, Joanna." Temple put his paper aside. "May I introduce you to Simone?"

Joanna put an arm around Temple's shoulders in welcome then moved over to pat Simone's shoulder. It pleased Temple to see the small token of affection bestowed by Joanna didn't startle Simone; that boded well for the bond he hoped the two would form.

"I am so very pleased to meet you," Joanna declared. "It's high time Temple found himself a wife." She plunked herself down in the chair beside Simone. "You and I shall be fast friends, I promise."

"That would be my fondest hope, Joanna," Temple said. "I fear Mother has not taken well to my new wife."

"Oh pooh," snorted Joanna. "Lady Frederica can be difficult. But not unmanageable," she confided sideways to Simone. "Oooh, those look good." She pointed to the sausages on Simone's plate. "Venison, I believe, from the country house." She scraped her chair back. "Will you excuse me while I get my own breakfast? I'm famished."

"Of course," Simone nodded.

"By all means," Temple said.

They both watched Joanna as she loaded her plate with much more than just the sausages. She manoeuvred back to her place beside Simone, dropping a scone in the process.

"I love breakfast," she announced to no one in particular as she took her seat. With one foot, she kicked the offending scone under the table.

Aye, thought Temple, *I would wager you love more than just breakfast.* He seemed to recall her love for cakes and sweets, too. Ah well, the poor girl had not much to look forward to, being widowed at a young age. She may as well take her comfort in food. Nonetheless she was a kind soul, good hearted and more than capable of taking Simone under her wing.

Despite her poor choice of mourning wear, she had a keen eye for the latest fashions.

"Joanna?" Temple waited for his sister in law to clear her mouth.

"Yes?" Lady Joanna dabbed butter from her chin with her napkin.

"Lady Simone needs clothing. We've been travelling and I'm afraid her wardrobe is sadly depleted."

"Wonderful!" Joanna clapped her hands. "There is nothing I enjoy more than a trip to the modiste's shop. Although that's been sadly curtailed." She cast a rueful glance down at her sombre dress and sighed.

"Joanna." Temple paused, carefully considering his next words. "Simone's upbringing has been rather unorthodox, shall we say. Are you game for a challenge?"

"The challenge being?" A mouth full of ham and bread muffled Joanna's words.

"Readying her for presentation to London society. I've done quite as much as I can but I'm not female and have a limited point of view on how some things are properly done."

"Of course," Joanna agreed before shovelling another forkful of ham into her mouth. Her chewing slowed as she scrutinized Simone. Joanna swallowed hard then pursed her lips before answering. "There is nothing more I enjoy than a good challenge." Her voice was doubtful, as if she had just now taken a thorough look at Simone.

"Splendid," Temple said, ignoring Joanna's scepticism. "What's the first step?"

"The first step?" Joanna paused and took another critical look at Simone. "As you suggested, decent clothing. That dress belongs in the rag bin."

Simone looked down at the blue seersucker, freshly laundered and pressed. "What's wrong with it?" she said defensively. "It's a pretty colour."

"Yes, well I'm afraid not even laundering can help that dress," Joanna said. "Frayed hems and cuffs are just not the thing this season. Neither is that particular shade of blue. This season we are leaning more toward yellow. Which may or may not look good with your colouring but we shall see what we can find at Mme Langlois' shop."

"Excellent." Temple picked up the paper again. "Now, if you ladies will excuse me, I have a bit of catching up to do with the going's on in Parliament these days."

"You men," Joanna exclaimed. "Why, your goings on bore me to tears. Now you, Simone," she patted Simone on the hand, "are going to be fun. We shall go to the dress shop this morning."

* * *

Jauntily swinging his umbrella, Gentry Ted strode briskly down Bond Street and the shops, a favourite haunt of his. A gent could get lucky if a lady needed help with her bags and earn a quid or two with deliveries.

He rounded the corner just in time to see a fine, shiny black carriage pull up in front of Mme Langlois' establishment. Perfect timing on his part—the fancier the carriage, the more items purchased. Disappointment filled him when he saw the two footmen standing on the footboard—they wouldn't need his help after all.

He pulled back to wait while one of the footmen opened the door to help a young lady with tousled blonde curls. She looked vaguely familiar and he inspected her for a few seconds.

Astonishment cascaded through him. Mona, was that Mona stepping down from that fine carriage? He sidled over to take a closer look. The face was clean, the hair curled and styled but indeed, it was Mona Dougherty.

He edged a bit closer to the young woman perusing the fabrics and gewgaws displayed in the shop window while her female companion was being helped out of the carriage by the footman.

"Psssst."

The young woman ignored him.

"Pssst. Mona, it's me, Gentry Ted."

The young woman deigned to glance at him. Recognition flashed through her eyes followed by a look of absolute horror, which offended him a tad.

"Ted!"

"Mona! Where ye been all this time? Me and the boys been worried about ye."

"Go away, Ted," she whispered, face scarlet red. "You'll ruin everything!"

"Why, Mona," Gentry Ted said shrewdly, looking at the fine carriage and the heavy gold signet ring she wore on her finger. "Ye've landed yerself a gentry cove, haven't ye?"

"Yes, now please go away. That life for me is over."

"Why of course, ma'am." Gentry Ted tipped his hat and bowed as three ladies drifted by, eying the pair curiously.

Mona had landed herself a plum gig. Well, he wouldn't expect anything else from her. That Mona, always landing on her feet. Far be it from him to ruin her chance at a decent life.

With another tip of his hat, he walked away, whistling his favourite tune. Wait till he told the boys.

And if he played his cards right, maybe he could count on her if money got tight. A pleasing thought.

* * *

A relieved Simone watched Gentry Ted saunter away. Oy, had anyone noticed him conversing with her. Her cheeks burned with embarrassment.

"Are you feeling well?" Joanna inquired. "Who was that fellow?" Her lips were compressed with concern. Or suspicion, Simone couldn't decide which.

"I don't know. Such a funny gentleman although I hesitate to call him such." She sent a thought to Gentry Ted begging his forgiveness. He would understand, surely he would.

"You look as if you've seen a ghost. You're flushed—are you catching a fever?"

"I'm quite well, thank you," she responded automatically. Yes, she had seen a ghost. A live ghost who could ruin everything for her before she even got started.

It had been a close call but if Joanna was suspicious, it did not show. For that, Simone was grateful—the always proper Joanna would be appalled if she knew the truth about Simone.

"Then shall we go inside?" Joanna asked. "I do so love this shop. Mme Langlois is the finest seamstress in London and pampers her clients with tea and cakes."

"How lovely," Simone murmured.

So passed a pleasant morning. While Simone pored over fashion plates of one high-waisted dress after another, Joanna, with a critical eye, offered her opinion and encouragement.

As luck would have it, Mme Langlois had several frocks from a cancelled order that only required a stitch here or there to alter for Simone to take that day: a butter yellow, soft twilled silk frock with stand-up collar and long, puffed sleeves tied with blue ribbons at intervals down the arms so that the sleeves ballooned between each ribbon; one of robin's egg blue muslin eyelet, collarless and with short puffed sleeves, its hem trimmed with fresh white ribbon and ruffles; and a pale lavender linen frock with long, tightly fitting sleeves, embroidered along the neckline with a pattern of pink beads above a low décolletage.

The latter Simone was sure was shockingly improper for, not only did the dress expose her back to the bottom of her shoulder blades, her breasts peeped over the neckline!

Not only frocks, but kid gloves, silk undergarments, satin slippers, even a satin-lined, fur-trimmed black felted cloak with matching bonnet found their way into the steadily growing pile.

At length, a weary Simone climbed into the waiting carriage and fell back against the cushions. She now had a wardrobe.

Maybe she wasn't quite yet comfortable with being a lady of quality but at least she would look like one.

Chapter Eighteen

"Look!" exclaimed Joanna as the two young women walked through the entrance hall of the Leavenby town house, followed by the footmen almost bowed under by the numerous boxes and brown paper parcels tied up with the distinctive striped ribbon that signified Mme Langlois' establishment.

"I must beg pardon?" A bewildered Simone looked around, not seeing anything.

"Calling cards." Joanna pointed to several creamy white cards and an envelope stacked carelessly on the silver tray on the table by the door. "Word has spread that the new Earl of Leavenby is in London."

Curious, Simone peeked over Joanna's shoulder. "I'm not certain what it all means," she admitted.

"Aha," proclaimed Joanna with satisfaction, picking up the envelope and turning it over to inspect the seal. "This is from the Lady Belmont, Duchess of Crossfield." She ripped it open eagerly and withdrew the page within, scanning it in a matter of seconds. "She's having a ball on Friday next and would like the company of you and Temple. The dear thing has also invited me but I shall have to decline."

"Not you?" Simone asked, hoping that Joanna would be there to bolster her courage.

"No, not yet. I'm still not ready for social engagements." She closed her eyes, and grief weighed on her features briefly, making her look old.

"I am sorry," murmured Simone. The show of sorrow surprised her. Joanna truly missed her husband but she hid it well under bright chatter. Simone squeezed Joanna's shoulder in understanding.

"But what fun it will be to get you dressed." Joanna's brief moment of melancholy had passed. "Was I not correct in insisting that we order you a ball gown?" She threw the invitation back onto the tray.

"I suppose." Simone's heart began to thump. How exactly did one dress for a ball? Too, presumably one would dance at a ball. Therein lay a problem: she didn't know how.

"Let's see what there is for tea." Joanna took her arm. "I believe Lady Frederica is out paying calls this afternoon. We shall be able to chat at our leisure."

They entered the sitting room to find it occupied. Temple sat, tea at hand, nose buried in a ledger.

Delight filled Simone at the sight. She gazed at him, appreciating the fine figure he presented with his crisply starched shirt collar, lawn cravat, brown tail coat and fawn coloured trousers tucked into glossy black leather boots. With every breath, her excitement grew. He was hers. And she would be accompanying him to an honest to goodness London ball!

She fair flew toward him, sliding to an unladylike stop beside his chair.

"We've been invited to the Duchess of Crossfield's ball," she said eagerly, dropping a hand onto his shoulder. Beneath her fingers, his muscles flexed as he closed the ledger with a snap, sending a thrill clear up her arm and stirring the butterflies of desire.

Temple remained silent, merely raised his eyebrows.

"It will be such fun, will it not?" Simone said uncertainly. The butterflies of desire fluttered off at his unenthused reaction. Puzzled, she took a closer look, noticing the set lips and tense expression.

"Oh yes, it will be an amusing evening. When are we invited?" His voice was dry.

"Friday next."

"Can you dance?" The stark question hung in the air like an axe waiting to fall.

"Oh." Simone shook her head. "No. No, I can't dance." She tried to keep the regret from her voice. "Do we need to dance? Could we not watch?"

Tears sprang to her eyes and she swiped at them impatiently. Silly tears, they popped up more of late. She stifled her disappointment. Of course they wouldn't attend the ball. Temple wouldn't want to take her out any more than he absolutely had to.

"You don't know how to dance?" asked an incredulous Joanna.

Simone nodded miserably.

"Where did you find her." Joanna poked Temple in the chest. "She arrived without a proper wardrobe and now she admits she doesn't know how to dance."

"I was lucky enough to find her during my travels in North America. I wager Simone never had the opportunity to learn how to dance." He quirked an eyebrow. "Speaking of the wardrobe, was your trip to the modiste's successful?"

"Yes, although just outside the shop, the strangest fellow accosted Simone. I thought she would fair faint when he spoke with her." Joanna shook her head in disgust. "Really, the boldness of the man was most uncalled for."

Simone jerked her head at the mention of Gentry Ted and her heart started thumping. Did Joanna suspect she and Ted knew each other? She sent an alarmed glance toward Temple. He shook his head imperceptibly as if to reassure her before turning to answer Joanna.

"Next time send the footmen to clear the riff raff. But enough of that." Temple patted Simone's hand. "Apparently the next item in your education shall be to teach you how to dance."

"Today is Wednesday, that gives us what, nine days of dance lessons. We'll start this evening," Joanna declared. "In my bedroom, Simone. I'll teach you the steps. When you know them, you can practice with Temple in the music room. I can play the pianoforte passably well, enough for dance lessons, I should say."

Pleased with her suggestion, Joanna snagged a square of pink frosted cake and several cookies and sat down, plate on her lap.

"Shall I pour?" Without waiting for an answer, she filled her own cup then those of Temple and Simone. "To the dance lessons." She lifted her cup. "Do not think for a moment you are getting off easy, Temple. In a day or two, Simone will need a real partner and you shall have to step in."

"As you say, Joanna." Temple inclined his head.

What could he do but acquiesce, he thought wryly. Joanna was doing just as he had asked of her—taking Simone under her very capable wing. A ball would be a challenge for Simone's first outing into polite society however he was a firm proponent of the sink or swim philosophy.

It really wouldn't matter where he first presented Simone—everyone would be curious about her regardless of the occasion.

* * *

A hesitant Simone rapped on the door to Joanna's chamber. At the muffled "Come in!" she twisted the knob and pushed open the door.

A visibly perspiring Joanna sat perched on the edge of a blue velvet foot stool; the matching chair had been pushed back against the wall, along with a small side table and foot warmer. The rug had also been rolled up, leaving a bare expanse of polished plank flooring.

"To give us room to move about," she explained at Simone's bewildered look. "We shall start with the contredans. Come stand beside me and watch while I pace out the steps. To start with, I'll show you two figures. Easy ones then we'll progress to the more difficult ones in the next few days."

To Joanna's count of "One two three four", a stumbling Simone tried to follow. Frowning, she watched Joanna's feet, taking a few hesitant steps of her own before stopping and placing her fists on her hips. Oy, dancing was not as easy as Joanna professed.

"I can't learn this." Dismay filled Simone's voice. The happy anticipation of attending the ball with Temple faded.

"You shall, if you wish to go to the Crossfield's ball as the Countess of Leavenby. Now stop looking at your feet," ordered an unsympathetic Joanna. "Lift your head and look at your partner. Remember, you must smile and flirt with all the gentlemen and one cannot do so unless one is focused on them, not your feet."

"Flirt?" Simone echoed stupidly. Did married women flirt with other gentlemen? She didn't want to flirt with other gentlemen—she wanted to flirt with Temple.

"Yes, flirt. Now look at me and dance."

The cherubic Joanna proved to be a harsh taskmaster and Simone, wanting to please her, obediently lifted her gaze and took several tentative steps.

"Talk to me while you practice" continued Joanna. "I should like to hear more about your life in Canada. There is an air of mystery about you I find intriguing. Temple has been naughty and scarcely answered any of my questions."

Simone had been dreading the moment when she would be questioned on her background. The moment had come and she was on her own, without Temple's comforting presence. To make matters worse,

Joanna posed the questions, the person Temple had assured her would be her ally.

In short, she wanted Joanna to like her.

Beads of sweat popped out on her forehead as she considered her answer and she stumbled again, knocking into the footstool and sending it flying.

"There is no great mystery about me. I grew up in Montreal with a dear family friend. My parents died when I was young."

"Oh dear, I am so sorry." Joanna's consternation was evident as she stepped away. "And a one two three four. I find your accent intriguing," she continued, her face red from the exertion.

"A mixture of French and English, I suppose," Simone replied. "The French were the original founders of Canada, you know." She hoped the explanation satisfied Joanna. It really had been difficult for her to conquer her east side accent. Even now, when tired or excited, she would let slip with an inappropriate phrase or word.

"What? Oh yes, I knew that." Joanna was beginning to puff. "Just one time more through each figure, Simone. I'm growing fatigued."

Simone obliged and finished with a final twirl that drew praise from Joanna. A wave of nausea overcame her and she leaned against the wall, swaying a little.

"Are you unwell?" Joanna's concerned face swam into her vision.

Simone nodded shakily. "I do believe I'm unaccustomed to the rich food."

"A spot of ginger tea is what you need. Let's move to the sitting room and ring Mrs Andrews, shall we?"

"What of Lady Frederica?" She blurted the question before she could stop herself. The nausea had passed yet she could not bear to face the intimidating woman.

"Oh, she has taken to her room with a fit of the vapours," Joanna said airily. "You and Temple have given her a bit of a comeuppance. Don't be afraid of her, she's harmless."

"Yes, Temple has said the same thing. That I must stand up to her." The old Simone would have defied the woman with a swagger and a curse that would have given the old lady a swoon. For Temple's sake, she wanted the dowager countess to accept her. She just wasn't sure how to go about it.

* * *

Her new gown arrived the morning of the ball. A few anxious moments had ensued when the matching slippers couldn't be found but eventually they had been unearthed in the bottom of the band box, beneath layers of tissue.

A bemused Temple watched from the comfort of his wingback chair as she twirled about their chamber, holding the swatch of ivory silk close to her.

"This is the finest dress ever," she declared. "It's a princess dress."

"Don't you think you should actually put the dress on before you make such a statement?"

"Well, then ask me again when I dress this evening. I'm so excited I don't think I'll be able to sleep this afternoon. Joanna told me that," she added. "A ball goes until the wee hours of the morning and I must rest for it."

"I could think of something to tire you out," he said, a wicked glint in his eye.

"Oh, you. I'm too excited for that now too." She tossed a throw cushion at him.

"I meant I have a new dance I want to teach you. What did you think I meant?" The glint in his eye belied his bland voice, leaving Simone no doubt he had another, more pleasurable dance in mind.

"A new dance?" She groaned. "Do we have time? What I have learned from Joanna has taken me days to conquer."

"Oh, it's easy enough. It's called the waltz." He demonstrated. "One two three, one two three. You step from foot to foot and let me lead you. Here." He grabbed her about the waist. "Let us begin. I start with my right foot forward, your left foot goes back. It's as simple as that. No, don't look down." He tilted her head up. "Just follow me."

Stiffly, Simone moved with him, looking him in the face as if the movements of her feet were reflected there. Her lips twitched in time, one two three, one two three.

"You know what's so delicious about the waltz," he commented as he twirled her about.

She clung to him, just barely managing to shake her head.

"I get to hold you scandalously close in my arms and the gossiping tongues can't say a thing."

And he did, pulling her even closer so that his thighs rippled against hers. His arm was tight against her back, and he squeezed her right hand with his left one. How heavenly, a floating dance, making her as ethereal as the butterflies that wafted through the rose garden by the stable.

"See?" he murmured against her hair. "Nothing to it." He leaned back to look at her. "Are you ready to rest now?"

"I shall do my best," she promised.

Much to her surprise, she did manage a small nap, awakening at the sound of Temple opening the door from his adjoining dressing room. He carried a cloth covered tray.

"Are you awake? It's time for you to call Joanna's maid." He strolled over to the wingback chairs flanking the fire place, placing the tray on the little side table before sitting down with a casual elegance.

"Thank you." Solicitous as always, she thought. She sat up and stretched before swinging her legs over the side of the bed. "Does Joanna mind sharing her maid with me?"

"What? Don't be silly, of course not. We'll find you a suitable candidate soon enough." He whipped off the cloth and pointed to the tray. "Mrs Andrews sent us a bite or two. Dinner will be late this evening. Will you pour, darling?"

Darling? She flipped him a startled look. He'd never called her darling before. It set her heart to fluttering. Perhaps he really did care for her, perhaps even loved her a little.

He seemed oblivious to her reaction, merely waited patiently while she poured. By now, she knew he took both cream and sugar in his tea and she prepared it just as he liked. She offered him the sandwich plate and he took two, propping them on the edge of his saucer against the cup.

As for her, anticipation for the evening's ball had dulled her appetite. She could barely drink one cup and eat one sandwich to please him; she had seen him scowl when she first passed the plate by.

He waited until she had finished her sandwich before he spoke again. "I must warn you, Simone. It's not going to be easy this evening. There will be gossip."

"I know," she nodded. "It's my first time in polite society." She picked up her cup and took a sip of the fragrant East Indian blend. Delicious; surely not even the Prince Regent drank finer tea.

"No, that's not what I mean. You shall fare splendidly this evening, I've no doubt." A rueful expression glided across his face. "No, it's me I'm referring to. I'm a pariah, the kind of man who mothers will cross the street to avoid."

"Surely you're joking, Temple. How could anyone think that of you? You are the Earl of Leavenby."

"Be that as it may," he shrugged, "let us just say I have an unsavoury reputation."

"Only because they don't know you," she defended him staunchly. "Perhaps I could spread a good word for you."

Her offer amused him, for he let loose a dry chuckle. "If only it were that easy, Simone. Nay, I fear my reputation is well earned. I haven't behaved in the most exemplary manner. At the time, it did not signify." He stopped.

And now, because of you, it does.

It signified now because he didn't want her tarred with the same brush for something that wasn't of her doing.

"What? And now it does?" She was truly astonished. "In my opinion, that does not signify. Mrs Featherstone told me once during our sewing lessons that what is in the past is past. Anyone deserves a second chance."

"They thought me a scoundrel. I thought I would oblige them." He lifted his hands, palms up. "I'm not who you think I am."

"Then who are you?" Her question was simple.

Apparently, the answer was not as simple, for Temple looked away from her deliberately. His eyes narrowed, and his hands, placed so carelessly on the arms of the chair, clenched into fists.

"I don't know," he replied at length, staring out the window at the hazy, late afternoon sky as if he could find the answer written there. "A rogue. A scoundrel." He turned his regard back to her, gauging her reaction. "I have done things I am ashamed of. You asked me why I would leave a life of privilege. Because I didn't deserve it. Because I wanted to turn myself into a man, a true man, a man of honour. A man who stands on his own two feet. A man who defends his loved ones."

A man who defends you, Simone, and our children.

She answered quickly, before he had a chance to consider that notion.

"You saved me, that means you're not a rogue. Or a scoundrel." She was staunch in her defence of him. "So do not be silly, I beg of you. What's done is done."

"Don't you want to know what it is that I've done?"

She looked at him long and hard before answering. "No. You're caring and compassionate, that's all that matters to me."

"Compassionate? Where did you learn that?" He raised his eyebrows, a familiar gesture she had grown to love. Her choice of words had obviously taken him aback.

"I've been studying the dictionary," she boasted. "It seemed to describe you perfectly."

"Ah, Simone, darling." He shook his head, closing his eyes until they crinkled at the corners. "You give me too much credit."

"You have warned me it will not be easy tonight. I appreciate that. However," she leaned over and brushed his hand with her own. "Do not worry for me. I don't care what they think of you."

I only care that I love you, she added silently. She desperately wanted to tell him but she held herself back. Why would he, a peer of the realm, want the love of an orphaned street urchin?

"Very well." A relieved smile creased his lips. "But don't say I gave you no warning."

"I promise," she vowed. "You shall not hear me grumble." She glanced over at the clock on the fireplace mantle. "Golly, look at the time. Joanna told me I should need several hours to ready myself. I should start."

"Yes, you should." He grinned, seemingly as if a great weight had been lifted from his shoulders. "Come to the sitting room when you're ready, I'll wait for you there."

* * *

An impatient Temple paced the floor, swirling the brandy in his glass first one way, then the other. Simone had taken his attempt at disclosure with aplomb but he sincerely dreaded the evening. Dreaded it, yet knew it could not be avoided.

Too, it did not bode well that Lady Frederica would be in attendance but had declined his offer to travel in the Leavenby carriage with them. Instead she was to be picked up by Lady Montford, her oldest and dearest friend who would support Lady Frederica until her dying breath. The gossip would fly before they even set foot in the Belmont's home.

"I'm sorry I'm late." Simone's breathless words were a welcome interruption. "What do you think?"

He turned to her and his eyes were literally pulled from their sockets as she did a slow pirouette for him.

She was breath-taking, her delight imbuing her with a radiance that reached into his very heart. He stood stock still, drinking in the sight of her as a parched man slakes his thirst with water.

He put down his glass and strode to her, bowing low and putting his lips to one ivory-gloved hand before raising his gaze to inspect her thoroughly.

Every inch of street urchin had been erased. Instead, an elegant woman stood before him, blonde curls piled high above a pearl encrusted headband and woven through with feathers. A few tendrils framed her face and he was hard pressed to tell if the flush in her cheeks came from anticipation or from a jar. The ivory silk dress, trimmed with pearls and feathers about the neckline and hem, gloved her body, hugging her bosom before flaring away from its high waist to drape about her hips and fall to the floor, from where ivory satin slippers peeped.

However, her eyes drew him the most, mysterious sapphires glowing with passion, with life, eyes that twinkled up at him. All he wanted to do was crush her to him and kiss the rosy lips curved in an impish smile. He resisted the urge, knowing she would squawk about him wrinkling her dress.

"Stunning," he murmured, instead pressing another kiss to her hand. "I shall be the envy of every man there this evening."

"Thank you, kind sir," she curtsied, a graceful motion that, unbeknownst to him, she had practiced for hours before her mirror with Joanna's critical advice.

She held out her shawl to him, a length of silk trimmed with the pearls and the same feathers as in her hair. He took it from her, draping it carefully over her shoulders before turning her around to suck in one last look.

Stunning. He had not lied—he would be the envy of every man there tonight—at least as far as her appearance.

The question was, would she pass muster? She looked so happy, so full of anticipation, the last thing he wanted was for her to be hurt by malicious gossip because of an unintentional misstep on her part.

He could not, nay, would not, let that happen.

Chapter Nineteen

Simone and Temple's carriage followed the long line of carriages jerking its way up the street, until at length they were able to stop and disembark. Gleaming lanterns lit their way up to the austere double doors. Once inside the front hall they waited again until it was their turn to be announced. Temple tossed his card into the bowl before they stepped forward into the archway leading into the parquet ballroom.

"The Earl and Countess of Leavenby," shouted out the footman.

One face after another turned to look at them, a flesh-coloured wave that flashed through the room until all looked their way. With each face that turned, the din subsided until silence reigned.

Simone's stomach plummeted. Oy, this was worse than she had imagined. They had already been tried and censured before even venturing into the ballroom itself.

Lady Belmont, properly sensing a disaster, pushed her way through the bodies until she reached their side.

"Lord Leavenby, how lovely to see you," she gushed. "And this is your new bride?" She turned to Simone. "I am Lady Belmont. Somewhere," she fluttered a hand sporting several jewelled rings, "is

Lord Belmont. Most likely in the card room, he does abhor dancing." She smiled, a motion that turned her rather ordinary features into something if perhaps not beautiful, then at least interesting. Her hazel eyes were inquiring as she scanned Simone from tip to toes.

"Enchanted." Simone curtsied. Oy, it was plain to see Lady Belmont was curious about the new Countess of Leavenby. Stomach knotted, Simone realized she must earn her position as such on her own merit and not on the coattails of Temple.

"On behalf of Lady Leavenby and myself, I must thank you for the invitation," Temple said.

"Delighted to have you here." With Lady Belmont's apparent stamp of approval, the buzz of voices began again, punctuated here and there with a raucous explosion of laughter. "The dancing commences shortly, the musicians are just warming up. As newlyweds, perhaps you would care to lead the first dance?"

"Of course, Lady Belmont, it would be our pleasure." A gracious Temple bowed.

"Off you go, then. There are refreshments in the dining room. Oh, there's Lord and Lady Bixby, do excuse me." She surged off through the guests, stopping to squeeze a hand here, or pat a shoulder there before reaching her intended quarry.

"She seems likeable enough," Simone commented, watching their hostess cordially acknowledge her other guests.

"Yes, well, it's not Lady Belmont I'm concerned about. As Duchess of Crossfield, she has good breeding and manners enough to overlook irregularities, shall we say. It's the rest of the ton that may be a problem. The society matrons can be vicious." He slanted a glance at Simone.

The concern in his eyes warmed her—he worried about her introduction this evening. She opened her mouth to reassure him, to tell him she would try her hardest, would keep her mouth shut and only smile and nod if need be but he continued before she had a chance to speak.

"Come, we need to speak to the musicians regarding our choice of music if we are to open with the first dance."

He pulled her along behind him, pushing their way through the crowd. Although several people tried to catch his attention, Temple ignored them all until they reached the sanctuary of the music salon at the far end of the ballroom.

"Wait here," he instructed, leaving her partly hidden by a potted palm placed by the doorway to the salon. "It's the contredanse we want, is it not?"

She nodded.

"This shall take but a moment." He left her there while he went to speak to the cellist.

The whispers started while she waited for Temple.

"Oh my." A woman nearby snickered. "Is that the little baggage Lord Leavenby married?"

"It is atrocious, is it not? So like him to flaunt her in polite company."

Heat suffused her face. Mercifully they couldn't see her standing behind the potted palm. She parted the fronds to peek at the two women tittering behind their silk fans.

Should she show herself? Nay, best to hear what was said about her, about them. Forewarned is forearmed, as Mrs Dougherty used to say. She let the fronds fall back into place.

"Yes, apparently he found her in Canada."

"What must Lady Frederica think? She must be appalled, poor dear. After the scandal of leaving Lady Susannah at the altar, not to mention his embarrassing military career."

"Well, what could one expect from Lord Scoundrel," interjected a third voice.

"Continued untoward behaviour shall be his downfall," sniggered the first woman. "I do hope the baggage is prepared for the worst."

The three burst into a fit of giggles, their laughter fading as they moved away.

A wave of dizziness hit her and she swayed a little, putting her hand on the wall for support. Baggage from Canada? Lord Scoundrel? She could only imagine what else was being said about them.

"Are you well?" Temple's solicitous voice filled her ears.

"What? Oh yes, yes of course," Simone stammered. She mustn't tell Temple what she had just heard—his reaction would only cause more fodder for tittle-tattle, of which there was already ample.

"The musicians are ready, at my signal they shall begin."

They moved back into the ballroom, taking their place across from each othe, waiting for others to form a line beside them on the dance floor. Rippling notes filled the air while the pianist played a simple scale to limber his fingers and the cellist and two violinists tuned their instruments.

Simone clasped her hands together to still them from trembling as the seconds ticked by. Silence fell over the ball room; the expanse of floor remained bare. Even the musicians stopped, a final, raucous squeak from a violin providing a punctuating note to the embarrassment.

Alone. They stood alone.

Not one couple had moved to join them. Censure hung heavy in the air, a palpable force pummelling them from all sides. Cheeks burning, forehead sweating, she glanced at Temple. A dull flush swept over his cheeks; a muscle twitched in the solid jaw.

Finally, he reached for her hands, prying them apart to pull her close to him, placing one damp hand on his black clad shoulder while slipping an arm behind her back. He grasped her other hand and gave it a reassuring squeeze.

"Let's really give them something to chatter about, shall we?" he muttered through taut lips. At his nod, music began again, the one two three beat of the waltz they had practiced only this afternoon.

Her gaze lifted to his and she found him watching her with encouraging eyes. Shuddering with nerves, she stumbled before he tugged at her hand, righting her. Together they began to whirl around the empty dance floor.

Her head spun, and it wasn't because of the waltz. Nay, it spun with incredulity over the cruelty of the assembled guests. She kept her eyes on Temple's face, at the mocking smile and rutted forehead. She took heart at the devil may care glint in his eyes. Let them look, he seemed to say, we shall enjoy ourselves with or without their approval.

He glanced down at her. "You are dancing splendidly," he whispered through stiffly smiling lips.

At his encouraging words, she relaxed to enjoy the rest of the dance. She even tossed her head once or twice when she caught the harsh stares as they spun past the other guests lining the walls. They twirled to a stop.

The pride in his eyes when he looked down on her flustered her a little and she had to glance away. He bowed low over her hand before placing it on his elbow to lead her off.

Straight away couples rushed to fill the dance floor now that they had vacated it. It hurt to see the mad dash.

"Are you thirsty? Perhaps we should take a beverage before we dance again," Temple said, mopping his brow. "I vow, I don't recall other balls being as warm as this one." His meaningless words were meant to distract her.

"It's because you are used to the New Caledonian cold," she laughed, giddy with relief the ordeal was over. "I would take lemonade. Shall I wait here?"

At his nod, she settled herself onto a bench. Curious, she looked about. The next set had begun and she watched the dancing couples step forward and back in time to the music, a twirling mix of rainbow colours. The chandeliers overhead glittered with candles, raining drops of light and drops of wax on the crowded room.

"Excuse me," said a feminine voice after bumping into Simone's legs.

"It's nothing," she replied automatically, watching the dancers and mesmerized by the lavish scene.

Someone else bumped into her, this time a little harder, the apology obviously forced. Simone glanced up but the woman had already moved on. Surely a coincidence in the crowded room, nothing else. She turned back to watch the dance.

Another woman strolled by, knocking into Simone and spilling a bit of iced tea on her lap.

Aghast, she looked at the brown splotch on the ivory silk. Ruined, her princess dress was ruined. She heard snickers and realization flashed through her. It was deliberate and had been done to embarrass her.

Face flaming, she stood up to find Temple. She had to leave. Now. They were hateful and she wanted no part of them.

She lifted her chin and began to make her way to the refreshments room, fighting back tears, scrupulously avoiding eye contact with anyone she passed. After taking one wrong turn and ending up in the cloakroom, where she garnered more than a few curious looks, she backtracked and found the dining room. A number of people milled about the food laden tables, obscuring her vision.

Where was he?

At length she spotted him at the far end of the second table chatting with a stylish young woman. As she watched, the woman, petite and dark, laid a familiar hand on Temple's arm and stood on tiptoe to whisper in his ear. The sight stopped her in her tracks.

He belonged here. She could see it in his aristocratic carriage, his manners, his casual yet confident manner as he conversed with his companion. Unlike her, he was born to this life. As was the woman he conversed with, a woman eminently more suitable to being his countess than Simone.

What had she been thinking, that she could move into his echelon? She swallowed hard against the knot in her chest threatening to steal away her very breath.

Aye, he belonged here but she did not. All the lessons, all the hours spent under Temple's tutelage had been for naught, had merely been time frittered away on an impossible task. The only thing she couldn't figure out was why he had gone ahead with marriage to her. Surely he had realized the unlikelihood of her ever fitting in.

She stayed as if rooted to the ground, unaware of the bodies jostling her, unaware of the muttered "excuse mes" and "beg pardons", unaware of the perfumes mingling with the scents of food into a cloying mixture.

For a seeming eternity she stood there until he noticed her. She saw him start, saw the small frown that made his face stern, saw him excuse himself and move toward her. What now? Would he acknowledge her? Or repudiate her?

"Simone," he whispered as he reached her, taking in with one look her distraught face and the stain on her dress before pulling her outside onto the balcony running the length of the ball room. "What happened?" He dabbed at the tea with his pristine linen handkerchief but the damage had been done – the stain had already dried.

She swiped at her damp eyes with a knuckled fist.

"They're horrid," she gasped. "The whispers, the pointing, now this." She gestured to the brown spot on her gown before the tears began in earnest, great gulping sobs that robbed her breath.

"Shhh, darling," he soothed, pulling her against his chest with one arm. "Where's the girl who braved the wilds of New Caledonia? Surely you aren't going to let a lot of long-nosed London society matrons get the better of you. Of us." He gallantly presented her with his handkerchief. "Take this, it's a bit more than the bits of lace you ladies employ."

She snatched it, dabbing at her eyes then scrunching it into a ball in her fist. "I don't belong here," she sniffled, shaking out the handkerchief again for the next onslaught of tears.

"Nonsense, you're the Countess of Leavenby, of course you belong here."

"No, I don't." Simone shook her head then looked him straight in the eyes. "I feel crude and vulgar."

"Utter nonsense."

"Is it? Have you heard the whispers? We are nothing but a joke." She wiped her eyes again and blew her nose. She stepped back and stiffened her spine though the wretched tears continued to fall. Somehow she had to escape.

"Simone, it's not like that." His protest sounded hollow to her.

"Aye, aye it is." She turned her head away, sick to her stomach. It had become clear to her this evening. What better way for Temple to flaunt his contempt of the ton than to marry an outsider? That was why he had married her, to defy his mother and the edicts of society. Feelings for her had had no part in it. He had tried to warn her earlier today but she had discounted it.

"Don't run away. Besides, if it's scandal they want, why don't we give it to them?" He stuck his head into the ballroom. "See, they've just begun another contradanse. We can fill the spot at the end. Perhaps we should time how long it takes for the lemmings to stampede and leave us." He gave her a lopsided smile and a sly wink in a transparent attempt to make light of the situation.

"No, no, I can't," sobbed Simone. "I want to go."

He stopped then, all jocularity gone. He stepped back and inspected her face. What he saw there must have convinced him it was better for them to leave for all he said was, "Very well." He lifted her hand and pressed a kiss into her palm. "Wait here, I'll get your wrap."

She nodded, relishing the cool night air on the heat of her face. She drifted over to the balcony's edge, tucking the soggy handkerchief into her sleeve before placing her fevered hands on the cool stone railing. Looking down into the dim gardens below, she spotted glowing lanterns and, here and there, couples, one or two locked in passionate embrace far from prying eyes while others strolled casually through the secretive darkness.

The minutes trickled away and still Temple didn't return. Perhaps she had misunderstood and he meant for her to wait in the front foyer where they had come in. She released her grip and gathered her courage. Hesitant, she moved back into the ball room, skirting the wall and trying to avoid notice.

It was not to be.

As she approached the plaster archway leading to the front doors, Lady Frederica walked past her, deliberately turning her face to give her the cut direct. The titters began again.

Anger spurted through Simone and she hurried after the woman, pulling on her elbow to turn her around.

"It was you, wasn't it," she accused Lady Frederica, not caring who heard. "It's not enough that you snub me within our home but now you must snub me in public?"

"Why, I do not know what you are talking about," replied Lady Frederica, a smirk on the rouged lips.

"Why yes, you do." Simone stabbed an index finger at the other woman's face. "Since Temple and I have returned to London, you have avoided me and avoided him. You've taken every meal in your room and only come out when you knew you would not see us. I know from Joanna you've tried to turn her against us as well but she would have no part in it." She paused and took in a deep, shuddering breath.

"Temple wanted to send you away but I said no, that it was your home too and you should stay. I thought you just needed to get to know me and perhaps then you would come to love me. But no, you had other ideas. And now I see what they were. You intended all along to destroy me, to destroy any chance I had for being accepted in polite society. Are you happy then, Lady Frederica? You ruined my coming out."

Simone threw back her shoulders and glared at the faces around her, some incredulous, some amused, and others openly embarrassed at the scene unfolding before them.

"Coming out? You?" The other woman hissed. "You don't deserve a coming out, you're nothing but gutter trash who somehow bewitched my son."

Gutter trash? Gutter trash? For an instant the hateful face disappeared in a red haze. The façade tumbled down.

"Aye, lady, I be gutter trash. From the workhouse on Bishopsgate Street. But I tell ye well, yer so called gutter trash is 'ead and shoulders above the trash ye call yer friends. Me friends be loyal and loving. What of yer friends," she said, sweeping her arms out to the crowd surrounding them. "Think ye that they would be yer friends if ye weren't the Lady Frederica, Dowager Countess of Leavenby. Think ye that they would be yer friends if ye did not have money?"

Someone laughed, a barking sound quickly shushed. The sound brought Simone down with a tumbling thud. Horror at what she had said penetrated the mist of anger. She clapped her hands over her mouth, looking around desperately for Temple. He was nowhere to be seen.

What have I done? Wide eyed, she looked at Lady Frederica. You've insulted Temple's mother in the presence of her peers, that's what. You let your temper get the better of you. You've just become the very thing Lady Frederica has accused you of—gutter trash.

She had to escape.

Now.

She bolted from the house, leaving the jeers and laughter behind her. What had she thought, that she could transform into a lady of quality. One angry word against her and she had lost all reason. One slip and she had thrown it all away. She had to run.

Back to where she belonged, far away from this artificial world.

And run she did, tripping down the stairs, dodging between waiting carriages, and dashing down the street to disappear around the corner before melting away into the comforting cloak of night.

* * *

It was his fault, thought a grim Temple. An ill-timed trip to the water closet, an unexpected encounter with Lady Susannah, who surprisingly bore him no grudge, and he had lost precious time. He knew Simone was upset yet he had been unable to politely tear himself away from Lady Susannah and her prattle on her upcoming nuptials to Lord Simpson.

He had returned just in time to catch Lady Frederica's snub of Simone. Simone and her refusal to be cowed by his mother filled him with pride but the pride had dissipated into dismay when Simone had dropped the charade and spilled the beans.

He must rescue her immediately and for her sake save whatever face he could. However, the crowd had tightened and by the time he had been able to push himself through, Simone had disappeared outside.

Shoving bodies one way and another, he darted after her, down the stairs and into the middle of the street. She was gone, disappeared like a wraith into the shadows of the evening.

Rage and despair mingled. Rage at his mother for her unprovoked and undeserved attack.

And despair for Simone's loss of innocence.

He looked down at the wisp of silk and feathers he still had in his hands, lifting it to his nose to inhale the scent. Her scent, the scent of sunshine and smiles and lemon verbena.

He had to find her. He had to make things right for her.

Chapter Twenty

"She's disappeared into thin air, my lord." Constable Wyndham Jones stood in Temple's library a week later, twisting his hat around and around in his slender hands. Tall and thin, he carried a forbidding presence, due in no small part to the scar that twisted his mouth into a half smile.

"How can that be?" Temple sat at his desk. Wearily he rubbed his eyes before leaning forward to prop his face on both fists. A smudged glass and half-empty decanter of brandy stood at his elbow, a mute testament to its deadening properties.

It had been a long seven days since Simone had disappeared from the Belmont's ball. Seven days that felt more like seven years. Seven days where he had paced the floor incessantly during the nights and searched the streets incessantly during the days.

He had even enlisted the help of the Bow Street Runners the morning after her flight; even the much vaunted detectives had not been able to find a clue as to her whereabouts.

Somehow she had dropped from the face of the earth.

"We'll keep searching for her, my lord. I'll report two days hence." The constable jammed on his hat and spun around on his heel. He marched to the door and swung around to sketch a brief salute before disappearing through the door. His footsteps clattered on the bare floor, the sound echoing and bouncing down the hall much like Temple's thoughts echoed and bounced within his mind.

If only he hadn't left Simone's side, if only the ball room hadn't been so crowded, if only his mother had left well alone. If only, if only. But he had. And it had been. And she hadn't. The deed was done, Simone had taken flight and he couldn't really blame her. The question was, where had she gone?

The obvious answer had been Mrs Dougherty's workhouse on Bishopsgate Street. However, that lady had been unresponsive, even hostile the day he had called the morning after the ball.

"Nay, milord, there ain't no one here by that name." She had tried to slam the door in his face, which he forestalled with one well-placed foot.

"Perhaps you know her better as Mona," he suggested, gracing her with a smile that would normally melt the most hardened of hearts. Particularly those of women. However, it appeared to have lost its charm for it had no apparent effect on her; if anything, the frown on her face deepened.

"Mona? Mona? That one ain't been here for nigh on two years. Skipped out one night, she did. Ain't never heard from her since. Now if ye don't mind, I am busy." This time, Mrs Dougherty was successful in slamming the door, leaving a somewhat bemused Temple standing on the front stoop.

Here he was, a week later and still befuddled over Simone's disappearance.

Perhaps he should try the workhouse again even though the Runner he had hired to keep the place under surveillance had not seen any evidence of Mona. Perhaps Mrs Dougherty's memory had improved in the intervening week.

There had been something about her manner that he had found shifty and evasive. Bloody hell, the woman knew something and he would wheedle it out of her one way or another. That's where he would go today, to pay Mrs Dougherty another visit.

"Tedham!" he bellowed as he charged out of the library, startling the butler who happened to be walking down the hall carrying a tray piled high with tarnished silver. "My coat and hat. Have my horse brought around immediately."

"Of course, my lord." Tray clanking, the butler scuttled away.

Within minutes, Temple galloped off, hat pulled low over his forehead, coattails flapping, face grim, the very picture of a hunter in search of his quarry.

* * *

Frenzied pounding on the door interrupted a harried Mrs Dougherty.

"I'm coming," she shouted as she climbed off the stool where she had been swiping at cobwebs in the corner of the dining hall with a twig broom.

"I'm coming," she shouted again as she waddled the length of the hall toward the archway leading to the front foyer. Whoever pounded the door, pounded with a ferocity that rattled it in its hinges and jiggled the latch. It continued unabated, setting her nerves on edge.

"Oh, oh, oh," she wheezed, "who is it this time?"

At length, she reached the heavy door. She pulled open the small grated window set within it to peer at the visitor, then, horrified, slammed it shut, turning to lean her back against the door.

"Criminy," she muttered. "It's him again. Mona told me he'd be coming back." The pounding started again, vibrating down her back. She rolled her eyes. Now this was an awkward set to. Not unseen, mind you, but still awkward.

"Mrs Dougherty! I know you're in there. Please let me in, I must talk to you."

"I must talk to you," she mimicked beneath her breath. *I don't think so, m'lord. Mona told me about you. I got nothing to say.*

"Open the door. Please."

The note of desperation in the 'please' softened her up a bit. She always was an easy mark for a heartfelt plea. "Only if ye quit yer pounding," she shouted over the din.

The pounding stopped. Silence reigned for a few seconds before she pulled back the latch. The door barely opened a crack before the gentleman barged through, almost setting her back on her bottom.

"Mona Dougherty, I know you know her. Where is she, I must find her." Temple grabbed the woman by her shoulders, barely restraining himself from giving her a good shake just to loosen her memory a bit. Just in time, he remembered his manners and dropped his hands.

"I told ye last time, she ain't been here for two years."

Mrs Dougherty was clearly not one to be intimidated. She hauled up her considerable bulk and crossed her arms, looking down her nose at the gentleman standing before her.

"She's my wife, where is she?"

"It seems to me a gentleman such as yerself should keep better tabs on his woman," she replied. "Anyway, ye wouldn't be marrying the likes of Mona."

"Simone. Her name is Simone."

"Simone, I don't know a Simone. And Mona?" Mrs Dougherty shook her head. "Mona ain't here."

Temple stepped back and took a long hard look at the obese woman. She was immoveable. Not only in her bulk but her mind.

Nonetheless, she lied to him. He could see it in the way she kept glancing away. Very well, she wouldn't talk. He would just have to wait around and see what he could see. This time he wouldn't be dissuaded by her refusal to help him.

"I must beg pardon, I seem to have made a mistake."

He let his scepticism show so the woman would know he saw straight through her. He swept her a bow that left her gape-mouthed before he moved out into the street, pushing through the crowded street until he found a convenient niche from which to watch the workhouse.

Simone was near. He could feel it in his bones.

* * *

"Insistent bugger," Mrs Dougherty sniped as she entered the kitchen. "As arrogant as the rest of them."

"Yes. Yes he is," said a weary Simone, leaning against the one and only table. She had spent the morning scrubbing the kitchen floor. Anything she could do to take her mind off Temple—the more laborious, the better, as if her very sweat could wash away the thoughts of him. "I told you he would come back. Thank you for not giving me away."

"Well now, Mrs Dougherty always looks after her own. Yer like a daughter to me, Mona. As long as ye need to stay here, ye can." She plopped down on the ladder back chair by the fireplace and began fanning her face vigorously. "Ale, if ye please."

Simone handed Mrs Dougherty a battered mug filled to the brim. "I'm grateful for your help."

"What are ye going to do now? He ain't giving up, you know." The other woman drained the mug and held it up to Simone. "That tasted like I need another one."

"Of course, ma'am." Simone again dipped the mug into the ale barrel by the door, wiping off the dripping foam with one sleeve before handing it back. "I don't know what I'm going to do." She sank to her knees in front of the woman and sat back on her heels.

"Aye, it'll be hard fer ye, having lived the life and all. I wager this house ain't so fine anymore. Not that I don't try to make it welcoming," Mrs Dougherty said with a self-deprecating grin, knowing full well her job was not to make the workhouse welcoming at all.

It wasn't meant to be a haven for the idle at the expense of the parish, but simply a temporary solution for those on hard times. Accordingly, the rules were strict, the life grim. No alcohol, no tobacco, no personal possessions.

"I know I can't stay here forever." Simone pulled off the chain and medallion from around her neck. "What do you know of this? Temple—er, Lord Leavenby thought this would be a clue for me." She handed it over.

"What?" The older woman squinted at it. "I suppose it could be a clue," she said slowly as she handed it back. "Ye had it on ye the day ye came to me. I had a mind to sell it but ye were such a sweet little thing, I didn't have the heart. I kept it for ye until I thought ye old enough to look after it yerself."

Simone nodded. She well understood how lucky she had been to have been taken in under Mrs Dougherty's wing.

"Any time yer ready to talk, I'm ready to listen. Ye been quiet since you came back, Mona. Yer hurting real bad but maybe it's time to let it out."

"I can't go back to him, I simply can't. I don't belong in his world." She clasped her hands in front of her and rested her chin on her knuckles. As much as she denied it, the heavy ring on her left hand was evidence she had been part of that world. "But I've been thinking."

"Aye, that ye have, I've seen it on yer face." The woman leaned over and patted Simone on the hand. "What have ye decided?"

"I'm going to go back to the street life. I want to open my own ale house and I need money to do it. I'm still the best there is at picking pockets. I know if I put my mind to it I can get what I need."

And if I can't, I shall retrieve the package I hid and see what it is. Temple had thought it valuable so it must contain something of value she could use. He hadn't asked about it after their arrival in London so it would be safe to assume he no longer wanted it—would it not?

"And then?"

Simone patted the medallion. "Then I'll hire a Bow Street Runner to find out what this means. Maybe it can tell me where I'm from."

"Yer sure? Ain't it a bit risky? Stealing money to open an ale house? What if yer fancy lord finds out? As much as ye ran away, yer still the wife of a peer."

"Well, he won't know, will he?"

"Wouldn't it be easier for ye to fight for him? To be his wife? Ye can do it, yer a bright little thing."

"No." Aghast, Simone shook her head. "I love him, Mrs Dougherty. I love him too much to be a constant embarrassment to him. After a lifetime of running, he finally has what he wants. A home, a position, a hopeful future. He deserves someone better than me." *Someone like the woman I saw with him the night of the ball.*

Mrs Dougherty gave her a searching look. "Yer not giving yourself enough credit. But I can see ye've made up yer mind." She nodded. "Yer welcome to stay here as long as ye like, then. Just be careful."

"Thank you, Mrs Dougherty, I will be. I promise I'll help you here in any way I can. If you don't mind, I need a little time to get back on my feet. I'm tired, so very, very tired." Fatigue haunted her every waking moment, a fatigue that pierced her very bones, a fatigue she couldn't shake.

"Of course, my dear, ye have all the time ye need. Just having ye back is help enough. I missed ye, ye know. Ye and yer twinkling blue eyes."

"'Like the blue skies of your country childhood,'" quoted Simone. "Whenever you said that to me, it always made me feel like I came from the country where the air was always fresh and the sun always shining."

"One day I have a mind to go back there. London's nice and all but it can be a dreary place, what with the smoke and stench."

"Maybe one day you will," agreed Simone. She vowed then and there she would help Mrs Dougherty return to her country roots. It was the least she could do for the woman who had been kindly to Simone in her own way.

* * *

Temple buried his chin in his collar against the chill evening air, unwilling to admit the day had been a fruitless one. Women of all sizes and shapes had passed through his view but none had been the one he sought.

Daylight had faded but not the bustle on Bishopsgate Street. The lamp lighter had been by long ago and the gathering darkness had been thwarted by the welcoming glimmer of street lanterns. Couples strolled by arm in arm, carts and wagons clattered over the cobblestones and watchmen passed by periodically, bellowing out the hour.

"Eleven o'clock," he muttered, needing a warm fire and a stiff drink. Simone wouldn't be out and about now, would she? Perhaps he should call it a day and return at first light tomorrow. His stomach rumbled as if in agreement. He stamped his feet and slapped his stiff hands together, trying to get some feeling in them. Bloody hell, but he had had enough for one day.

He moved out from his niche, joining the flow of humanity. He had left his horse at the public mews a street or two away so didn't have far to go. He adjusted his hat and jammed his hands in his pockets, using his arms as a shield against the bodies jostling around him.

"Well, if it isn't Lord Wellington."

His skin crawled at the familiar voice—the voice that had driven him away from London, the voice that he had hoped never to hear again.

The voice of Peter Mortimer-Rae.

Pretending not to hear, he hastened his pace, reaching his intended street in a matter of seconds. He turned onto it and began to jog the last few yards toward the relative safety of the stable.

A hand clamped down on his shoulder, slowing him. "What's your hurry?"

He tried to pull away but a second hand joined the first, only this one grabbed his arm, twisting it around behind him. Pain shot through his elbow.

"I'm afraid you have the wrong man." He didn't turn around, didn't want to see the hated cold grey eyes.

"Oh, that could be right, then couldn't it, my lord. I heard you're now the Earl of Leavenby. That's right, that would make you Lord Leavenby, not Lord Wellington. My mistake."

The sneering tone set up waves of loathing. Peter Mortimer-Rae, the man who had sucked a very vulnerable and very naïve Temple Wellington onto the road to ruin.

"What do you want?" Temple demanded. "I have nothing to say to you." He stood stock still to avoid any pull on the elbow twisted back at an unnatural angle.

"Is that how you speak to old friends, my lord?"

"I do not consider you a friend." He deliberately made his voice cold.

"Really." The other man clicked his tongue. "And here I thought we had a good friendship. I'm disappointed in you, my lord."

"Release me." Temple ordered, knowing full well he wouldn't be but hoping that if he stalled along enough, a watchman might pass by and come to his aid.

"You think you can order me about like the lackeys that run your estate and your house? I think not." The man pulled on Temple's arm, the movement sending spears of pain up into his shoulder.

"The lackeys that run my house are good, decent people. Unlike yourself."

"Oh, now you seek to insult me? Really, my lord Leavenby, time has changed you." Mortimer-Rae leaned into him to whisper in his ear. "Not for the better, I might add."

"I suppose that would be a matter of opinion."

"Actually, your opinion doesn't really matter to me." Temple felt the other man shrug. "What matters to me is the bit of unfinished business we have between us."

"We have no business together. You and I are through."

"Is that so? I wager others would not be so quick to agree with you. Come, we've wasted enough time standing here in idle chit chat. I should like proper compensation for the package you stole from me."

Pain shot up Temple's arm again as his companion manoeuvred him into a dark alley beside the mews. Several shadows moved to surround him, familiar shadows, the shadows of Mortimer-Rae's henchmen.

The unmistakable prickle of fear raced over Temple's skull and he began to struggle, ignoring the throbbing in his arm.

"I don't have it," he snarled, impotent rage burning in his breast. "Unhand me."

He lashed back with one booted foot, colliding heavily with what he surmised to be a shin. He took grim satisfaction in the corresponding grunt of pain but his satisfaction was short-lived.

An explosion of stars ricocheted before his eyes and   all   went   dark.

Chapter Twenty-One

"Tedham?" The querulous voice resounded through the grand entrance hall of the Leavenby townhouse as Lady Frederica picked her way down the grand staircase. "Have you word of my son?"

"No, my lady." The butler stood at the bottom, watching his mistress conquer a step at a time, railing in one hand and walking stick in the other. "May I help you, my lady?"

"No, on no, thank you, Tedham," she snapped. "I am more than capable."

"Very well." Tedham bowed, not wanting to rouse his lady's temper any more than it already was.

"What of Lady Joanna?" The dowager countess puffed once she reached the ground floor. "Has she word of him?"

"I think not, my lady. Shall I fetch her for you?"

"Yes, if you please, Tedham. Send her to the sitting room." She started to limp away then turned back. "Have you seen that Runner that Temple engaged?"

"I do believe he will be coming by today."

"Yes, well, when he does, send him in to me. I wish to speak with him."

"Of course, my lady."

A very resigned Tedham watched his mistress make her laborious way toward the sitting room and, no doubt, her favourite settee.

Temple's disappearance two days ago coupled with his unseemly marriage had sent the dowager countess into a funk such as he had never seen. Shaking his head, he walked away to ring for the Lady Joanna. Lord Temple couldn't return soon enough, in his opinion.

* * *

"You sent for me, Lady Frederica?" Lady Joanna bustled over to sit in the armchair opposite the settee, needlework in one hand, pattern in the other. She plopped herself down and held out the linen she was working on. "What do you think, is that not a lovely lavender shade for the violets in this piece?"

"What? Oh yes, lovely." Lady Frederica barely deigned to look. "I didn't call you here to discuss your latest project. It's about Temple."

"What about him?" Joanna was cautious, knowing that Temple and his mother had been at constant odds since his return.

Odds that had reached a peak after the scene that had marred Lady Belmont's ball. All London had been a twitter over it, so much so Joanna sincerely regretted not being there to witness it for herself.

"Temple has disappeared. He left two days ago in search of the baggage he claims as wife but he hasn't returned."

"Oh, you know Temple. No doubt he has holed up in some club somewhere to get his bearings. I shan't worry about him if I were you."

Lady Frederica sent her a piercing glance. "That is uncharacteristically callous of you."

"All I know, he was distraught over Simone's disappearance. If he is searching for her, doubtless he doesn't wish to waste time returning home each night."

"Well, he didn't do that for the first week. He was home every evening while he sent the Bow Street Runners out to look."

"They didn't find her, did they? I expect he has taken matters into his own hands."

"Excuse me, my lady." Tedham knocked before shuffling into the room. "Constable Wyndham Jones is here."

"What? He is here already? Yes, send him in, please Tedham."

Within a minute or two, an obviously uncomfortable constable stood pinned in the gaze of a formidable Lady Frederica and to a lesser extent, the interested gaze of Lady Joanna.

"He's not here?" he stammered in response to the dowager countess' query. "What a shame, I found something of his wife." He held up a pair of ivory slippers and Simone's ivory gown, or what was left of it. The beading and feathers had been removed, leaving only the tea stain as identification.

"Why yes, I believe that is hers," said Lady Frederica, eyes narrowed. "Where did you find it?"

"In a pawn shop down in Cheapside. The shop's owner said a young woman had brought it in and when I asked him to describe her, he said she had blonde hair and blue eyes." He shrugged. "It had to be her, my lady.

Apparently she wore a gold signet ring which was much more to the shop owner's liking. She denied him however, telling him it held special meaning for her and was not available for pawn."

"That's odd. I know that piece, it's very valuable."

"Therefore we know she was not after money. She sought to get rid of the dress," said Lady Joanna. "Otherwise, why keep the ring?"

"Why, indeed," muttered Lady Frederica, unwilling to let go of her image of Simone as a money grubbing tart. "What of my son?" She changed the subject.

"What of your son," asked the surprised constable, "Is he not here? I was scheduled to report to him today."

"No, he left two days ago to search for his wife. We have seen neither hide nor hair of him since."

"Why, I was here two days ago to report. He didn't mention anything to me about searching for Lady Leavenby."

"No? Then we must assume it was a hasty decision on his part. Where do you think he would go?"

"Well, if it was me, I would return to the only London home his wife has ever known. The workhouse on Bishopsgate Street."

Lady Frederica inhaled sharply at this tidbit. The chit had grown up in unsavoury surroundings. Hardly surprising considering her outburst at the ball.

As much as Frederica wanted to gloat over the fact her suspicions had been correct, she needed to focus on the matter at hand—Temple, the current Earl of Leavenby, was missing. "May I engage you to expand your search to include my son?"

"Of course, my lady." A visibly pleased Constable Wyndham Jones bowed. "It would be my pleasure."

"And if I'm paying you," she added, reaching with her walking stick to poke him in the midriff, "I shall expect you to report daily."

"Nothing would please me more, my lady." The constable bowed.

"Very well, you are excused."

"Do you think he will find Temple?" Joanna waited until the constable had left the room before posing the question.

"I don't know. We shall just have to hope for the best, won't we?"

Joanna darted a glance at Lady Frederica. Did she imagine it, or was there a hint of capitulation in the usually distant voice?

* * *

Easy, ridiculously easy, thought Simone, pocketing the coins she had spirited from an unsuspecting gent while he watched a couple of young lads engaged in fisticuffs. A slight jostle as she pushed her way past him to hide the hand slipped into his pocket, a wide-eyed innocent glance and a heartfelt "I am so sorry" when the frowning gentleman looked her way and then she was on her way, no one the wiser. He wouldn't know until he reached home that he had even been picked.

Oy, Simone, you are the best, she congratulated herself, *simply the best.*

She continued down the crowded street, darting around the corner into a lane leading to the customs houses down by the Thames. Counting coins in her mind, she didn't see the man lounging in the door of the Royal Swan until he stepped out in front of her, scaring her half out of her wits.

"Mona, how ye been?" Gentry Ted adjusted his cravat and swept her a bow. "I heard ye were back on the streets but I didn't believe it. To tell the truth, I didn't think ye would leave the rum situation ye found for yourself."

"Ted! Whew, you gave me a start." She couldn't hide the pleasure in her voice. "But if you knew I was back working, why didn't you stop by?" She deliberately ignored his reference to her "rum situation". It really was none of his business.

"Because that Mrs Dougherty runs a tight ship. She don't like me coming around. Thinks I'll be a bad influence on the residents." Gentry Ted winked. "I only influence the ones wanting to be influenced."

Simone laughed. "I suppose you would be referring to me. You know it was the only way to support myself without giving in to some man's advances."

"Is that still holding true for ye then? About the unwelcome advances, I mean."

Her laughter died. "I suppose it is." Images of Temple flooded her mind and with great resolve, she pushed them away.

He was gone. To all intents and purposes, he was dead to her. She closed her eyes and swallowed hard against the lump that rose in her throat at the thought of him.

"Mona, are ye well?"

"Aye." She nodded. "I am. Just a memory that had no right popping into my head."

"Ye look like ye could use a pint. Here, let's go inside and have one. Talk about old times."

"What? Oh. Certainly." She trailed after him into the crowded public house.

He headed for the farthest, darkest corner; she had no choice but to follow.

"You're a careful one, Ted." She settled onto the stool he pulled out for her. "But you've never been on the wrong side of a jail cell door, have you?"

"Aye," he boasted, "never been nabbed for nothing." He signalled to the blowsy bar maid and sat down. "Ye've changed," he commented, squinting at her. "Not just your talk and your clothes." He pointed to the fashionable outfit she wore—a moss green muslin gown with a matching velvet spencer and fringed bonnet.

"It's easier to get closer to my marks if I'm nicely dressed."

He let loose an appreciative guffaw then slipped into silence, searching her face with perceptive eyes before speaking again. "Do ye know how ye've changed the most?"

She shook her head.

"You're sadder." And he punctuated it with an index finger held up like a lone sentinel.

"Am I?" She pasted an artificial smile to her face. "I don't think so."

"Aye, you're sadder. It's to do with your fancy gent, ain't it?" he said shrewdly.

She gave up trying to pretend. "Yes." Her shoulders sagged and she propped her elbows on the upended barrel that served as table.

"Tell me about him."

"What do you want to know?"

"Start at the beginning." He signalled for a second pint. "I can tell this is going to be a long story. May as well make myself comfortable." He leaned forward. "Now, start."

"The watch was chasing me. I hid in his trunk. He found me before he set sail. He was going to Canada. I asked him to take me with him. He said yes." She recited it as if she had said it a hundred times. Which she had, trying to make sense of it all.

"Ye've been in Canada?" Gentry Ted's eyes were round, matched by the 'O' of his mouth.

"Yes." She nodded, memories flooding back. Oy, why had she agreed to talk to Ted? It didn't help, rather, it aggravated the ache in her heart as if a tiny dagger embedded within it had been twisted.

She clamped shut her mouth to stop from bawling. She couldn't go on, Ted would understand.

"Tell me his name," he suggested. "Forget the rest, just tell me who he is. Maybe I can help or something."

She looked at him, his concerned visage distorted by her welling tears. Concern for her. The tears started to fall. "Lord Wellington," she choked out, "Lord Temple Wellington, the Earl of Leavenby."

"Lord Wellington, why does that name sound so familiar to me?" He tapped his fingers on the barrel table. "Lord Wellington, Lord Wellington." Recognition flooded his eyes. "Ye don't mean to say you're married to Lord Scoundrel?"

"Lord Scoundrel?" The name puzzled her. She had overheard it at the ball that evening. "How do you know of Lord Scoundrel?"

"Only that he was tied up with Peter Mortimer-Rae. That one, he's nasty. Your lord was in over his head right from the start."

"What did he do?" Interest flashed through her; she was on the verge of discovering the secret in Temple's life.

"Lord Wellington was the bully cock of the gang. Being as he was gentry and all, he could go into any of the men's fancy clubs. He'd find a likely mark with a fat pocket, pick a quarrel and when they stepped outside to fight, Mortimer-Rae's crew would be waiting to rob the poor fellow."

He paused to slurp some ale, swilling it in his mouth before swallowing it. "Worked fine until one day he picked a quarrel with the wrong gent. This one fought back and he was killed in the scuffle. Mortimer-

Rae's cronies ran off, leaving your lord to deal with it. With a smooth tongue and a bit of greasing the right palms, Wellington managed to place the blame on Mortimer-Rae, who didn't take too kindly to it even if it was true. He swore to kill Wellington. Wellington disappeared but before he did, he nicked something that belonged to Mortimer-Rae. He's got a long memory, that one."

Stunned, she said nothing. She knew exactly what it was Temple had nicked. And where it was.

"There's more, Mona. Er, Lady Leavenby." He stumbled over the words, as if it were difficult to reconcile the Mona he once knew with the stylish woman who sat with him in the boisterous environs of the Royal Swan.

"Yes?"

"Mortimer-Rae's been searching for two years with nary a hint of luck but word has it he has him. Wellington is his prisoner."

"How—how can that be?" Her stomach plummeted.

"I dunno," Ted shrugged. "Yer lord was snooping around in parts he shouldn't have been. Heard he was looking for something. Or someone." Sharp grey eyes impaled her. "You, I wager."

She gaped at him. She didn't doubt Gentry Ted—if he said Temple was being held prisoner, then it was true. Had he been captured because he had been searching for her in the areas of London he thought she might be? Exhilaration exploded within her quickly followed by dismay. It was her fault he was in trouble.

"But Temple is alive?"

"I think so or I would've heard. I fear Mortimer-Rae is going to extract his pound of flesh before doing away with him."

"You don't mean—"

"Aye, I do." He nodded his head emphatically. "Torture."

"Where is he? We must rescue him!" The thought of Temple in trouble brought waves of nausea. She had thought him securely ensconced in his London townhouse, doing whatever a gentleman of means did.

Nay, instead he faced peril, death even. She couldn't allow that to happen. She could rescue him; she would rescue him. Then they would be even. "Will you help me find him?"

"Aye, I'll help ye, Mona. Ye always was my little girl. Still are," he added. "Wait." He reached in his jacket pocket and pulled out an orange. "Look what I have for ye."

She took it from him, cradling it in both hands. Her nose caught the tangy scent and she was transported back to the morning she had eaten an orange and tossed the peels into the ocean for the sea gulls. Then she had been hopeful, excited over the new land and new life that beckoned, had even entertained daydreams of loving him.

Sadly, the daydreams were over, dashed by words spoken in anger to the dowager countess, words witnessed by countless others.

The chasm between her and Temple was simply too great to cross.

However he was in danger and the very chasm separating them would serve her well now. This was her world, not his. He was the stranger here, not her. For him, she would put her well-earned talents to use.

She lifted her eyes to the grizzled man who regarded her fondly. "We will save him, won't we Ted?" She tucked the fruit into her reticule. "I'll take this with me for luck. When shall meet again?"

"I'll come by the workhouse for you tomorrow after I do a bit more nosing around."

She nodded in understanding. "I'll be ready." She rose and gave him a gracious nod. "Until then."

As much as she chafed at the thought of waiting, it would give her the time to retrieve the packet. Surely Mortimer-Rae would trade Temple's life for its return?

* * *

In the privacy of Mrs Dougherty's kitchen, a stunned Simone kneeled, not feeling the rough stone pressing into her knees. Temple's box lay on the scrubbed floor in front of her. The knife she had used to pry it open lay beside her, blade bent with the force.

Gold coins glittered in the firelight—more gold than she had ever imagined existed. Along with the deed she had found inside, there was more than enough for her to start a new life.

Inadvertently, Temple had given her a chance— if she still wanted it.

Chapter Twenty-Two

Simone sat back on her heels and chewed her lip. Nay. She shook her head. She couldn't walk away from Temple. If there was the slightest possibility the box and its contents could save him, then that's what she would do.

With trembling figures, she re-wrapped the box in the oiled cloth and tied it up with twine.

* * *

"What do ye want?" A scowling Mrs Dougherty barred Gentry Ted's entrance to the workhouse.

"I'm here for Mona."

"She's too good for the likes of ye, now bugger off." She shook her fist at him.

"Leave him be." Simone moved up to stand beside the older woman. "We have business together."

Mrs Dougherty threw her a look plainly indicating her doubt at the wisdom of Simone and Gentry Ted doing business together. Nevertheless, she stepped back. "Watch yer backside," she said with an audible sniff. She continued to glower at Gentry Ted, who, not intimidated in the slightest, gave her a cheerful grin.

"I will," Simone assured her then marched down the steps to link her arm with Ted's. "What did you discover?"

"Yer lord is in a warehouse by Blackfriars Bridge. We may have to search one or two 'cause I couldn't figure out exactly which one. But we'll find him," he assured her.

Poor thing, the news on Temple had taken its toll on her. Worry lines scored the parchment of her face; black smudges pooled beneath eyes faded with fear and anxiety.

"Mind ye take care of her or ye'll have me to answer to." Mrs Dougherty's words swirled after them as they moved away to join the throngs on Bishopsgate Street.

"Of course I'll take care of ye," Ted muttered. "She don't need to remind me." He patted Simone's hand where it lay upon his elbow.

"Pay her no mind," soothed Simone. "She's feeling protective of me. Now, where do we have to go?"

"Upriver from Blackfriars."

Simone shivered. "Not the most pleasant neighbourhood."

"Ye just need to keep yer wits about ye, Mona. Er, Lady Leavenby."

"Mona is better. Not as pretentious." As if she had any right to be pretentious.

"Speaking of pretentious, your cloak won't do." He shook his head. "It's too fine to be wearing in this end of London."

"I know," she sighed. "But it was just to get away from Mrs Dougherty." She pulled it back to reveal a stained and tattered skirt coupled with a rough woollen shawl. A heavy linen sack hung over one shoulder, carrying Temple's box; she hoped it didn't show beneath the shawl. "We'll stash my cloak once we get closer to the bridge."

The two continued at a brisk pace, heading toward Cheapside and St. Paul's Cathedral. Now that she actually did something, the helpless feeling over Temple's predicament fell away. Aye, as difficult as it had been to do nothing the past hours, Gentry Ted had come through for her in her quest to rescue Temple. That is, if he still needed rescuing and not a burial.

Of course he does, she scolded herself. My heart tells me he's still alive.

"Here." Gentry Ted said at length, stopping at a narrow lane that twisted away from the thoroughfare they were on.

Dilapidated brick warehouses lined it, each one leaning into its neighbour as if they propped each other up. Simone had the fanciful notion that if she pushed too hard on the first one, the street would tumble like dominoes.

"Are you certain?" Dubious, she peered down the haphazard row. Save for two burly porters struggling with a sack-laden cart lodged in a mud hole, the lane was empty.

"Give me your cloak. We'll hide it here." Ted stuffed it into a crack.

"Won't they see us?" She gestured toward the porters.

Ted shook his head. "They'll think we're looking for a quiet place to conduct business, if ye get my drift." He winked at her.

"Of course," she nodded, flushing. It was just a game. As abhorrent as it was, she could play the part.

"This way." He pushed her ahead of him. "Closer to the river."

The porters lifted weary heads as they approached.

"What are ye buffle-headed gents lookin' at," Simone sneered as they skirted the hapless pair. "Ain't ye ever seen a workin' girl afore?"

"Give us a kiss, luv," teased one.

"Can't ye see I'm busy? But I could come back for ye in a bit—" She pursed her lips suggestively, squeezing her upper arms together to enhance her cleavage.

"Come on," Ted pulled her arm. "Yer mine, I paid for ye."

"Ta, boys, I'll be back for ye." She blew them a kiss.

"Now they'll be looking for us to come back," Ted grumbled as they trudged on.

"Then we shan't return this way."

"Sauce box." However the smile on his face softened the curtness of his words.

They followed the alley, which crooked toward the river. Overhead the buildings almost touched and made it difficult to distinguish the slop ditch in the growing darkness.

"Aren't we there yet?" Simone groused when her foot slipped into the malodorous muck for the third time.

"I see the place." Gentry Ted stopped in front of a crumbling edifice, indistinguishable from the rest in Simone's opinion.

"How do ye know?"

"That." He pointed to a painted barrel dangling precariously from the heavy beam extending from the peak of the building. "They told me to look for a red barrel."

"Or it could be that one." She waved her arm to the adjoining building. It too had a red barrel, only this one was wedged beneath the latch on the double doors. "What's in these buildings, do ye think?"

"Empty. Or so they told me. " He rattled the latch on the first warehouse. "Let's try this one."

He rattled it again vigorously with both hands before stepping back to inspect the door. "Hell's bells, that ain't opening. Look, it's been nailed shut and for quite some time, judging by the rust. I doubt he's in here."

"Try the other one." She walked over to tap the barrel blocking the door to the second warehouse.

Ted put his shoulder to it. "It's moving," he grunted. He shoved again with enough force that the barrel, with an indignant squeal from the latch as it broke free, tipped upright.

Ted stood up, mopping his face. "I tell ye, that barrel ain't empty."

A burst of crazed laughter echoed behind them.

"Some one's coming," she hissed then ducked behind the barrel.

A decrepit cart piled high with a mound of what appeared to be rags lurched its way into view. Simone didn't know which was sorrier: the swayback nag pulling it or the hunchback hobbling along beside.

Ted grabbed her hand to pull her from behind the barrel and shoved her around the warehouse corner. "Wait here."

Nonchalantly pulling a pipe from his pocket, he strolled away from view back to the front of the warehouse.

Simone sagged against the wall. On jelly knees, she slid down to a squat, leaning her head back against the bricks. Her heart had leapt into her throat at the sight of the rag cart and she breathed deeply, trying to quell the nerves roiling in her stomach. With straining ears, she listened to the exchange between Ted and the carter, chafing at the delay.

"Good day." Ted's pleasant voice drifted through the dank air.

"Leave me be," replied the carter, his querulous voice demonstrating his displeasure at being interrupted. "If I were ye, I wouldn't be spending time here. The gent that owns this warehouse don't like street scum hanging about."

"I took a wrong turn. Thought I'd stop to catch me breath before I headed back."

"Don't say I didn't warn ye. The gent, he's a vicious one. I've seen with me own eyes what he does to them he don't like," he cackled. "Now leave a working man be and get out of my way."

Simone exhaled heavily as the cart creaked away from view.

"That were close," Ted remarked as he slouched back to join her.

"Where do you think he is going?"

"Eh?" Ted shrugged. "That way leads to the river. The poor bugger must have a place to call home somewhere down there."

"Do you think it's safe now to go inside?" Simone's voice quivered.

"Aye," Gentry Ted nodded. "I took a closer look at the latch. It's unlocked."

"Then let's not waste more time. I don't like it here." Simone stood, wiping her gritty palms on her skirt.

"Come on." With a cautious peek around the corner, he motioned her to follow him.

By the time she reached the front doors, he had already slipped inside. She glanced about the empty alley then scooted in. Ted closed the door and the wedge of light disappeared, throwing the room into gloomy darkness. She stood disoriented for a second while her eyes adjusted to the murk.

The smell hit her like a workhouse bully. It smelled of oil and tea, manure and wool. Her nose ached and her skin crawled with it.

Worse, it smelled of something else: rats. As if to confirm her thoughts, she heard a rustle and a muffled squeak behind her.

Rats. She shuddered. She hated rats, had hated them when they ran across her bed at night, hated them for the filth they left behind. Nay, it was beyond fear. It was terror, irrational terror. Bile rose in her throat and she fought the urge to flee. They were here to look for Temple and nothing could dissuade her from that task. She swallowed hard, forcing the bile back into her stomach.

"We don't have much time," warned Ted. "We don't have a lamp and it's getting dark."

She nodded. They started forward, Simone clinging to Gentry Ted's arm.

The room was long and narrow, lit only by what light managed to filter in through a series of narrow windows high on the walls. For the most part, it was empty save a few barrels and crates piled in the farthest corner. They scuffled along the dirty floor, littered with straw and mouldering bits of cloth and rope.

But other than the shadows darting along the perimeter, they found naught, saw naught.

"The rats are following us," Simone quavered, pointing to the moving shadows.

"Pay them no mind, they're curious animals. They want nothing from us."

At the far wall, they stopped and stared at each other.

"He's not here," she said, sick with disappointment.

"Don't fret, there's another door." He pointed to their left. Sure enough, behind the crates, Simone could see a narrow door.

"It has a padlock. There must be something of value behind it," Ted surmised, "or it wouldn't be locked."

"We don't have the key, how can we get in?" Frustration coloured Simone's words. It had been one obstacle after another, each wasting precious time.

"Before we worry about that, why don't we take a peek and see what we can see. There's an opening near the roof. I'll give ye a bit of a boost. "

"Very well," she agreed, glad to be off the floor and away from the rodents scurrying past with disconcerting frequency.

"Ye ready?"

At her nod, he linked his fingers together, holding them low enough for her to step into. With a grunt, he lifted her up.

She reached up for the sill with taut, hooked fingers, trying to find enough purchase to pull herself up. It was no use.

"I can't see anything, I'm not high enough." Sobs formed in her chest and pressed against her throat. "I don't think he's here."

"How do ye know if ye can't see? Step on my shoulders and try again."

His voice, calm and matter of fact, had the desired effect. After a few calming breaths, she did as he suggested.

Teetering, she clung to the sill with every ounce of strength she possessed. Resolutely ignoring the fact the floor was farther below than it had any right to be, she looked through into the next room.

It was darker than the rest of the warehouse. She strained her eyes, trying to see what lay in the gloom beneath her.

Nothing.

She scanned the floor. Still nothing, save for an indeterminate shadow against the wall.

No, not a shadow. A body!

The body of a man.

Temple.

Horror struck, she gazed at his inert form lying in a pool of blood.

And at the blade protruding from his back.

Chapter Twenty-Three

A sob rose in her throat. They were too late.

Her head swam, the room spun around her. The unthinkable had happened. Peter Mortimer-Rae had killed his quarry. She closed her eyes and leaned her forehead against the sill.

"What do ye see?" Ted pinched her ankle. "Ye've not said a word."

"He's dead." She heard the words as if they came from a far-off place rather than from her own throat. "Temple's dead."

"You're sure?"

"Yes. There's—there's blood."

"Blood." Ted clicked his tongue. "Blood always looks worse than it really is."

"And a knife," she whispered.

"I'm bringing ye down." Ted's sharp, authoritarian voice crashed through the haze in her mind. "When yer ready, let go and I'll catch ye."

She loosened her grip and slid down.

"Now," he said when she was safely on the ground, "Give me a hairpin."

"What?" The question made no sense to her befuddled mind. Surely Ted was not about to pin his hair?

"A hairpin," he said impatiently. "I ain't never seen a padlock that can't be picked."

She fumbled in her hair for a pin and handed it to him. A lock of hair fell across her cheek and she tucked it behind her ear.

"While I'm doing this," he suggested, "why don't ye pinch a few rags from the ragman. If there's blood, we'll need 'em to sop it up. Besides, it'll just make me nervous if yer watching over my shoulder." He gave her a little push. "Go. Get a bit of air, Mona, I don't want ye collapsing and leaving me with two bodies on my hands."

"Rags? You want me to get rags?" She resisted the urge to break out into hysterical laughter.

"Yes. Go." He pushed her again.

"No." She shook her head. "I'm not leaving. I won't watch you, just get on with it." Turning away, she drew a shuddering breath. "Do as I say, get on with it."

Ted grunted, already fiddling with the lock. The minutes ticked by in silence save for the scrape and scratch of the pin against iron.

Clasping her elbows, she girded herself for the ordeal of facing Temple's body. Don't cry, she ordered herself. He wouldn't want you to cry. She stared into darkening space. Dark as death.

"Aha, I got it."

She turned back to see a triumphant Ted hold the padlock aloft. Without waiting, she flung herself past him, wrenching open the door and darting to the comatose body curled face down on the floor. She knelt and cradled Temple's head. Desperate, she leaned down to hold her ear close to his mouth.

Did a breath disturb an errant curl?

"Temple? Temple? Can you hear me?"

She lowered her ear again. Yes, a breath! Faint but a breath nonetheless.

"He's breathing," she shouted over her shoulder, elated. "Ted, he's breathing!" She rained kisses on Temple's head, careful not to jostle him.

"Splendid," Ted patted her shoulder. "What did I tell ye? Don't judge by the blood."

"We must get him out of here."

"Aye, we'll do that. Seeing as how ye wouldn't get the rags, I'll do one better and fetch the whole cart." He winked at her.

"He's alive," she repeated, tears streaming down her face to drip onto Temple's head. "Hurry, before anyone comes back."

Ted gave her a big smile. With a tip of his hat he hurried off with clattering footsteps that disappeared abruptly once he reached outside.

In the quiet, she sat and held Temple's head, placing a cool hand on his fevered forehead. She forced herself to look at the knife handle jutting from one shoulder. It didn't look too bad. It looked as if most of the blood had actually seeped from a wicked gash on the back of his head.

"Breathe," she ordered. "You're not going to die now, Temple. You must live. You must keep breathing."

She could barely see him in the dimness. Did she imagine it or did one side of his mouth twist into a smile? Nay, he must be dreaming.

She dropped a multitude of kisses on the top of his head. "Don't die on me, do you hear me? I should like to waltz again. " She lifted her head. The moon had risen—a harvest moon burning its way through the sooty skies and sending slivers of light into the warehouse.

His face was clearer now in the moonlight and her eyes roved over it greedily, devouring every detail, every hair, every pore.

"I love you, Lord Temple Wellington, Earl of Leavenby." She was unafraid to say the words, cocooned in the dark as she was, secure too that he could not hear her. "I love you." She leaned down to whisper in his ear.

In the shadowed corner, a rustle.

The rats had followed her. Oy, now she had to keep the rats at bay. A wounded man was fair game for the disgusting creatures.

"I shall keep them away from you," she promised, stroking his stubbled check. "But only if you don't die."

Time dragged on.

Her skirts grew wet with blood where she sat. Temple's blood, from the still seeping gash on his head. He needed a doctor's attention. Where was Ted? Surely he should be back by now?

She strained her ears but could not hear the cart's creak. Had something happened to him?

She slapped her hands on the floor to scare away a rat that had come too close.

The rats grew bolder, darting over Temple's legs and stopping just out of arm's reach to leer at her. Her hands grew sore from slapping at them. Desperate, she looked around for a weapon of any kind to scare the creatures away but could find nothing. She pulled away from Temple and flailed at the rats with her feet.

Still Ted did not come.

Chapter Twenty-Four

Temple drifted in and out of consciousness.

Demons peopled his dreams, demons that bound him and beat him. Demons prodding and pinching and howling for revenge, demons laughing maniacally.

Then an angel appeared. An angel who smoothed a cool hand over his brow. An angel who professed to love him. An angel who wanted to waltz with him. What utter nonsense, what angel would ever love him?

And the dark. Where was he, that it was always dark? Was it actually dark or was it his mind that was dark?

His treacherous mind teased him with thoughts of sunshine and smiles and lemon verbena yet when he opened his eyes, all he saw was blackness. Sinister, murky shadows. Dark, swirling mists.

He couldn't pull himself free from the black that consumed him, sucked him down, pulled at his legs and wouldn't let him reach the light.

He gave up and let it take him.

* * *

Voices? Simone cocked her head. Did she hear voices on the evening breeze? Had help finally arrived?

"Maybe Ted has come back," she whispered to a comatose Temple. "Forgive me for leaving you but I must see who it is."

She pulled out the orange Gentry Ted had given her in the Royal Swan and rolled it away. It wasn't much for rat bait but it would have to do. Then she drew off her shawl and laid it over Temple's face as best she could, anything to deter the rats if only for a few moments.

Fumbling with the linen sack, she managed to extract the package to place it on the floor beside him. A weak offering and perhaps too late, but would Mortimer-Rae not be pleased at its return? And if leaving the package meant the end of her dream of an ale house, so be it—saving Temple was the only thing that mattered right now.

Simone got to her feet and lurched through the door, taking a single step before stopping. Her heart thumped so, she was certain it would leap from her throat.

A lantern shone through the door at the far end, outlining two figures. Could one of them be Ted? Had he found someone to help them? Nay, the one was too tall and the other too portly to be Ted.

It wasn't Ted. But who? Terror stabbed her. It had to be Mortimer-Rae or his henchmen.

She ducked behind the crates and crouched, holding her breath. Blood pounded in her ears and she swallowed hard in a vain attempt to still the hammering. Willing herself not to faint, she placed her palms against the crate in front of her, concentrating on the slivered wood pricking her hands.

The two men ambled into the deserted warehouse, lantern swinging crazily, throwing distorted shadows against the walls and ceiling.

"We killed Wellington, what should we do with him?"

"I say leave him, who's going to find him here?"

"I say throw him in the river," argued the first. "The Thames has a way of disposing of unwanted garbage."

A shout from outside interrupted them.

"What the…!" The two chimed in unison before sprinting for the door. The lantern light blinked off and then came the echo of pounding hooves.

Simone didn't hesitate. She got to her feet and tore the length of the warehouse.

At the entrance, she stopped to listen.

Silence. She poked her head out. A lantern lay tipped on the ground, glass smashed and oil puddled. The lane was empty—whoever had left, had left in a hurry.

She sidled out and throwing caution aside sprinted down the lane toward the river to find Ted. Shadows chased her, clutched at her. Cobblestones caught her toes and she fell once, hard on her hands and knees, so hard her breath jarred in her lungs. She ignored the pain, stumbling to her feet to continue her frantic flight. Panic stricken, she turned the final corner and fled toward the shimmer of moonlight on black water.

Chest heaving, she pulled up at the river quay. There, under the shadow of the bridge, stood the ragman's cart. With cocked ears, she edged closer, searching the gloom until her eyes ached.

Neither Ted nor the ragman were there. Only the ragman's bony nag stood, forlornly picking at a few stalks of hay.

She couldn't risk shouting, couldn't risk spending more time on what appeared to be a fruitless search. Ted had disappeared. The onus was on her—she must get help for Temple. She must go to his townhouse and enlist the aid of Joanna.

She spun on her heel and pelted back the way she came, stopping only long enough to retrieve her cloak before making her way westward toward Mayfair. Grateful for its warmth against the chill of her sweat-stained blouse and the thickening evening air, she hurried as best she could down Cheapside Street.

She had just reached St. James Palace when a burly hand literally yanked her off her feet. She tripped, wrenching her ankle.

"Well, well, who do we have here?" The hand clamped down on her shoulder, squeezing with such force pain shot down her arm.

She turned. A sickening wave of terror welled up from her belly when she saw who it was.

Constable Carstairs. Dismayed, she shook her head. What a dreadful coincidence. Why now?

"Mona Dougherty, I've been looking for you. You made me look a fool but I knew your luck would run out sooner or later."

"Let me go." She tried to wrestle free from the ham-handed fist. "My husband, Lord Wellington, the Earl of Leavenby is hurt and close to death. I must save him."

"Sure, and you think I'm going to fall for lying words from a gallows bird? No, I've been waiting for you to make a mistake. Heard you were back in town. Eh, what's this?" He turned her about to see her better in the lamplight, pushing back her cloak as he did so. "Looks like blood. Have you added murder to your list of crimes then?"

"No, let me go or my husband will die! They've come back for him, let me go!"

"Save it for the magistrate, Miss Dougherty. I don't believe a lying word that passes your lips."

"No! No!" Simone wailed, struggling to pull free. It was no use. She was no match for the constable's bulk.

He dragged her down the street, mindless of her kicks and screams. No one paid attention to just another piece of street riff raff.

"No," she moaned, tears spurting down her cheeks. "I must help my husband. No." The hubbub on the street drowned her wail.

"Shut your mouth," he snarled. "It's prison for you and in prison you shall rot."

* * *

Newgate Prison.

The name struck terror into the hearts of those who might find their way there with or without the help of their own transgressions. Dark, evil, its stone walls were permeated with desolation and defeat, permeated with the stench of human waste and unwashed bodies, permeated with lost hope and lost souls.

With each step that took Simone deeper and deeper within its bowels, her despair grew. It flooded her mind and drowned all reason.

At length she was shoved into a narrow cell, which although barely wide enough to stand with arms outstretched, was not empty. Vacant faces stared at her in the brief flash of lantern light before the door clanged shut. She turned and clutched the iron bars in the tiny window while unknown terrors scratched at her back.

"No!" she shouted, trying to force her face through the bars. "I am innocent, let me go!" She battered the heavy door with her feet.

No one could hear her over the din of moans, screeches and wails. Still she battered at the door until, spent, she clung to the bars and leaned her head against her fists.

In her mind, she lined the facts up: rightly or wrongly, she was in prison. No one knew she was here. Temple was hurt. Only Gentry Ted knew where Temple was. Gentry Ted had disappeared.

Her stomach rebelled at the stark hopelessness of the situation and she vomited in the rotting straw at her feet.

Someone shifted behind her and goose bumps pimpled her arms at the sound. In her initial frenzy, she had forgotten she wasn't alone. Shivering, she pulled away from the door, wrapping her hands in her cloak to pull it tight around her before turning to face her cellmates.

"Welcome to our hen club." A low pitched voice sounded out of the murk. "I am Tess, and here is Bonnie and beside her is Elizabeth."

She could barely make out her companions in the dim light. Tess appeared to be a woman of generous proportions. It was difficult to see much of Bonnie and Elizabeth, however, for they huddled together beneath a shredded blanket. All were of an indeterminate age as if the prison air had sucked the vigour from their skin leaving a wrinkled, sagging mass in its place.

She drew in a shuddering breath. "I am Simone Wellington. Countess of Leavenby," she added.

It may not be wise to tell them her name but she had nothing of value on her. Perhaps if more people knew of her identity then word would spread beyond the prison walls.

Tess hooted. "Countess, you say? Why, we're all countesses here, aren't we, girls?"

"It's true," Simone protested.

"Well, Countess Leavenby, no one cares about you here. You're just another prisoner awaiting your turn with the judge. Mind telling me what you are in for?"

"Thievery." Her shoulders slumped. What was the use, Tess was right. She was just another prisoner. Who would believe that she, with her blood stained skirt, unkempt hair and dirty, broken fingernails, was the Countess of Leavenby?

She forced herself to look at Tess. "And you? You are educated, why are you here?"

"I had a position as governess to a fine family. A lovely posting it was, until I caught the lord's eye. The lady did not like it in the least and accused me of stealing her silver comb. Of course, the comb was found in my room." A ribbon of bitterness twined through her words. "Who would believe me, a child's governess over the lady of the family?"

"So why don't you believe me, then? I speak the truth."

"If I may be so rude, you hardly look the part."

"Well, it is true. I am the Countess of Leavenby." She spoke boldly although inside she quaked. Temple had told her once it was all in the mannerisms. Project an aristocratic air and like as not people will believe it. "I am certain this is all a misunderstanding."

"That's as may be," Tess said with a knowing smile. "But it will be difficult to convince the magistrate. He's not very sympathetic to the plight of the prisoners."

"How long have you been here?"

"I don't really know. Long enough to know there's no getting out of here. Unless one has money, perhaps. You may be able to send word to your count. He may be able to bribe your way out." Her sarcastic tone lacked conviction.

Simone's brief surge of hope dissipated and she sagged to her knees, fingers curled into fists. Her left hand felt bare; she missed the comforting mass of Temple's signet ring. It lay beneath the workhouse floor boards where she had hidden it before embarking on this mad venture this morning, in the same spot where she kept her medallion when not wearing it.

"Aw, Tess, don't scare the poor thing. She'll find out soon enough what it's like here." A thin voice, scratchy with ague, joined the conversation.

"When I want your opinion, Bonnie, I shall ask for it." Tess turned back to Simone. "I'm not lying about the money. Having it makes life in here more bearable. We can buy better food and drink with it. Do you have anything we could barter or sell? You would share with your cell mates, wouldn't you?"

Simone shook her head. "I have naught." Without thinking, she fingered the medallion hanging between her breasts.

Tess' sharp eyes missed nothing. "What is this?" she said, yanking at the chain. It gave way and the medallion tumbled to the floor.

"No!" Simone swiped at it but Tess beat her to it.

"This will buy us a day or two of comfort." The other woman pocketed it. "Tomorrow, when the guards come, we shall see what we can get."

"Please no, it's the only thing I have that ties me to my past."

"Don't worry," Tess cackled, "A few days in here and your past won't matter anymore. Neither will your future."

Tears trickled down Simone's cheeks. "Please. Give it to me." It wasn't that she didn't want to help Tess and the others, it was the chance the medallion gave her, however slight, to be able to somehow barter it for her freedom.

Tess ignored her and made her way to the stone bench in the far corner, flopping down on the stained mattress and turning her back.

Anguish buried Simone in an avalanche of brutal finality. The tears flowed unabated, wetting her wretched cheeks. She was lost, confined in an underworld more cruel than anything she had ever imagined.

Aye, Newgate had been an ever present threat but she had always been careful. Thanks to mischance, she now lived her worst nightmare.

Nay, being in Newgate wasn't her worst nightmare. Losing Temple was.

Even now, Temple could be dead. She would never be able to love him, to hold him, to tease him to coax forth the boyish smile.

Regret pierced her. Fool that she was, she had only told an unconscious Temple she loved him. Why hadn't she told him before?

Because she had felt unworthy of him.

Yet he had never made her feel that way. He had always treated her with charm and consideration. Always, she had felt his equal.

Why had she doubted him? He had rescued her from her miserable street urchin life, taught her how to be a lady, had married her, had brought her back to London society. He hadn't been ashamed of her.

And what had she done? Let her insecurity turn her into a shrieking harridan against his peers. Then she had fled, even though he had wanted to stay at the ball and show them all for the fools they were.

And it was in his search for her that he had been captured and tortured. The blame lay squarely on her shoulders but she couldn't help him now.

She couldn't even help herself.

Great hacking sobs rose and she couldn't hold them back. Her howls of misery disappeared into the din that was Newgate.

Chapter Twenty-Five

"Enough, my lord, you'll hurt yourself."

A firm hand pushed against Temple's chest. Scowling, Temple looked up at the narrow, angular face of Dr Arthur Simon, the long-time physician of the Wellington family, before collapsing exhausted against the pillows.

"Blast it, I'm weak as a newborn babe."

"You've lost a lot of blood. It will take time to recover your strength. Rest assured you'll be good as new but only if you obey orders and rest."

"Very well," Temple grumbled. He relaxed against the bed linens, burrowing his shoulders into the feather pillows until they formed to his body. He tipped his head back to the headboard, wincing as he inadvertently bumped the gash. "How long have I been unconscious?" Despite his best efforts, his eye lids fluttered close. He ignored the pounding in his bandaged shoulder to concentrate on the doctor's answer.

"The better part of two weeks. I dare say you were found in the nick of time."

Bloody hell, he'd been unconscious for nigh on two weeks. Simone. Where was she? How was she? He slammed a fist against the bedclothes in frustration. Here he lay, a useless bed-ridden oaf.

"Where was I found?" He opened his eyes.

"Face down in a rag cart and how you got there is anyone's guess. Hold still." Dr Simon leaned over and placed his ear against Temple's chest. "Splendid rhythm," he commented as he pulled away. "If nothing else, your heart didn't suffer from the beating you took."

"So I was found under rather mysterious circumstances." Temple winced again as the doctor prodded his bruised ribs. "You could just ask me if they still hurt or not," he muttered. "No need to keep poking about."

"What? Oh, sorry, of course. Yes, mysterious circumstances indeed." Dr Simon nodded his sandy blonde head. "But all's well that ends well. The wound in your shoulder has healed nicely as has the gash on your head, although your head shall ache for a week or two. As long as you do as I say, you'll make a fine recovery."

A fine recovery? A bitter smile bent his lips. What did the doctor mean by "a fine recovery"? Aye, a fine recovery for his body perhaps but how did one define "a fine recovery" for one's heart?

The doctor stood there with an expectant air; Temple quelled his sour thoughts. "Of course. I shall follow your instructions to the letter."

"Splendid," said the doctor, snapping shut his leather case. "I've left you laudanum for the pain. Until tomorrow then." He bowed and left the room in a cloud of peppermint and antiseptic.

Laudanum. The irony of the situation smacked him straight in the chest. Laudanum. With grudging desire, his eyes opened and he turned his head to search his bedside table for a familiar glass vial. There it was, among the bandages and jars of liniment. Without wasting time on thought, he raised his hand and knocked it off the table.

It fell, shattering into a hundred shards as it hit the bare wood of the floor. He stared at the shards; they vaguely resembled a heart shape and irony smacked him again.

There, for all the world to see, lay his broken heart.

* * *

Sorrow sat heavy on Simone's shoulders, pushing her into a pit of desolation. Sorrow held her face taut and her heart still, sorrow trapped her in hopeless misery. Time was meaningless to her, had become a futile passage of one empty minute merging into the next. How long had she been incarcerated? A day? A week? A month? She had no way of knowing in the constant grey twilight.

Too, her heart ached for Temple. She missed him dreadfully, missed his teasing smile and the lively glint in his eyes, missed the way he whistled when he thought no one was listening, missed cuddling against his warmth at night. Was he even still alive?

To add to her misery, just this morning, she had had another drowning nightmare which if nothing else, had garnered sympathy from Tess.

"Not that I blame you for having a nightmare in here," Tess said, patting her shoulder.

Simone nodded miserably. She sat hunched over, head between her knees, cloak drawn tightly about her.

"You know, you might be able to sell that cloak of yours for a favour." Tess fingered the fabric. "The wool is very fine."

Simone turned toward her companion. "What would that get me?" she said, her voice listless. "Food and drink for a day or two? Only to prolong this misery?"

"I thought you might sell it for a note."

Simone looked at her, suspicious at the sudden change of heart of the other woman.

Her suspicion must have shown for Tess hastened to explain herself. "It's just that if you are who you say you are, you're probably of more benefit to us if you're on the outside. "

Ah yes, purely selfish motives on Tess' part. However it sparked a flare of hope in Simone's breast. She opened her mouth to answer but before she could utter a word, Tess spoke again.

"And it would be of more benefit to the baby you're carrying."

Gape mouthed, Simone stared at Tess. "What? What did you say? No, oh, no," she protested, shaking her head emphatically. "I'm not carrying a child."

"Suit yourself," Tess shrugged. "But to me it appears as if you're suffering from morning sickness."

"Oh no." Simone shook her head again. "It's the food in here. It doesn't agree with me." That and the sickening knowledge she had failed Temple.

"When did you have your last monthly? You haven't had it while you've been here and that's been two weeks already."

"Why, it can't have been much before then." She wracked her memory. On the ship, her last monthly had been on the ship. Three weeks later, they had reached London, then two weeks at the Wellington townhouse, a week back at the workhouse, now two weeks here. She ticked them off on her fingers.

Aghast, she raised her head to look again at the other woman. "Eight weeks," she whispered. "It's been eight weeks."

"Well, I would say that's as much confirmation as one would need. Isn't that right, girls?" She looked over to Bonnie and Elizabeth. They giggled and nodded their heads in agreement.

"I can't have my baby in here," Simone whispered. Shock numbed her mind, reducing her thoughts to only one—a child. She carried Temple's child.

"Sell your cloak, then. It should buy you a note."

"A note? What do you mean? I have no means to send a note."

"The guards will do it, providing you can pay. They lower notes from the windows to the street outside."

"Do you think it could work?"

"I don't know." Tess scratched her lice ridden head. "But it's the best chance you have."

Being cold or having her child, their child, in Newgate. The choice was easy.

"Here," she said, ripping it off her shoulders and handing it to Tess. "What do I have to do?"

* * *

The past two weeks, decided Gentry Ted, had been an unmitigated disaster. It had started with the disappearance of Simone, his certain ticket to financial reward. That evening, he had started down the alley to retrieve the cart when he heard men approaching from the opposite direction. Instinct told him their arrival did not bode well for Simone and her lord, so he had successfully diverted their attention, leading them on a wild goose chase back toward St. James Palace. When he returned to the warehouse, he discovered, much to his puzzlement, Simone had left, leaving behind her lord.

Then he had tried to take Lord Wellington back to his home. He had almost succeeded, however, within a few houses of reaching his destination he had been drummed out of the posh district by the local constabulary, barely escaping with his hide intact.

To make matters worse, the past few days had been slow, with nary an easy mark to be found.

Consequently he sat in his favourite corner of the Royal Swan with just enough in his pocket to pay for a couple of pints and a bit of food.

"Have ye heard the news?" the barmaid said as she plunked down a plate of bubble and squeak.

"News?" He frowned, trying to recollect what the woman might be referring to.

"Yer favourite, Mona Dougherty. She's in Newgate."

"No." He shook his head. "Mona's too good to be caught. How would you know, anyway?"

"There's a note from her. The puff guts over there has been bragging about it." She pointed to a chubby gentlemen holding court in the centre of the crowded pub.

"I see." Ted narrowed his eyes. The man, William Merriweather, was well known to him. A braggart with a bit of a mean streak, he made his living hanging around Newgate preying on the misfortunes of the inmates.

Ted ate his meal slowly, watching and listening to Merriweather as the other man made a show of waving the sheet of paper clutched between pudgy fingers.

He stopped chewing as an idea hit him with the stunning precision of a prize fighter's fist.

Choking down the food in his mouth, he pushed the half-empty plate away and sprinted toward the door, snatching the note from Merriweather's hand as he charged past and out the door. Ignoring the shouts behind him, he darted down the street and disappeared into the seething crowds.

Head down, he hurried on, not stopping until he reached the steps of the Wellington townhouse. He squared his shoulders and adjusting his cravat with one hand, reached up with the other and grabbed the knocker, banging it with a ferocity that echoed down the street.

The door swung open on well-greased hinges to reveal a cadaver-like man. He stifled a smile. The butler appeared more suitable for opening the gates to Hades rather than a house of the upper crust.

"We'll have no beggars at the front door," said the haughty butler. "Off with you."

"I am no beggar, sir. Rather, I have information regarding the Earl's wife." Ted patted the pocket where securely sat the folded note. "His lordship should see this."

"What nonsense is this?" The butler looked down his rather large nose. "His lordship is in no state to accept visitors."

"I wager he'd be happy to see me," Ted said confidently. "I have news regarding Lady Simone's whereabouts."

The butler started at the mention of Simone's name and blinked several times, obviously considering whether or not the shabby man on his doorstep spoke the truth.

"What have you got to lose?" Ted spotted the butler's indecision and pressed his advantage. "I have a note from her ladyship. Asking for help."

Being unable to read, Ted was not absolutely certain the note contained a plea for help however, he made his voice confident. "Please see that Lord Wellington reads it." He handed the precious paper to the butler. "Er, may I come in while I wait?" Without waiting for an answer, he brushed past the stunned butler and sat down on an embroidered bench.

The butler scuttled off, holding the note between two fingers as if it were a noxious substance rather than simply a piece of paper.

Idiot, Ted thought, he's run off and left the front door open. He leaned over and gave it a push. It swung back and closed with a lazy click. Ted found himself alone inside the rather impressive entryway of Lord Temple Wellington's town home.

A satisfied smile crept across his lips. Hell's bells, it looked as if the rotten luck of the past two weeks was about to turn.

* * *

"Leave me, Tedham. I'm in no mood for company." Temple's voice was querulous. His head ached, his shoulder ached, and his heart ached. All in all, he was in a foul mood. He opened one bleary eye to see a flushed Tedham standing beside his bed.

"A, ahem, gentleman brought this, my lord." The butler's tone clearly indicated the man was no gentleman. He held up a greasy, folded square of paper.

What rubbish. For that, he had been disturbed from his rest? Temple groaned and closed his eye. "And?"

"He claims it's from Lady Simone, my lord."

"What?" Temple sat bolt upright in the bed. Stars prickled his eyes and he swayed for a moment before he reached over to grab the paper. It reeked of stale ale and cooking oil and his first inclination was to drop it. With shaking fingers, he unfolded it and read it, once in disbelief, twice to make sense of it all.

"My lord? What shall I tell the gentleman?"

"Tell him I shall be right down." An unsteady Temple lurched to his feet, grabbing his robe before jamming his feet into his slippers. Bloody hell, according to the note, Simone sat in Newgate prison. How could that be, he had sent Constable Wyndham Jones there to inquire for her. It must be a lie.

But maybe, maybe, it wasn't.

With pounding head, he staggered his way downstairs to confront the shabby man sitting in the entrance foyer.

"How can I be sure this isn't a ruse?" Temple waved the note in front of the stranger's nose.

"Why would it be?" The man jumped to his feet and adjusted his dirty cravat before thrusting his chest forward. "Are you accusing me of being a liar?"

"I'm accusing you of taking advantage of a sad situation. How did you know my wife had disappeared?"

"Because I know her as Mona Dougherty."

Temple's jaw dropped. The man had called her Mona. Maybe this wasn't a ruse, after all.

Gentry Ted bowed. "My name is Gentry Ted. I've bin looking out for Mona for years. I saw her on the street a few weeks ago and she told me the whole story, about you taking her to New Caledonia, and marrying her and all."

Scarcely believing his ears, Temple said nothing. With bated breath, he waited for the rest of the explanation.

"I put two and two together," Ted hastened to explain. "That you were one and the same as Lord Scoundrel. I knew ye were in the clutches of Mortimer Rae. I told her that and she insisted on finding you. Mona has a heart of gold," he added. "That and she loves you. Yer a lucky man."

"She loves me? A woman who loves her husband does not run away at the first sign of trouble." His mind tumbled with the news or perhaps it was just being on his feet for the first time in days that affected his equilibrium. He stood there, swaying. Bloody hell, his head throbbed so, he couldn't reason properly. What had Ted just said? Simone loved him?

Then he realized the enormity of the words. A thrill of joy coursed through him—Simone loved him! But why hadn't she told him?

"Believe me or not," Gentry Ted continued, "it's true. In any case, Mona, er, Simone and I found you. We had a spot of trouble and by the time I got back to the storehouse with a cart to move you, she'd disappeared."

"Are you the one who brought me home?"

"Aye." Ted nodded. "The constables didn't take too kindly to me hanging about. I had to run."

"How did she end up in prison?" Temple rubbed his forehead; his shoulder ached abominably, making it difficult for him to concentrate. And one thought kept beating through his mind: she loves me, she loves me, she loves me—making it even more difficult to concentrate.

"I don't know." Ted shook his head. "I only know, she's been gone for perhaps a fortnight. And Newgate ain't the most pleasant place. I'm guessing you'd like to get her out of there and the sooner the better." He stopped talking and leaned back on his heels.

Temple read Ted's expectant attitude correctly and reached into his pocket, pulling out a sack of coins. "For your trouble," he said, tossing it toward Ted before hobbling over to the door to pull it open. "Thank you for informing me of my wife's whereabouts."

With a pleased expression, Ted pocketed the coins. "It were my pleasure. I always had a soft spot for her."

"Perhaps you should be on your way." Temple pointed out the door. He didn't mean to appear ungrateful but there was not a moment to lose. He must rescue Simone.

"Thank you," replied Ted. With a broad smile and a tip of his hat, he bounced out the door. He walked away with a spring in his step. His little Mona had a fine husband who cared for her. Aye, he would miss her but she didn't need him anymore. Whistling, he turned the corner and headed toward the friendlier environs of the east side.

An elated Temple closed the door and leaned against it for a few seconds to catch his breath.

For the first time in weeks, he had firm proof of Simone's whereabouts. Newgate Prison. Nasty business, that, but with the help of his solicitor, he should have his wife home by the end of the day.

Gritting his teeth, he mounted the stairs one agonizing step at a time. Bloody hell, all he wanted to do was race to his wife's rescue but his body wasn't cooperating in the slightest. Sweat prickled his forehead and dampened his palms but he ignored it. Simone needed rescue and his physical discomfort was of no consequence.

* * *

White-knuckled, Simone gripped the railing and stared at the grey-bewigged magistrate who sat before her.

Put to death? Me?

Moisture trickled down her thighs; her armpits grew wet. A roaring filled her ears. Her knees buckled and she sat down, hard, on the bench in the prisoner's dock.

Put to death.

By hanging.

The object of ridicule for the hundreds of people who came by to watch the spectacle at the gallows in front of the prison each and every Monday morning at the hour of 8:00 a.m.

Sometimes she had trolled the fringe of the crowds gathered to watch the poor unfortunates taking their last breaths in sight of the jeering mob. She had never watched, instead had taken the public executions only as an opportunity to make some easy money. She hadn't given much thought to the lives that ended so brutally, assuming they deserved their fate.

Now her life was to be snuffed. Her life and the life of the babe within her womb. Aye, she had stolen but only for good purpose, to feed herself and others in the workhouse. For that she would die?

Perhaps she deserved it, with her flippant ways and cocksure attitude. But the innocent baby within her did not deserve that fate.

Rough hands grabbed her and dragged her away, toward the dismal passageway leading to the holding area.

"You cannot hang me," she shouted over her shoulder, digging in her heels in a vain attempt to slow her removal from the courtroom. "I'm with child."

"Unhand her."

A stern voice boomed through the court.

Astonishment rippled through the room; the grip on her loosened and Simone took the opportunity to pull herself free.

All heads, including that of Simone, turned to see a dark, imposing figure push his way through the benches of spectators.

Temple.

Incredulous, she watched as he limped toward the magistrate's raised bench. A slight, stooped man carrying a leather folder followed him.

"That woman is my wife, the Countess of Leavenby." Temple raised his voice against the murmurs. "Unhand her, I say, she is innocent of any and all charges against her."

Disbelief mingled with hope coursed through her. Temple had found her. Temple would put things right.

A grey mist rolled through her mind and in a dead faint, she toppled over.

Chapter Twenty-Six

Thin, painfully thin, even more so than the evening she had stowed away in his trunk. Concern filled him—she weighed nothing on his lap, a wisp of skin and bones and once again, rags. Her hair was a tangled, matted mass and great black shadows hung below her eyes; her cheeks were hollow smudges. She smelled of grease, perspiration and urine, an odour born of the deep seated fear that stains one's clothing and stains one's soul.

Newgate had not been kind to her.

He tucked the blanket around her shoulders as if, by doing so, he could tuck away the horrors she must have endured. With gentle fingers, Temple traced the contours of her gaunt face. Each time the carriage hit a bump, a groan trickled from her lips. His heart squeezed at the sound and he pulled her close against his chest as if he could stop her pain by sucking it through his own skin.

He lifted his gaze and let it wander out the window, looking without seeing the gas lamps that patterned the interior of the carriage with shadows as the drove past.

"Temple?"

He looked down; her eyes were closed. It must have been his imagination. He looked away again.

"Temple?"

This time he knew she had spoken. Elation filled him and he leaned over to kiss her nose.

"Hush, I'm here," he murmured against her pallid brow. He relished the feel of her in his arms. A shiver crept along his spine at the realization of how much he had missed her and how close he had come to losing her forever.

"Are you cold?" she whispered through chapped lips. She must have felt him shiver.

"Nay, I'm not cold." A smile twisted his lips. "I have you on my lap, how could I be cold?" He meant it as a jest and relieved, he saw the corners of her mouth lift slightly.

"Am I so very warm?"

"Yes." He brushed away a stray wisp of hair that clung to her forehead.

The exertion of speaking even a few words cost her for she closed her eyes again and lapsed into silence. The shudders started then, great, wracking convulsions distorting her face and jerking her arms and legs about. He gathered her close, holding her tight so she could not hurt herself. It must have helped, for the convulsions subsided to tremors.

"Hurry!" He rapped on the wall and shouted to the driver. "Hurry!"

The horses picked up their pace and the coach swayed and bumped on the cobblestones. After what seemed an eternity, they pulled up with a jerk. The screech of the brakes must have alerted Tedham, for the door swung open as Temple galloped up the stairs carrying his listless burden.

"Send for the doctor!" Temple barked to the surprised butler. "Have the maids bring hot water, soap and towels to my bed chamber."

He carried a limp Simone upstairs. Tenderly, he laid her on his bed. He stripped off her clothing down to her shift, inspecting the bloodied skirt with narrowed eyes. Her blood? If not hers, then from whom?

A knock sounded. "My lord, we are here with the water."

"Enter." He shouted and even to his ears, his voice sounded harsh. "Over there." He waved to the washstand. "Anna, fetch a clean night gown."

"Of course, my lord." The maid dropped her stack of linens and scooted off.

The door closed behind the parade of chamber maids, leaving behind pails of steaming water and an assortment of scented soaps. He searched through them until he found the scent he sought. Lemon verbena. He held it close to his nose and inhaled. Lemon verbena. And sunshine and smiles.

He began to wash her, dabbing at the pale skin time and again. Her eyelids fluttered but her eyes remained closed.

A knock sounded again. "My lord, I have the night gown." He stalked to the door, yanking it open and grabbing the gown from the hand of a very startled Anna.

By the time he had washed Simone and slipped on her night gown, Dr Simon burst through the door.

"Forgive me for not knocking, Lord Wellington, however Tedham impressed upon me the urgency of the situation."

"It's my wife," a grim-faced Temple said. "She needs medical attention. A very unfortunate set of circumstances landed her in Newgate and I fear for her health."

Before he had even finished speaking, the unperturbed doctor had set his bag beside his patient and begun his examination.

Temple sagged against the foot of the bed, swiping a hand against his sweat prickled forehead, wincing at Simone's every moan or twitch as the doctor poked and prodded.

"She's fine." Dr Simon pronounced at length, turning to face him.

"The tremors? It's not gaol fever?"

"Oh no," the doctor declared. "The tremors are simply the result of stress. Hunger, too, I would wager."

"She should make a full recovery?"

"Oh yes." Dr Arthur nodded head confidently. "One thing, however. I should be the first to congratulate you on your impending fatherhood."

"I beg your pardon?" Temple gaped at the smiling face.

"Your wife is with child. Due in about seven months, I would say. Not that we have anything to do with that. It rests entirely with the whims of the baby." He rummaged about in his bag and pulled forth a small bottle. "A spoonful in the morning and evening of this tonic should help her regain her strength. Start her with a hearty broth for a day or two. After that, make sure she eats plenty of fish and red meat."

"Of—of course," stammered a stunned Temple. He moved to sit down beside Simone, not noticing as the doctor excused himself and quit the room.

A father. He was to be a father. A new life, created by him and Simone. A smile spread across his face; laughter burst from his throat.

A father.

* * *

No matter how hard she tried, she couldn't open her eyes. Her eyelids refused to obey, as if lead weights sat on them. She puzzled on this a moment or two before lifting one hand to brush the weights away. To her surprise, a warm hand caught hers. Something soft brushed against her fingers, something like … lips?

"Simone? Are you awake?" The whispered query battered her brain.

Awake? What was awake?

"Simone, open your eyes." The whisper became authoritarian and rebellion rose within her. She would open her eyes when she was good and ready to open her eyes.

"Simone, please open your eyes." The tone changed, becoming more pleading. It caught her attention.

Oh, very well, she thought crossly, if only to stop you from pestering me.

Eye lids quivering with effort, she tried to open her eyes. She wanted to give up. But something in the voice compelled her to try again. Slowly, her eye lids obeyed her.

She blinked against the light. A very tired, very bedraggled, very unshaven Temple came into focus.

"Where am I?" Her voice was scratchy, her lips wooden. She tried to look around the room but he loomed over her, restricting her view.

"Home. In my bed. In our bed," he corrected himself.

"I'm not in Newgate? This isn't a cruel joke, is it?"

"Not a joke." He shook his head. His dark hair was tousled, as if he had run his hands through it time and again.

"I am sorry," she whispered, "for causing you so much trouble."

"See that it doesn't happen again, young lady," he said with mock severity.

"Not to worry." A ghost of a smile crossed her face. "I have had more than enough of prison." Her eyelids drifted shut then fluttered open. "You searched for me?"

"Yes. I would have found you sooner but the constable who visited Newgate inquired for Lady Simone Wellington, Countess of Leavenby, not Mona Dougherty. I, distraught as I was over your disappearance, didn't think of it at the time. " He dragged his free hand through his hair. "I am sorry."

He had looked for her! Joy bubbled within her at the realization. "How did you persuade the magistrate to release me?"

"In the end, it was easy enough. I simply explained to him you had been dressed for a masquerade ball, we had a tiff and you ran off. You were picked up in a case of mistaken identity. He was a bit suspicious of the blood on your skirt, though." He paused and looked at her sharply. "How did you get blood on your skirt?"

"Oh that." She paused to think. "It is your blood. From the warehouse. We found you and I stayed with you while Gentry Ted went for a cart to bring you home."

The shadows in his memory parted and he remembered. "It was you? You were my angel?" He lifted her hand again, turning it over to place a feather light kiss in her palm. "I never believed angels existed," he murmured against her palm before lowering it. "Now I do."

The warmth in his voice embarrassed her. An angel. He thought her an angel. Before she could consider the implications of that, Temple spoke again.

"Gentry Ted tipped me off on your whereabouts. It puzzled him that you had run off without him."

"He didn't come back." A sigh escaped her lips. "I waited for him but I was almost discovered by Mortimer-Rae's henchmen. It scared me and I realized it was up to me to save you." A lone tear trickled down her cheek. "I was on my way to Joanna. I didn't know I would run into Constable Carstairs or I would have been more cautious." She wiped away the tear with her sleeve.

"Rotten luck," Temple growled through clenched teeth. His fingers twitched. "I should like nothing better than to wring the constable's neck."

"The prison was horrid," Simone whispered. "The noise, the stench, the dreadful people." She stopped to swallow hard.

"You must not think about it," he soothed. "You are safe now and forever with me."

She nodded. "It is wonderful, you know." He gave her a quizzical look. "To be warm and clean," she explained. "I had not realized how lovely that really is."

He chuckled. "That's quite a come around from the day I met you," he teased gently.

He still held her hand in his and she relished the feel of his fingers clasped about hers. A small touch, really, but it a touch promising sanctuary and it warmed her all the way to her toes.

Her eyelids drifted shut. *The baby. I must tell him about the baby.* She jerked them open. "Temple? There is something I must tell you."

He shook his head. "Rest," he said, placing a finger against her lips. "We'll talk later." Reluctantly, he loosed his grip and laid her hand across her chest.

They would talk later, he thought, there was still much to say and unfinished business between them. He leaned back in his chair and watched her innocent face as she slept.

* * *

The windows were dull, the sky pewter grey, when Simone next awoke. A cheery fire flickered in the grate, casting its glow onto the oak panelled walls and its warmth into the room.

She sensed rather than saw Temple sitting by the bed and turned her head to look at him.

He sat with legs extended, eyes closed, dark head propped on a book, chin lifting and lowering slightly with each breath. He had taken the time to wash, shave and change into a clean shirt. The collar lay open, exposing the crisp black curls of chest hair. She longed to run her fingers through it and of its own volition, her hand reached toward him.

The small movement woke him and his head jerked upright.

"Hello," she whispered.

"Hello," he whispered back, leaning over to drop a kiss on her forehead. "How do you feel?"

"Famished," she admitted wryly. She struggled to sit and he helped her, throwing one firm arm about her shoulders and shifting her knees with the other. He pulled up the bedclothes, patting them into place.

"I have just the ticket," he said, reaching for the tray on the night stand and placing it carefully on her knees. "Eat," he commanded as he whipped off the linen cloth covering the tray, "or the cook shall be sorely disappointed."

She briefly contemplated chiding him for his overbearing manner but decided against it as the tantalizing odour of soup, roast beef and freshly baked bread hit her nostrils. Manners be damned, she thought, and she tackled the tray with gusto, not stopping until every last crumb was eaten.

"That was lovely," she sighed, licking a bit of butter from her fingers. "Although not a display a lady of quality would put on."

Because I'm not one, she added to herself, *and somehow I must make Temple understand that.*

"I shouldn't worry about ladies of quality, if I were you. Only about regaining your strength."

Simone snorted. "Who are we fooling, my lord? I am what I am." Her full belly made her bold and so she continued. "I don't belong in your world and we both know that."

"Now who came up with that conclusion? Certainly not I."

Her heart leapt at his brash assertion. However, she must not allow herself to be dissuaded from the decision that had formed in her mind over the past days and weeks. She simply did not fit in the upper class and never would.

Furthermore, she wouldn't hold him to their poorly conceived marriage. If she left now, before he knew of her pregnancy, she could have his baby. It would be hers and hers alone and at least she would have something of him.

She sucked in a deep breath. "I do not wish to embarrass you further," she blurted. "Perhaps we could have our marriage annulled."

"Annulled? I vow that is the most scatter-brained suggestion I have ever heard. Besides, how would you explain the child?"

"The child?" Her head spun at his words. "How do you know of that?"

"The doctor told me." He looked at her as if she had grown two heads. "How else do you think I would know? Which brings me to another matter." He tapped her on her nose with a well-manicured index finger. "Why didn't you tell me earlier?"

He knew. He knew about the baby.

Her dreams came crashing to the ground and, defeated, she hung her head. She clutched the sheets in her fists to quell the trembling before lifting her face to look at him. "Because I do not wish you to be ashamed of your child's mother," she cried out at length.

"Ashamed? Of you? Wherever did you get that notion?"

"I've been in Newgate. How could you explain that?"

"Why do I have to? No one knows. All we shall say is you've been at the country house."

"But all of London knows I grew up in a workhouse. I am a common thief. That, my lord, is beyond explanation."

"Pffft," he snorted. "The next incident has already taken hold of the wagging tongues. Not to disappoint you," he tickled her under her chin, "but you're not the scandal of the moment anymore. I do believe it is Lord Wrigley being discovered on the street outside of White's naked as the day he was born."

His calm, matter of fact manner irked her. He simply did not, or would not, understand.

She threw out her last argument. "But what of your mother? She dislikes me intensely."

"My mother?" He rolled his eyes. "How does my mother enter into the conversation?"

"She snubbed me at the Belmont's ball. Her social clout is enormous."

"No more so than yours. May I remind you, Simone, you are now the Countess of Leavenby."

"But she doesn't like me," she wailed. "In all likelihood, she never will."

"You are guilty simply by association with me." Hurt flashed through his eyes to be replaced by contempt. His lips twisted. "My mother despises me, ergo she despises you."

Surprise at his words blazed through her. "Why is that," she prodded. The hurt she could understand. But contempt?

"My crime? I'm not Richard. She never wanted me, never wanted more than one child." He stopped for a minute, looking up to the ceiling in an obvious effort to collect his thoughts. "She denied my father his rights as a husband," he continued, battling his emotions. "She claims he took her against her will one night and I was the product." He stopped again to swallow hard. "When I realized that nothing I did would ever change her opinion of me, I decided I may as well live up to, or down to, as the case may be, her expectations of me. I simply did not care anymore."

"What of your father? Surely he could see the unfairness of it all."

"No." A harsh smile twisted his lips. "I was a reminder to my father of his unhappy marriage. He couldn't wait to be rid of me the second I was old enough to be shipped to boarding school."

In a blinding instant she knew: he craved his parents' acceptance. She held her tongue, knowing nothing she could say would ease the hurt of a child neglected.

He must have seen the sympathy in her eyes for his manner changed abruptly.

"She may or may not come around regarding me," he said brusquely. "But I have the suspicion an impending heir would do a lot for changing her opinion of you."

Of course. He did not wish the marriage annulled to protect his first born child. It had nothing to do with her. Her mouth turned to ash.

It was as if he read her thoughts. "Do you think I don't wish our marriage annulled to stop my son from being born a bastard? Don't be daft."

A son. His assumption that the child would be a boy amused her bitterly. She squared her shoulders before replying. "I understand," she declared over the lump in her throat. "I understand because I never had a mama and a papa. I had Mrs Dougherty, oh, and I had Gentry Ted," she added, thinking of him and his never failing gift of an orange, "he looked out for me but it's not the same as having a mama and a papa."

"Staying together is not because of the baby." He leaned over and took her hands in his. "You make me want to be a better person. I don't want our marriage annulled because I love you, Simone. It's a simple as that."

Speechless, she looked at him. "You—you love me?"

"Yes. Be prepared, for my purpose right now is to make you love me too, even if it takes me the rest of my life.

"That battle is already won, Temple," she whispered shyly, looking at him with adoring eyes. "I love you too. I've loved you since that morning we first saw North America. I realized then I wanted to be with you, no matter where your adventures took us."

"Simone, my life is different with you at my side. You're jolly good company and fun to be with. You care nothing for the material trappings and you care nothing for my title. You are happy to be warm and clean and safe."

She held her silence and considered what he said. He thought her fun, enjoyed her company. And he loved her. How could that be, she of the workhouse upbringing? But he had declared himself so it must be so. The idea made her light headed with joy; a smile crept across her lips.

"Anyway," he continued without waiting for her response, "the doctor has suggested we retire to the country house away from London's foul air."

"Yes, I should like that." Still she smiled. She must look a fool, bemused by his admission as she was, but she couldn't help herself.

"Incidentally, I have something for you." He reached in his pocket and pulled out a velvet pouch. "I had it polished and a new chain put on."

Simone took the pouch and released the draw strings, tipping it over so its contents fell onto her lap. It was her medallion.

"Where … how did you get this?" Startled, her grin dissipated; she turned her gaze to him. "I traded it away for the note."

"I happened to notice it around the neck of one of the guards. I passed him a few guineas and he was more than happy enough to part with it." He snagged it from her lap and draped it around her neck. "I couldn't leave it, it's the only clue we have of your identity."

"You shall help me?"

"Of course. Everyone deserves to know from whence they came."

She looked down at the medallion then raised her gaze to his. "What of Mortimer-Rae?" she blurted. "I hope you are not angry with me but I left the package behind in exchange for you. I know how important it was to you but I had hoped it would dissuade Mortimer-Rae from pursuing you further."

"It's not important to me anymore." He gave her a crooked smile. "That part of my life is over. As far as Mortimer-Rae, he may have retrieved it, I don't know. However, it's another good reason to leave London for a time. I have the constables looking for him and I provided the necessary information regarding his nefarious activities. It shall be he who spends his time in Newgate."

"Good." She nodded her head. "It is what he deserves."

"On a better note, Joanna is here and anxious to see you. I told her she must curb her impatience until the morning," he chuckled, "which made her rather cross with me. And," he squeezed her hand, "I told Mother she would not be needed. She is away on an indefinite visit to her cousins in Northumbria."

Relief flashed through her. Facing Lady Frederica was not a task she wished to undertake just yet.

A blaze of the setting sun pierced the gloom, shining bronze into the room, illuminating a glass bowl on the mantle.

A bowl piled high with oranges.

Surprised, her gaze darted about the room. There were oranges everywhere—baskets of them, on the floor, on the hearth, even oranges made into a bouquet on the side table.

"Oy," she managed to gasp before tears began to slide in earnest down her cheeks. "For me?"

"Aye," he nodded his head. "For you." He reached down and plucked one from the basket by the side of the bed. "They are your lucky charm, are they not," he said as he handed it to her.

She took it, cupping it in both hands. A tremulous smile broke through the glistening tears. "You are my lucky charm now, Temple. I love you."

"And I you." He leaned over to kiss her very, very thoroughly.

As she flung her arms about Temple's neck the orange dropped from Simone's hands to land in her lap. It lay there nestled securely in the bed clothes, next to the life growing within her.

Chapter Twenty-Seven

"Are we there?" Simone couldn't keep the excitement from her voice. At last, she would see Leavenby Manor, where Temple had spent his childhood. Dr Simon had not given his permission for her to travel until she was well into her fifth month of pregnancy; the wait had been unbearable. "Is it very grand?"

"You shall see soon enough. I vow, you are like a child awaiting Father Christmas," Temple chuckled. "Look, there are the gates, just ahead."

Simone poked her head out of the carriage. "I don't see any gates," she complained, settling back against the squabs. "You are teasing me, I know."

"You looked in the wrong direction." He pointed out the other side. "See, there are the gates to Leavenby Manor now."

Simone half rose to poke her head out again. Temple resisted the urge to pinch her very attractive, very proximate, bottom. He opted instead to pull her onto his lap.

"Scoundrel," she pouted. "You could leave a girl alone." She swatted him with her fan and wriggled off to sit beside him.

"A girl, yes," he agreed mildly. "But my girl? Never."

"Oy," she said, fanning herself vigorously. "I saw the house. It is ever so large."

"A bit more comfortable than Stuart Lake Outpost," he remarked. "Nonetheless, the lifestyle here is much more relaxed than the season in London."

But she wasn't so sure about that when the carriage finally rocked to a stop on the gravelled drive in front. After Temple helped her from the carriage, she stood back to look, massaging her aching back as she did so.

The house was every bit as grand as the town house, in fact much more so for it was at least double in size. Two mismatched wings, both of mellow red brick, spread out from the central block of light-coloured stone. Marble steps ran the entire front width, centred by panelled mahogany doors. By her estimation and judging by the array of mullioned windows, there must be dozens of rooms inside.

The grandeur made idle words of Temple's assertion that country life would be a lot simpler. She tapped his arm to catch his attention.

"I thought Leavenby Manor was a country cottage. Not this—this—," she swept both her arms wide while she searched for the proper word, "behemoth."

"Don't you like it?"

"Of course I do but I fear I have been sadly misled."

"If a cottage is more to your liking, there are several about that may please you."

"Are you teasing me?"

"Not in the slightest. If the manor house is not of your taste, we'll reside elsewhere on the property.

But first do let us go inside to greet the staff. They are doubtless dying of curiosity to meet the new countess."

She nodded and picked up her skirts, girding herself for her first test here as countess. The doors swung open as they mounted the stairs to reveal a double line of servants standing at attention within the entrance hall.

Temple and Simone crossed the threshold to move into the marble-floored hall. The doors snicked shut behind them and a rotund, bald pated man dressed in butler's clothes scuttled over.

"Rathwell." Temple nodded pleasantly to the butler.

"My lord, it is an honour to have you and my lady here at Leavenby Manor."

"The honour is mine. The season is tiring and one is best well away from it." He pulled forward a very reluctant Simone, tucking her hand through his elbow for encouragement. "I should like to present your new mistress, Lady Simone."

"Welcome, my lady," the butler bowed so low Simone imagined he would tumble over. "May I introduce you to the staff?" He began to rattle off names so quickly that Simone could not keep track.

"Enough, enough," she gasped at length. "My head is full of names." She smiled and inclined her head to Rathwell. "I shall remember them all, I promise you."

"Come." Temple gripped her hand. "To the sitting room. And refreshments if you please, Rathwell."

As Temple pulled her along, Simone peered every which way. Here the dining room, there a library, here the hall stretching both ways to the wings, and at the back of the manor house looking into a walled garden, the sitting room.

"I'll never find my way about," she blurted as she lowered herself carefully into a forest green and cream brocade chair by the mullioned windows of the sitting room.

She gazed into the garden, rich with spring bulbs, rubbing her swollen abdomen. New life grew in the garden, like the new life growing within her.

"Not to worry, only one wing is open. The other is used for hunting parties and the like."

They were interrupted by the arrival of the butler's wife, who served as housekeeper. "Pleased to meet you, ma'am," twittered Mrs Rathwell as she bobbed a quick curtsy. "My lord," she put down her tray to pluck a creamy envelope from her apron pocket, "this came just this morning." She handed it to him.

"Thank you. That will be all."

The house keeper curtsied again and left.

Temple pried the seal on the flap and pulled forth a card. "Lord and Lady Pendleton wish to ride over tomorrow with a gift for us," he said after scanning it. "Do you feel up to it? I must confess, darling, I wrote them several days ago to inform them of our arrival. Lady Pendleton is French and I thought to show her your medallion."

Simone held her tongue.

He correctly interpreted her silence. "No whiff of scandal has followed you here. They don't know who, or what you were. They're a lovely, well respected family. Shall we agree, then?"

She nodded and forced a smile to quivering lips.

Temple brushed a stray curl from her cheek. "If tomorrow still finds you fatigued, we'll postpone the Pendletons' visit. Agreed?"

A grateful Simone nodded. "Thank you, Temple. Please forgive my silliness."

Was the fluttering in her stomach from the baby moving within her womb? Or was it nervous anticipation over perhaps at last solving the mystery of her medallion?

* * *

"You'll find Lord and Lady Pendleton an interesting couple," Temple remarked the next morning. "The first Lady Pendleton died and his lordship married her sister. Quite the talk at the time but they truly are fond of each other. And fond of their dogs. They breed pointer spaniels and the dogs are well known within hunting circles."

Sure enough, when Lord and Lady Pendleton rode up the drive later that day on matched bay hunters, they were accompanied by two dogs, both with silky white hair and brown patches over their eyes.

Lord Pendleton helped his wife off her mount and grabbed the saddle bags from the back of his horse before the two turned to a waiting Temple and Simone. Arm in arm, they climbed the marble stairs.

Lady Pendleton, a tall, slender, silver haired woman, spoke first. "Good day, Lord Wellington," she said in an accented voice, holding out her hand to Temple for him to kiss. She turned to Simone. "You must be the new countess of Leavenby, Lady Simone Wellington. I am Lady Isabella Pendleton."

Only with her accent, it came out more like Ladeee Eeesabella.

The other woman presented the picture of elegance in a gold riding habit and feather plumed top hat, leaving Simone feeling gauche and insecure. Even far from the confines of London, she felt a social outcast.

Oy, she sighed to herself, will this never get easier? Unsure of what to do, she curtsied.

"Oh non, ma chère, I can see right away you are enceinte. Please, let us go inside so you can sit."

Their dogs made as if to follow but with a stern "non" and firm hand signal, the two immediately sank to their haunches. "They are my children, please excuse them."

"Worse than children," growled her husband, a tall, white-haired gentleman with snowy moustache. However, the adoring glance he bestowed on his wife more than belied his gruff words.

"Lord Randolph Pendleton," Temple said, extending his hand. "Welcome."

The two shook hands. "Good to see you again, Wellington," he harrumphed then turned to look at Simone. "This is your lovely wife, I presume?"

At Temple's nod, he moved closer. He stopped stock still at seeing her.

"Simone," he gasped. His face blanched and he swayed slightly, mopping his suddenly perspiring face with a very crumpled handkerchief.

"How do you know my name?" Puzzled, Simone turned to look for Temple. "Did you tell him?"

"No, I did not."

Lord Pendleton continued to stare at her at length before he spoke. "Forgive me," he said in a voice barely above a whisper. "You greatly resemble my late daughter-in-law, Simone de Bergeron."

"Your daughter-in-law?" Temple's voice was incredulous.

"Yes, she drowned in an unfortunate boating mishap." He closed his eyes.

"So terribly sad," whispered Lady Pendleton to no one in particular, "Not only did he lose his son and daughter-in-law but he lost a granddaughter as well." She clucked sympathetically behind one gloved hand. "Only two bodies were ever recovered—that of his son and daughter in law. The body of the granddaughter, a little girl of three, was never found. It was assumed the river took her."

Lord Pendleton's anguish made a palpable force. With a face devoid of colour, he continued to stare at Simone. The saddle bags slid from apparently nerveless fingers and piled on the marble landing beside him.

Distraught, Simone pulled the medallion from within her bodice and began to fiddle with it.

It caught Lord Pendleton's attention. "Where did you get that?"

"I have always had it," she replied.

"Yes," interjected Temple. "Simone has had it since the day I met her. It's the medallion I wished to show your wife."

"May I see it?" Lord Pendleton held out his hand.

"Of course." Simone handed it over, watching the man take it and look at it carefully through his quizzing glass. His face blanched again.

"It's hers," he muttered. "It's Simone's coat of arms, of the de Bergeron family, of your family, my dear," he said, turning to his wife. He handed her the medallion. Lady Isabella turned it over and over in her hands.

"Mais oui," she whispered. "It is ours." She too turned an anguished gaze toward their hosts.

"I'm afraid I don't understand," Temple said.

"The de Bergerons were French émigrés who fled France during the horror," Lord Pendleton said. "This is their crest. Tell me, how did you get it?" He faced Simone and grabbed her shoulders with trembling hands as if to shake the very truth from her.

"I don't know," she said, trying to push his hands from her. She couldn't be his granddaughter, she had grown up in a workhouse. Should she tell him the truth about her life? Temple had assured her no one here knew of her past but if she spoke of it, all would know. She looked to Temple for guidance.

Temple's eyes were narrowed, his stance aggressive. "Simone, you had the medallion with you the day Gentry Ted brought you to Mrs Dougherty?" His voice was tight.

Simone nodded.

"You were three at the time? Did Ted ever mention where he found you?"

"Close to the river Thames," she said. "And that my clothing stank of river water. Oh my." She clapped a hand to her mouth. "You do not mean to tell me…." Her voice trailed away.

"Your dreams, Simone. Your dreams of drowning. They weren't dreams at all. They were memories of the day your parents drowned."

"Grand-père? Are you my grand-père?" Without realizing it, she spoke in French. She sagged against Temple.

"May I suggest we move to the sitting room," drawled Temple, "before I find my wife in a heap on the ground?" He picked up Simone and against her protestations, carried her inside. "Follow us."

* * *

"I cannot believe this day," Lord Pendleton professed. "Finding my granddaughter is a gift from the heavens." He glanced skyward, tears glinting in his eyes.

"Nor I," echoed Lady Pendleton. "We had thought you dead and now…." A brilliant smile lit her face. "It is a miracle."

The two were on either side of Simone, Lady Isabella perched on the arm of the Simone's chair, Lord Pendleton kneeling, each holding one of her hands.

"Ma chère." Lady Isabella suddenly pulled her hands free and clapped them over her mouth, looking in dismay at her husband. "Your saddle bag, where is it?" She sprang to her feet and dashed away.

A bemused Simone, one hand tightly secured in her grandfather's tight grasp, looked over at Temple. He raised his eyebrows and shrugged at her unspoken question.

Lady Isabella burst into the sitting room and made a beeline for Simone. "In all the excitement, I forgot about our gift to you both." She thrust a shivering white and brown bundle into Simone's arms.

"For you," said Lady Isabella. "His name is Trumpet."

"A puppy, I've always wanted a puppy," Simone breathed. "A puppy and a grandfather. What a wonderful day this has been."

A chorus of agreement echoed about the room. She looked at Temple. His gaze, so full of love, trapped hers, enveloping her in a warm cloud of wellbeing.

Yes, it had been a wonderful day.

Epilogue

Children of all sizes and shapes tumbled about the play yard of the Leavenby Home for Unfortunate Children. And playing amongst them, a golden-haired, blue-eyed girl of perhaps three years.

"Papa," squealed the moppet running toward her father as fast as two chubby little legs could carry her, "Papa, catch me!"

"Bloody hell," Temple groaned. "I vow that one will put me in an early grave." He got to his feet.

"Temple," Simone teased, "wasn't it you who told me running after Isabella would keep you young?" One hand on Trumpet's head, she rocked lazily in the garden swing that hid in the dappled shade of the tree at the corner of the orphanage yard.

"Up, papa, pick me up." The golden-haired moppet held out her arms.

"True," Temple said wryly. "But I hadn't anticipated being run off my feet every waking minute. And you, Bella," he said to his little girl as he swung her high overhead, "must learn to say please."

"Your fault." Simone flashed him a saucy grin. "You could allow Tess to fulfil her duty. That is why we have a nanny," she added, "so you could give over your duties as papa."

"What? And miss one precious second? Never." He shook his head and propped the little girl on one hip.

She wriggled and squirmed until he set her down whereupon she darted away only to promptly return to hug Temple's knee. She stuck a thumb in her mouth and looked up with adoring eyes at her papa.

"What shall you do when her sister arrives?" Simone looked down and rubbed her swollen stomach. "You can't be in two places at once."

"Let us cross that bridge when we come to it, shall we?" Temple smiled. "Why are you so sure it's a sister? What about a brother for Bella?"

"This one kicks just as much as Isabella. Therefore, it must be another girl." She gave him a triumphant look at her reasoning.

"Papa, come with me," Isabella pleaded. "There's a pony." The little one darted away again toward a plump black pony being lead toward the orphanage by one of the Leavenby Manor stable lads.

"Yes, Bella, Papa's coming. And you," he said, tweaking Simone on her nose, "must rest."

"My, you are impossible. I will rest but not until I speak with Mrs Dougherty about the new schoolmaster for the children."

"Darling, I see her coming now."

"Go." She gave him a little push. "Or you shall lose Isabella somewhere in the milling crowd." It was true, shouting, clamouring children now surrounded the patient pony.

"Lady Leavenby," Mrs Dougherty said, dipping her head.

"Please, call me Simone. Lady Leavenby makes me sound like Temple's mother."

"Nay, it isn't proper. Ye be the Earl's lady and that is just how it is. Speaking of your mother-in-law, how is she?"

Simone sighed. "I don't suppose we shall ever be fast friends. But at least now and again she comes to visit. More so for Isabella than Temple or me, I am sad to say, however, it's a beginning. Enough about me. What about you?" She leaned over and squeezed Mrs Dougherty's hand. "Is being the matron of the Leavenby Home for Unfortunate Children all you had hoped?"

"Oh, aye," beamed the other woman. "All that and then some. The children are content and so excited about the new schoolroom. As for me—" She tipped her head back to look at the blue sky. "I'm back where I'm the happiest, away from the smut and smudge of London city."

"You have a home here as long as you wish."

"I second that," Temple chimed in as he strode up, a red-cheeked Isabella sitting on his shoulders. "The children love you."

"Oh. I love them too. It is so different here than the Bishopsgate workhouse. Here the children are valued."

"Thanks to your excellent care," said Temple. "If I may claim my wife? Lady Joanna arrives this evening and Simone needs her rest."

"Of course, my lord, if you would excuse me." A visibly pleased Mrs Dougherty plodded off in the general direction of the mayhem surrounding the pony.

"You do so enjoy ordering me about, don't you?" Simone pretended to pout.

"Indeed I do and that shall never change so you had better become accustomed to it."

"I suppose I shall. One day."

"Who would think Lord Scoundrel would leave behind his wild ways and become a gentleman farmer and proprietor of an orphanage," Temple mused as they began the trek back to Leavenby Manor.

"And who would think Mona Dougherty would leave behind her thieving ways and become a proper lady?" Simone teased.

"Well, thanks to those thieving ways, you have plucked the one prize I never thought to lose."

"That is…?" Her question drifted on the breeze, mingling with the nonsensical burbling of Isabella.

"My heart. You have stolen my heart."

"For now and forevermore, I hope."

"Aye." He clasped her hand, raising it to drop a kiss on her fingers. "For now and forevermore."

The End

Author's Note:

New Caledonia is now known as Washington State and British Columbia. Stuart Lake Outpost, the administrative centre of New Caledonia for the North West Company, is modern day Fort St. James in the province of British Columbia. In 1820, the North West Company merged with its chief rival, the Hudson's Bay Company, which is still in existence today.

Daniel, Lisette and Polly Harmon, Baptiste Boucher and Chief Kwah were all real people. Many of the details about daily life in Stuart Lake Outpost I learned from Daniel Harmon's journal.

For the sake of the story, I've glossed over some facts. The first white woman did not live in Stuart Lake Outpost until the late 1800s. Also, the journey from Montreal to Stuart Lake Outpost took nine months and I didn't wish to impose a trip of that length on Simone and Temple!

About the Author
From vikings to viscounts, join the adventure, live the romance.

Living by the motto "You don't know unless you try", A.M.Westerling started writing historical romance because she couldn't find the kinds of stories she enjoyed. After all, she thought, who doesn't enjoy a tasty helping of dashing heroes and spunky heroines, seasoned with a liberal sprinkle of passion and adventure?

Westerling, a former engineer, is a member of the Romance Writers of America and active in her local Chapter. As well as writing, she enjoys cooking, gardening, camping, yoga, and watching pro sports.
Visit her at:
http://www.amwesterling.com
www.facebook.com/A.M.Westerling
www.Twitter.com/AMWesterling

Note from the Publisher

Thank you for purchasing and reading this Books We Love Book. Books We Love and the author would very much appreciate you returning to the online retailer where you purchased this book and leaving a review for the author. *Best Regards and Happy Reading, Jamie and Jude*
http://bookswelove.net